CU01034293

THE EAST HAM GOLEM

By Barbara Nadel

Bright Shiny Things
Displaced
A Time to Die
Web of Lies
The East Ham Golem

THE EAST HAM GOLEM

BARBARA NADEL

Allison & Busby Limited
11 Wardour Mews
London W1F 8AN
allisonandbusby.com

First published in Great Britain by Allison & Busby in 2025

A CIP catalogue record for this book is available from
the British Library.

First Edition

ISBN 978-0-7490-3135-0

Typeset in 10.5/16 pt Sabon LT Pro

The paper used for this Allison & Busby publication
has been produced from trees that have been legally sourced
from well-managed and credibly certified forests.

FSC
www.fsc.org
MIX
Paper | Supporting
responsible forestry
FSC® C171272

Printed and bound in the UK using 100% Renewable Electricity at
CPI Group (UK) Ltd, Croydon, CR0 4YY

To all my crime writer friends especially Derek Farrell, Valentina Giambianco, Quentin Bates, Nicola Upson, Mandy Morton, Elly Griffiths, Tom Mead and everyone who leans to the side of the weird

PROLOGUE

Prague, Czechoslovakia. 1938

'Rudolf!'

The small, balding man ran over to his slightly staggering colleague and took his arm.

'My God, you look terrible!' he said as he led the tall, darker man over to a seat by the window.

Then, calling out to a young man sitting at a desk, he said, 'Janos! Get Herr Baruch a glass of water!'

'Yes, Herr Rozenberg.'

The young man left and Levi Rozenberg sat down next to his friend and colleague, Rudolf Baruch.

'Was it difficult?' he asked.

His colleague nodded.

'Did you manage to get anything from Voss?'

Rudolf shook his head. 'He can't get anything now, not even aspirin. They're strangling his business.'

Levi Rozenberg shook his head and then he said, 'All the

more reason we need to act fast. Today the pharmacy . . .'

The young man returned with a glass of water, which he gave to Rudolf Baruch.

'Thank you.' He drank and then said to the young man, 'Is everything prepared, Janos?'

'Yes, Herr Baruch.'

'And the family?'

'They want to visit as soon as it's over,' he said. 'I told them to come this afternoon.'

'Good.'

And then the young man, Janos Horak, said, 'Herr Baruch, if you don't mind my saying, you look unwell. Are you sure . . . ?'

'I will finish attending to Frau Zimmer and then I will go home,' Rudolf said and then he stood. 'Levi, are you ready?'

His colleague also rose to his feet and said, 'As I will ever be, my friend.'

And then the two of them left their office and repaired to their laboratory.

ONE

Plashet Jewish Cemetery, East Ham, London. March 2023

'Is it me, or does everyone think that whoever did this should be strung up by his nuts?'

The group of uniformed police officers standing beside the tall, middle-aged man struggling to keep upright on the uneven ground beneath his feet looked at each other, but said nothing.

''Cause, you see, I find I don't really give a shit whatever the thinking was behind this – far-right nationalism, religion, madness – I just want to punch whoever did it until his spleen falls out.'

Still nobody spoke. Detective Inspector Tony Bracci was generally a likeable old geezer – family-orientated, friendly, fair. But he had 'views' which, if challenged, could land the challenger in a place they wouldn't like. In other words, Tony had a temper he wasn't afraid to use.

Looking around the recently desecrated cemetery, he said,

'Vi's got family buried here. Don't know how the hell I'm gonna tell her . . .'

A female officer said, 'You mean Detective Inspector Collins, guv?'

'Yes, God love her,' Tony said. 'If she was still in the job she'd be effin' and jeffin' and kicking your arses to get hold of every Nazi fanboy and would-be *jihadi* in Newham.'

'So why aren't you?' the officer continued.

Tony shrugged and then he said, 'Where to start these days, Siddiqui? Seems to me there's some sort of two-for-one deal on extremists these days. Can barely turn round for the bastards. No, it's SOCO slog for now, see whether we can get anything useful from the site, then house to house where we'll no doubt learn that no one has seen or heard fuck all.'

He lit a cigarette while all but one of his team dispersed around the group of shattered and desecrated tombstones in the middle of the cemetery. Rather closer to the main entrance than the rest, Detective Sergeant Kamran Shah was minutely examining the most egregious offence against the dead, in the shape of a coffin which had been dug up and its lid smashed. Fragments of what could have been the corpse's shroud stuck up from the broken lid like tiny off-white sails. If the body of Rudolf Bennett – the name he'd finally managed to make out on the scuffed metal plate once attached to the coffin lid – was to be reburied, it had to go through the hands of a police pathologist first. So Shah, as well as examining the site, was also waiting for Dr Gabor, the latest recruit to the tribe of specialists assigned from time to time to Forest Gate CID. He'd never met Gabor before, but he'd been told by his boss that the latest 'path' looked about twelve.

Tony Bracci ambled and stumbled his way over to his sergeant and said, 'So what's the score then, Kam?'

'Can't see much without disturbing it, guv. Path phoned to say he wants to transport the whole thing to the lab so he can maybe see why they picked on this particular bloke.'

'I can tell you that,' Tony said. 'Because he was there and because they're twats.'

'Yeah, but . . .'

Tony put a hand on his sergeant's broad shoulder and smiled. 'I know – look for all and any possible motives. Dinosaur I may be, but I'm not stupid. Just pulling your leg, Kam.'

The younger man smiled.

Kamran Shah had joined Forest Gate CID back in 2018 on an accelerated graduate programme. His now-boss had then been a sergeant who had worked with the legendary Detective Inspector Violet Collins. Tall, skinny and foul-mouthed, Vi had retired back in 2019, along with her signature Chanel suits, Opium perfume and famous preference for younger male lovers. What she hadn't taken with her was the dark sense of humour she had shared with Tony Bracci. It was something Kam Shah had learnt to appreciate – especially during the frightening days of the recent Covid pandemic. Like most police officers, Tony and Kam had worked all through what became known as 'the virus', trying, often in vain, to get people to obey the heavy quarantine restrictions that had been in force back then.

Kam said, 'But they are twats anyway.'

''Course.'

The entrance gates to the cemetery swung open and

a black transit van reversed in. When it finally stopped, a young man with flaming-red hair and Harry Potter glasses got out and opened up the back doors. Dr Benedict Gabor, police pathologist and, it was said, a practising pagan, was not a man who waited for 'inferiors' to do the donkey work allied to his profession. Pulling a trolley out of the van while two of his mortuary attendants looked on, he nodded at the coffin and said, 'This our man?'

'Yes, Doctor,' Kam said. 'Called Rudolf Bennett.'

Dr Gabor liked to have names for his 'people' where possible. Observing the shattered coffin, he said, 'Makes you wonder, doesn't it?'

'Wonder what?' Tony said.

'Why . . .'

'As I said to Kam here earlier,' Tony said, 'it's because they're twats.'

Gabor nodded and then said, 'It's as good an explanation as any.'

While Tony Bracci and his team were searching Plashet Jewish Cemetery for clues to who had desecrated the site, Private Investigator Mumtaz Hakim was drinking *masala chai* at a house that backed onto the graveyard. The owner of the house, a Mrs Meera Dhawan, had invited her to talk about her younger sister, Lakshmi.

'She's what my husband calls an "airhead",' Mrs Dhawan said as she crossed one elegant leg over the other. 'Thirty going on seventeen.'

It was nice to be given a cup of proper home-made *masala chai*. The spice-flavoured milk tea was ubiquitous all over the entire Indian subcontinent – though in the UK, as Mumtaz knew all too well, a lot of British Asians now opted for pre-mixed spice blends. But then Mrs Dhawan was the proprietor, with her husband, of three Indian restaurants across the London borough of Newham, as well as the 'star' of a highly regarded Asian cookery blog. Her masala chai was heavy on the ginger, which Mumtaz loved.

'Maybe,' Mumtaz said, 'that is why she is attracted to this much younger man.'

'You could have a point,' Mrs Dhawan said. 'But to want to marry an eighteen-year-old! I mean, who does that?'

'Other teenagers? If as you say your sister is still behaving like a teenager herself, she may very well find this boy appealing.'

'Yes, but she's a lawyer!' Mrs Dhawan said. 'I mean think about the optics of that? What on earth will her clients think of her? Lakshmi works with our father at his solicitors' practice in Chingford. Together with our brother Dev, they have some very important clients, high-profile people in our community.'

Unlike Mumtaz, a Muslim, the Dhawan family were Hindus. Meera and Lakshmi's father Dilip Dhawan was a well-known and respected solicitor across east London, especially amongst Hindu families. It must have come as a huge shock when the younger of the two Dhawan sisters announced that she wanted to marry a white teenage boy she'd met at the gym.

Shouting voices from the nearby cemetery insinuated themselves into Meera's smart, very grey living room and she looked towards the patio doors. There was no way she could see anything, but the police had been in there since very early that morning and their presence was unsettling – because it probably signified that the cemetery had been vandalised again.

Mumtaz, who had noticed the clutch of police vehicles at the entrance to the cemetery, said, 'It must be worrying for you when people get into the old graveyard.'

'It is,' Meera agreed; then she turned back to Mumtaz and said, 'All this hatred these days. Even levelled at the dead. Just because they were Jewish. I mean look at us. You are a Muslim, I a Hindu, but we get along with each other, we do business, talk like rational human beings.'

'It's men mainly, who do these things,' Mumtaz said. 'Most women don't have time for such things.'

'Oh, that is so true!' Mrs Dhawan said. 'Men and boys chewing betel all day long and talking about politics they barely understand. They want to try raising children, keeping house and pandering to the orders of men like themselves all day long!' Then she shook her head. 'Sorry, Mrs Hakim, ridiculous men are my *bête noire*. Like you, I'm a working British Asian woman who really doesn't have time for the prejudices of men. And I don't just mean Asian men either. I told Lakshmi, this white Christian boy of hers will be no better. I give it a year before he's got her picking up his dirty socks and then leaving her to go down the pub.'

Mumtaz smiled. Her own on-and-off lover was white, but he'd never made her pick up his socks and he had certainly never left her alone to go to the pub. Lee Arnold, for all his faults, was teetotal.

'Anyway,' Mrs Dhawan said, 'I'd like to find out more about this Danny Hall my sister has taken up with.' She passed

14

Mumtaz a photograph of a slim, dark-haired teenager who wore a slightly challenging expression on his finely chiselled face. 'He lives in Canning Town with his parents and, so my sister says, seven younger brothers and sisters. Given the size of the family, I do wonder whether they're Travellers. But you'll probably find that out.'

Mumtaz bit her tongue. Prejudice against Travellers and Roma was rampant and she really didn't want to get into that with this woman. Maybe Danny Hall did come from a Traveller family, but if he did, so what?

'Danny himself attends that New Vic College doing some course or other – when he's not with my sister,' Mrs Dhawan said. 'His mother cleans for a living, which is honourable, but the father is unemployed. Sick apparently.' She rolled her eyes. 'I want to know whether they're in debt. I don't want my sister used as a human bank and I want to know whether they're involved in crime. I'm not a fool, I know that not everyone involved in crime has a record. I could follow the boy myself, make forays down to Canning Town and ask around about these people, but you're better than I am at all this, and you have contacts.'

Mrs Dhawan was right. Although the next time Mumtaz would be in the vicinity of Plashet Jewish Cemetery, in three months' time, it would be in connection with what the police were doing in there right at that very moment.

By that time, Lakshmi Dhawan and Danny Hall would have been married for three weeks.

The whole process was recorded as well as individual photographs taken, from the time the shattered coffin was placed onto plastic sheeting on the floor. As each piece of broken wood was carefully removed it was numbered, photographed and laid in its approximate place on top of the coffin, but now on a bench. Just removing the lid took over an hour. And when the final piece was removed, Benedict Gabor had to decide whether to remove the shroud in situ or once his team had lifted the whole thing onto his examination table. While the table itself was covered with plastic sheeting, the doctor wanted to avoid any residual clumps of earth and other outside elements contaminating his work area. However, to remove the shroud in situ did mean pulling it from underneath the corpse, which could create damage.

In the end his team of technicians removed the enshrouded body and placed it onto the examination table. Gabor noticed that they struggled with the weight and wondered what, if anything, the body might have been buried with. The only woman on the team, Rosa, was left temporarily breathless.

When she could speak again, Rosa said, 'Weighs a ton!'

Her male colleagues all nodded their agreement while Benedict changed his nitrile gloves and then, with the aid of tweezers, began to pull at one corner of the shroud. From the date on the brass coffin plate, it would seem that Rudolf Bennett had died in 1940 and so he was probably way beyond liquefaction. But even when dealing with desert-dry skeletons, it was still surprising how fabric particularly could stick to a corpse. And this skeleton was heavy, or something was. As Benedict began to peel away the upper layers of the shroud, he sensed that what was underneath was rather more substantial than a skeleton.

Had the family of Bennett had the body embalmed? And

if so, to what degree? When Benedict's own father had died, he had been subjected to a high level of preservation. At the behest of his only surviving sibling, his sister Eszter, the body of Viktor Gabor had been mainly formaldehyde when he'd been buried. Benedict had been surprised. He hadn't thought that Jews were big on body preservation. But then what did he know? With Benedict brought up a Gentile by his Gentile mother, Viktor's original identity as a Jewish Hungarian was, and remained, a mystery to his son.

Benedict asked his team to lift the body while he disentangled the shroud from the underside of the corpse. This happened three times before first the head and then one shoulder came into view. And while the face, as might be expected, was covered by thick if discoloured gauze, there was something about the shoulder than made the doctor take a step back for a moment and breathe.

Benedict recapped. Not only was the corpse unusually heavy, but the shroud appeared to have been wrapped around it in a haphazard way. That, or maybe those who had attempted to remove or destroy Rudolf Bennett had rewrapped him after they'd finished whatever ghastly thing they had done to him. And yet the gauze over the face was intact and, when he pulled at one corner of it, it came away easily.

Benedict looked. Then he blinked several times to make sure that what he was looking at was real. A long aquiline nose dominated a grey-tinged face whose startlingly vivid blue eyes looked up at Benedict with . . . what? Stepping back from whatever this was, Benedict said, 'Christ!'

'What the hell is it, Doctor?' one of the technicians asked.

Quickly, as if more protracted contact with Rudolf Bennett might taint him in some way, Benedict pulled the shroud down to the body's mid-section – and then they all looked, with a mixture of horror and confusion, as the moulded chest of what looked like a tailor's dummy came into view.

TWO

June 2023

'They called it the East Ham Golem, unofficially like.'

The small, dark man sitting in front of her wore a soft brown hat and a lot of thick gold jewellery, especially on his left arm, which was probably an attempt to cover the huge scar there. He told her straight off the bat that some of his neighbours called him a 'pikey' behind his back. 'I actually like the travelling folk myself,' Bernie said. 'So I don't take it badly.' Turned out that Bernard Bennett was, at least in part, Jewish.

'Back in March I got a call from the Old Bill,' Bernie said. 'Now I know you probably look at me and think, geezer like him is a dead cert for a visit from the law—'

'Lee has told me you work at Newham General,' Mumtaz said.

'Yeah, I'm a cleaner.'

Sixty-year-old Bernard Bennett lived in the same street as

the mother of Mumtaz's business partner, Lee Arnold. Lee, a former soldier and copper, had started the Arnold Private Detective Agency when he'd left the Metropolitan Police. When business picked up, he'd employed Mumtaz, a psychology graduate, as a trainee investigator. The two of them had been together, both as business partners and sometimes lovers, ever since.

'So you clean at the hospital . . .' Mumtaz prompted.

'Yeah. Right,' he said. 'So I get this call from the police. It's about me grandparents' graves in the cemetery up Plashet. Apparently some bastard's been in there desecrating the graves.'

'I remember,' Mumtaz said. 'I was actually with a client who lives in one of the houses that back onto the cemetery the day the police began their investigation. Your name was never made public, was it?'

'No. Wouldn't have it.' Bernie leant forward in his chair and said, 'Do you mind if I have a fag, Mrs Hakim?'

'You can't smoke in the office but if you don't mind going out on the steps outside, that'll be OK,' Mumtaz said.

'Oh,' he said. 'Only Rose, you know, Lee's mum, she told me it was alright to have a snout in his place.'

'It's against the law, Mr Bennett,' Mumtaz said. 'We could get shut down. I tell you what, it's nice and warm outside – we can sit on the metal stairs if you like and I'll make us both a cup of tea.'

The Arnold Agency's one office was over a kebab shop at the Forest Gate end of Green Street, Plaistow. The office was accessed via a back alleyway and a steep flight of iron stairs, with the windows at the front looking out onto the large, modern Forest Gate Police Station building. Lee Arnold had worked there back in the day, and it was partly because he was an ex-copper that Bernie Bennett had come to see him now.

'I'm sorry Lee can't be here today, he had to be in court,' Mumtaz said as she gave Bernie a cup of tea and then sat down beside him on the iron stairs.

'That's alright, love,' Bernie said.

Mumtaz wondered what, if anything, Rose Arnold had told Bernie about her. When he'd arrived she'd got the feeling Rose hadn't told Bernie she wore hijab. He'd looked a bit shocked.

Now with a cup of tea in one hand and a fag in the other, he continued, 'So I had to go up Plashet Cemetery and have a look. I own the gravesite now my dad's dead. By the way, his grave wasn't disturbed at all, just my granddad and grandma's.'

'I know the detective who worked on the case, Tony Bracci,' Mumtaz said.

Bernie smiled. 'He's a bit of a sort, in't he?'

Mumtaz could imagine Tony ranging around the cemetery, swearing.

'It was Granddad's grave where they found the statue. Properly weird, I can tell you!'

'You saw it?'

'Yeah. Police asked me whether it looked like him, but how the hell should I know? He died during the war when my dad was just a baby. No photographs of him I know of. This statue was a man, dark hair, blue eyes, made to look quite young, like Granddad would have been. You know what a golem is, Mrs Hakim?'

21

Mumtaz had looked the word up when the story had been in the news.

'As I understand it, a golem is a clay figure,' she said. 'Created by rabbis to protect the Jewish community.'

'Magical,' Bernie said. 'I don't know how, I don't believe in all that stuff. I don't believe in nothing. Dad'd put down he was Jewish on forms and that, but me mum wasn't Jewish and so I never went to synagogue. I knew nothing about it until all this business come up. But now it has come up . . .'

'What do you want from us, Mr Bennett?' Mumtaz asked.

He sighed. 'They found my grandma's body, the police,' he said. 'Chani Bennett she was called, but Granddad's still out there somewhere.'

'The police never recovered his corpse?'

Mumtaz hadn't seen Tony Bracci for months, time during which the story of the Golem of East Ham had just sort of faded away.

'No,' Bernie said. 'Size of that golem they found in his box, there was no room for the body. The statue they've got in some storage place somewhere, but Granddad has never shown up. But then he wouldn't. Must've gone before his funeral. Unless of course someone took him out since at some point. I dunno, but it bothers me. Rudolf Baruch was his real name and the way my dad used to tell it, he was a brave man. He come here on his own from Czechoslovakia in 1938 when the Nazis took control. He worked doing anything he could get, but Grandma was always the real breadwinner. She was born here and worked as a dressmaker. Chani outlived Rudolf by thirty years, never married again, and when she died she was buried alongside him because that was where she wanted to be. Now me dad's in there an'all, but with me granddad gone, it ain't right.'

'So you want us to . . .'

'Find Rudolf,' Bernie said. 'Something about him, who he was, if you can. And his body. Police don't say they've given up, but they have and I understand it. Why look for a dead bloke who maybe went missing in 1940, when the living need so much help? Don't make no sense. Rosie told me I'd have to pay and I will. My wife died three years ago and me daughter's married with kids so I work most of the time. What else is there to do?'

'Mr Bennett—'

'Bernie,' he said.

She smiled. 'Bernie. I'm Mumtaz, and of course we will try and find out as much as we can about your grandfather. Whether we will be able to locate his body is less certain. No arrests were made in connection with that crime and so it's not as if we can ask the perpetrators where they put Rudolf's body – even if they took it, which looks unlikely.'

'I know it's a long shot.'

'But for the time being,' Mumtaz said, 'let's see if we can find out more about Rudolf. Do you know whether he had any other family members in the UK?'

'No, like I said, he come here alone. I've still got some paperwork of me dad's at home so there might be something in there, but I don't think there's anything about me granddad,' Bernie said. 'Chani's family name was Freedland. I do remember her from when I was a kid, but I dunno what family she had. I know she died in the Jewish Hospital in Stepney Green because Dad took me to see her before she passed. But I don't remember anyone else being there. Don't mean they weren't. I was just a kid at the time, and 'course there was the look of her too what took my mind away from anything else.'

'The look of your grandmother?'

'Yeah,' he said. 'Like a living skeleton she was, and her skin was the colour of nicotine. Cancer.'

Lee Arnold leant back against a listing weeping angel and lit a cigarette. 'Death by Misadventure' was the verdict the coroner had handed down. It had satisfied Kathy's dad, who had travelled from Ghana for the hearing. Ninety years old, he'd just wanted closure. Not so Kathy's brother, Ezra Appiah. He had walked out after the verdict and Lee didn't blame him. Anyone who'd known Kathy Appiah even slightly during the last year of her life knew full well she'd killed herself. Or rather been murdered. The trouble was that Kathy's killer had been nowhere near her when she died. He'd been in Russia.

Kathy Appiah had been a nurse at the London Hospital in Whitechapel for nearly twenty years when she died. A committed Christian, sixty-year-old Kathy had lived alone in a one-bedroom flat in Plaistow, sending half of what she earned to her family in Ghana, mainly towards the education of her sister's children. Everyone who met Kathy had loved her. Her patients, her neighbours, the people at her church. Always happy when she made contact with her relatives via the internet, Kathy had also met a lot of other, apparently like-minded, family-orientated people online. A lot of them were not as fortunate as Kathy, and she soon became aware of how much misery there was in the world outside her immediate circle. Over the years she sent small amounts of money to a single mother in Lebanon, an animal refuge in Syria and a man who needed to save up for surgery in Cameroon. Then she met Vladimir.

Vladimir was twenty-six, tall and blond and really didn't want to go to war against Ukraine. He had nothing against Ukrainians and wanted nothing more than to leave Russia and make a new life somewhere in Western Europe. At first Kathy merely commiserated with 'Vlad', but as their communications became more frequent, she realised that she was falling for him. He was so kind and respectful, never pushy or inappropriate. For her part Kathy looked upon Vlad as the young son she'd never had – at least that was what she'd told herself. That was what she'd stuck to until one night she got a phone call from Vlad. In tearful broken English he'd told her that he'd been called up to the army and was now on the run. He feared that if Putin's people caught him, they'd kill him. He wasn't, he said, asking for money, but if Kathy would just reciprocate his feelings of love, at least he'd be able to die happy.

Kathy was nobody's fool. She knew about internet scams. But she'd built a relationship with Vlad; she'd spoken to him on the phone and he'd told her she was the only person in the world who cared about him. She'd sent him five thousand pounds via Western Union to the place where he was hiding: Ekaterinburg in the Ural Mountains. Vlad had been so happy. But then they'd caught up with him yet again and so he'd had to move on. Her 'lovely boy' had travelled to St Petersburg, Kazan, Nizhny Novgorod and Perm in the months that followed, never asking for money. But she gave it to him anyway. Then her brother found out what was going on.

Ezra Appiah was Lee Arnold's neighbour; he knew what Lee did for a living and had asked for his help to try and discover who this Vladimir was. Lee had put his most internet-savvy investigator on the job, who had discovered that 'Vladimir' was actually a bus company in Ekaterinburg. Hurt, humiliated and angry, Kathy had, against Lee's advice, confronted 'Vladimir' online. The reply she'd received had told her she was a stupid, pathetic old woman who deserved everything she got, and asked why the hell she would think that a young attractive man like Vladimir would want her. Showing this to no one, Kathy mulled his response for a couple of days before she took a handful of sleeping tablets and threw herself down the stairs leading up to her flat.

Lee had just given evidence at Kathy's inquest. Held at the Coroner's Court at Walthamstow Cemetery, it had been a sad end to a life of selfless service. But in retrospect the verdict had been the right one. Nobody was going to bring 'Vladimir' to justice any time soon, and had the coroner handed down 'suicide' it would have meant more pain for her father who, like Kathy, was a committed Christian. But Lee also knew why Ezra was angry. His sister's death had been needless and a waste and, as he'd told Lee, 'If this carries on unpunished, how many other vulnerable women will send money to these bastards? How many more will take their own lives?'

He was right, of course. But how did you police the internet? Now that the genie of mass 'democratised' communication was out of its bottle, putting it back in wasn't an option.

For Lee personally, Kathy's death was just one more

example of what he was coming to see as a run of bad luck for him. In the past six months he'd been pistol-whipped by a young gang member on whom he'd tried to serve court documents, his wayward daughter had gone to live with a violent cage-fighter, and his on/off relationship with Mumtaz had broken down – again. And money was tight. He needed a win. But PI work was thin on the ground, mainly because nobody had any money. He just hoped that his mum's neighbour, Bernie Bennett, had something he could actually have a chance of solving. Not that he'd make a mint out of a man who worked as a hospital cleaner.

When Mumtaz had called DI Tony Bracci, he'd invited her for coffee. They met at what he told her was his favourite chai place on Katherine Road. When he arrived, Mumtaz could clearly see why Tony had prefaced this meeting by telling her he was 'addicted to their Karak coffee cakes'. This was a much bigger Tony than the one she'd seen eight months ago.

Tony ordered for them both – chai latte for Mumtaz, spicy Karak coffee for him plus two helpings of delicate Genoise sponge soaked in coffee – the famous Karak coffee cake.

'I'm in here almost every day now,' Tony told her while they waited to be served. 'And at the moment I can't say I can justify it by needing to keep me caffeine levels up.'

'You're not busy?'

'Well, we are,' Tony said. 'Antisocial behaviour has been with us since the dawn of time and will outlive both of us with no bother. But, as you know, one person's antisocial behaviour is another person's just living his life. 'Course, it can get serious if blades are involved but, contrary to what you hear in the news, crimes involving blades don't happen on every street every day here in Newham.'

'It's terrible the way the stigma never detaches from east London,' Mumtaz said. 'Way before Jack the Ripper, the East End had the reputation for crime it still has to this day.'

'Funny, innit,' Tony said. 'In spite of all the rich kids moving into the borough with their olive oil tastings and artists' ateliers, some people still think it's like the Somme down here.'

Their food and drink arrived. One bite of Karak coffee cake was enough to convince Mumtaz that Tony's addiction was completely understandable.

After some moments of gastronomic bliss, Mumtaz said, 'So, Tony, the East Ham Golem . . .'

She'd told him on the phone that Bernie Bennett had been in touch, and so he was prepared for it.

'Nothing so far,' Tony said. 'The thing itself is down at our storage facility in Belvedere. I can send you some photographs. Just between us, like.'

'Thanks Tony, that would be useful.'

She knew he wasn't supposed to do that, but she'd already found one photograph online that had been leaked to one of the local free papers back in the spring.

'What's Bennett actually want you to do?' Tony asked.

Mumtaz finished her cake and was tempted to go for another piece, but just settled herself to her very good chai.

'Well, of course he wants his grandfather's body put back in its grave,' she said. 'But he's a pragmatist, luckily.'

'We may never see that,' Tony said. 'All I can tell you is whoever opened that grave got in and out of the cemetery via the High Street North entrance. We found some fibres on the gate which could have come from the shroud that was around the statue. There was a piece missing. But unless we catch 'em . . .' He shrugged. 'Probably in some scrote's shed somewhere. Some lone Nazi thinks he's got one over on the Jewish Illuminati by nicking a shroud. I blame the fucking internet.'

Mumtaz smiled. Lee ranted about the internet in just the same way. The proliferation of conspiracy theories, like the one about a sinister cabal of Jewish bankers known as the Illuminati, who were planning to take over the world, was out of control.

'Bernie is aware that you guys have got more important things to do than go looking for a dead man,' Mumtaz said. 'I mean, unless Rudolf's body and the statue were in the coffin together, then the actual bodysnatching must have happened years ago. What he's after is information about Rudolf Baruch. He knows why he came to the UK and when, but he's no real notion of who he was. His father's dead and Bernie's pretty much cut off from that side of his family. The only lead I've got so far is the name Chani Freedland. She married Rudolf in 1939. She was British and came from Stepney Green.'

'A lot of Jews in Stepney Green back then.'

'But from what Bernie told me, it seems that when she married Rudolf, Chani lost contact with her family for some reason.'

'Maybe the Freedlands didn't like him.'

'Maybe. Rudolf was killed during a Nazi bombing raid on London on 26th September 1940,' Mumtaz said. 'Chani was eight months pregnant with Bernie's father, Morris, who

29

of course never knew Rudolf. From what Bernie has told me, it seems that Chani brought the boy up alone, working as a seamstress, although I don't know where.'

'The old East End was full of sweatshops back in the day,' Tony said. 'And of course some women worked from home. Where did Rudolf Baruch come from?'

'What is now Czechia. Prague. I've told Bernie that if we have to make contact with the authorities over there, it won't come cheap.'

'No. Any idea what he did for a living?'

'None. He got out just before the Nazis invaded. He was twenty-seven.'

Tony shook his head. 'Well, if I pick up anything about Rudolf, I'll let you know.' He sipped his coffee. 'How's Lee?'

She sighed. 'He's at Walthamstow at the coroner's about Kathy Appiah. When I spoke to him this morning, he said he couldn't work out what verdict he was hoping for. In spite of no note it was almost certainly suicide, but her family are devout Christians and so he hopes for their sake it's declared misadventure. I mean, I guess that suicide would make people think more.'

'Would it? I don't see it, Mumtaz. It's all based on hope innit, the internet romance thing. Everyone wants to believe it's real, even when they know deep down that it ain't. We all want to be loved, don't we. Even if it could destroy us.'

Mumtaz knew. She'd wanted, against all evidence to the contrary, to believe her husband had loved her, even when he'd abused her. Ahmet Hakim had died leaving her alone with his teenage daughter Shazia, whom he had also abused. And in spite of the fact the girl had hated her stepmother at first, the two of them had made a life together and now Shazia was a trainee detective constable with the Met. Mumtaz was the only female British Asian PI in east London, as far as she knew. She was also engaged in an on-and-off affair with her white British boss, who did love her. She in turn loved him too, but at the moment, he wanted commitment while she wasn't ready. Mumtaz had done marriage once and hadn't liked it.

Her legs were bad and so Bernie Bennett knew he'd have to let Rose Arnold in rather than trying to talk to her on his front doorstep. He lived in one of the older houses on Shipman Road, while Rose was in a council place at the top of the turning. Knowing how slow she was now, he reckoned it must've taken her ten minutes to get to his place.

'How'd you get on with my Lee? He sort you out?' Rose said as she stepped painfully into Bernie's hallway.

After settling Rose down on the sofa in his living room, Bernie made tea for them both and brought some clean ashtrays. While Rose lit up, he said, 'I never saw Lee, saw Mumtaz.'

'Oh. Where was he then?' Rose asked.

'Court. But didn't matter. I told her about it, and she said she'd try and help. She's nice, in't she? But you never told me she covered her head.'

'Oh, yeah,' Rose said. 'I don't get it, Bernie. Schtupping my boy and yet she wears that. I like her. Lee's besotted, but I think he's on a hiding to nothing. She'll end up marrying one of her own.'

'You never told me they was schtupping,' Bernie said.

'Oh, yeah.'

As children of Jews, albeit on only one side of their respective families, both Rose Arnold and Bernie Bennett lapsed into Yiddish from time to time. Besides, 'schtupping' sounded so much better than 'fucking'.

'So what'd she say, Mumtaz?' Rose asked.

'Said she'd give it a whirl,' Bernie said. 'Try and find out as much as she can about me granddad. But she was not hopeful about his body.'

'Oh, Lee'll help you with that, love,' Rose said.

'Don't know that he can,' Bernie said. 'Like Mumtaz said, the coppers can't waste time looking for a dead bloke, can they?'

'Ah, but my Lee knows people, Bernie.'

'What people?'

'People you wouldn't want to meet down a dark alley.'

Bernie took Rosie home when he left to do his shift at the hospital. It was a nice sunny evening by that time, but rather than feeling better now that he was actively seeking Rudolf, he felt depressed and a little bit paranoid. What was he going to find out about Rudolf – if anything? His body was long gone. It had probably been missing for decades. Did the golem look like Rudolf, or was it just a statue of some other man? Had Rudolf even died in 1940? Bernie got on the bus and tapped his Oyster card. As he sat down, he looked at the man sitting behind him for a moment and then slumped down with his chin on his chest. If only it were winter, he could hide in his overcoat.

THREE

The face, if not the body, was well made. A man with black hair, a long Roman nose (rather like Lee's) and startling, aquamarine-blue eyes. Its mouth, whose lips looked fleshy, was slightly open, leading Mumtaz to wonder whether the artist who'd created it had put a slip of paper into its mouth.

While keeping the photographs Tony had sent her on her laptop screen, Mumtaz had also opened up various windows containing more information about golem legends. Created by Kabbalists – sort of magicians – to protect the Jews in places like Prague and Vilnius, they were 'mud men' made of clay which, via a succession of spells, could be animated to disable or kill the enemies of the community. As far as she could tell, a golem could only be killed or deactivated in one way, and this was where the paper in the mouth came in. On the paper, the magician, who was also usually a rabbi, would inscribe the word *emet* – meaning truth – prior to performing the ceremony of activation. So if the golem began to go out of control, the magician/rabbi could take the paper out of its mouth, cross out the initial 'e' (aleph in Hebrew) which would leave the word *met*, meaning death. At this point the golem would 'die' and turn to dust.

This thing had been dubbed 'the East Ham Golem' by the press. But was it a golem or was it just a mannequin made out of clay? Because it had been found in a Jewish cemetery, 'golem' had probably been too tempting a term to avoid. But in reality it was simply a statue of a man. What made it unsettling was where it had been found. Someone had buried it, probably with all due ceremony, in a grave meant for a real corpse.

Mumtaz sent Tony Bracci an email with some further questions.

Her phone rang, and without looking at who was calling she picked it up.

'Mumtaz,' she heard Lee say. 'Are you busy?'

'I'm looking into Bernie Bennett's case,' she said.

She was, but also she didn't want to talk to Lee – not unless it was in the office, about work.

'I was wondering whether I could come round?' he asked.

She'd spoken to him briefly, just before she left the office, and knew that Kathy Appiah's inquest had upset him.

'I'm really into this golem thing,' she said. 'Is it urgent?'

There was a pause and then he said, 'No. Just . . .'

'How are Ezra and his father?' she cut in.

'Ezra's taken the old man down the pub,' Lee said. 'They wanted me to go with them but . . .'

'So go if you're lonely,' she said. 'I'm sure they'd like the company. Where have they gone?'

'The Holly Tree.'

'That's a lovely pub,' she said. 'And just down the road from you. Lee, they asked you to join them for a reason. Ezra probably needs some support with his dad. I'd go.'

'I wanna talk to you!'

That was quite an outburst, if not unexpected. Five months ago when she'd told him that she wanted to take things more slowly, Lee had been devastated. Had it been the first time she'd pulled away from him, it wouldn't have been so bad, but it wasn't. Their relationship was conforming to a pattern that wasn't healthy. And although Lee didn't have a psychology degree like Mumtaz, he knew it. They'd start their relationship as friends and sometimes lovers and within weeks Lee was asking her to move in with him. Then talk quickly turned to marriage. Then Mumtaz stopped it.

Again, she would explain how her years of marriage to her violent husband Ahmet had made it very hard for her to trust any man, which Lee would counter by asking her whether she was going to let a dead man define her life for ever. But Mumtaz's reluctance to commit to a relationship with Lee was about more than memories of the horror of her marriage. It was also about the fact that now she was free, she valued that. As a stepmother devoted to her stepdaughter, as a professional working woman and as an observant Muslim, Mumtaz did all these things in her own way, not asking anyone's permission. Her life wasn't easy, she was often skint, but she was free and she loved it. She also loved Lee Arnold, but at a distance.

Eventually it was Mumtaz who spoke.

'Lee, I'm busy. I want to get Bernie Bennett's case kicked

off, which means I have to work out who may and who may not be able to help me. The Jewish community in this part of London is small now and—'

'Vi,' Lee said. 'Her mum was Jewish, speak to Vi.'

Mumtaz had thought about contacting ex-Inspector Violet Collins. Now retired from the Met, Vi had been Tony Bracci's old boss and, for many years, Lee Arnold's lover. Consequently, for Mumtaz to contact Vi had always been a bit problematic. But in spite of this, it was a good idea. Although she hadn't been brought up Jewish, Vi knew a lot of the old families who either still lived in the East End or in nearby Essex.

Mumtaz agreed she would call Vi and then said to Lee, 'Go to the pub with Ezra and his dad.'

Then she put the phone down.

Bernie often walked home after work. It wasn't far. The only problem was crossing the A13, which involved several sets of traffic lights, road islands and a lot of twitchy drivers. Also the Custom House end of Prince Regent Lane, near where Bernie lived, could be a bit dodgy at night. It wasn't so much the kids hanging out round the chippy or the alkies peering through the window of the offie – it was those you couldn't see that were the problem. Men mainly, hanging back from the street lights in side alleys, lurking down behind Jay's General Store, talking in hushed voices, passing things to one another.

You didn't dare look. If you did, if you were lucky, they'd just tell you to 'mind your fucking business'. If you weren't lucky, they'd accuse you of 'disrespect' and kick the shit out of you. So Bernie kept his head down, eyes to the ground as he made his way off Prince Regent Lane and into Shipman Road. As he passed the Arnolds' house he could see that the kitchen light was on. But Rose was unlikely to still be up. That would be for her eldest boy, Roy. He'd died a while ago, but Rose still kept a light on for him. An alcoholic, like his father, Roy Arnold would have been Bernie's age, although no one would ever have guessed it. Unlike his younger brother Lee, Roy had always had a face like a smacked arse. Rail thin, he'd had a massive drinker's hooter and had been beginning to turn yellow when he died. The only consolation for Rose was that now Roy was dead, no one smashed her place up any more. It was also said that his brother had helped put an end to all that too. When Roy had threatened their mother, Lee had given him a good hiding. Kicked the shit out of him.

Bernie took his door key out of his pocket and opened his front gate. Usually when he was on late shift, he made himself something to eat when he got home. But this time he was too knackered to think about food. There had been a lot of blood on the floor in A&E this evening, and also talking to that private investigator had taken it out of him. Just off to bed for him. Bernie went to put the key in the door, but found that he couldn't. Because it was already open.

'You can sleep in the box room if you want to make a night of it, Vi,' Mumtaz said.

Even over the phone, she'd been able to tell almost immediately that Vi Collins was bored shitless and gagging to get out.

'So if I bring a bottle of Malibu, a couple of cartons of

pineapple and a packet of fags over to yours . . .'

'It's a lovely warm evening, we can sit in my garden,' Mumtaz said.

'You're a sweetheart. Here, do you like Turkish delight?'

'Yeah.'

Vi had just got back from a holiday to Turkey. No doubt she was going to bring a lot of *lokum* she'd bought there, together with almost certainly many salacious stories about her encounters with waiters and taxi drivers. Although Vi and Mumtaz couldn't be more different, they got on well and enjoyed each other's company.

An hour later Vi arrived carrying bottles, boxes of Turkish delight and an overnight bag. Mumtaz had told her she needed her help in the full knowledge that if there was one thing Vi Collins craved, it was being needed.

After organising drinks and snacks and putting on the fairy lights in the garden, the women sat down to talk. Mumtaz had lived in her current home for three years. Situated in Sebert Road, Forest Gate, it was an upstairs flat in an Edwardian house overlooking Manor Park Cemetery. An old man lived downstairs but he rarely went out, and so most of the time Mumtaz had the small, flower-stocked garden to herself. A stone's throw from the great open space known as Wanstead Flats, this part of Forest Gate was quiet and almost rural.

'There were a few Jewish girls went to my school,' Vi said after she'd lit up a fag and taken a gulp of Malibu and pineapple. 'Not religious types. Sarah Bonnell was a bog-standard comp.'

'Still is,' Mumtaz said.

'There you are,' Vi said. 'I never took much notice of what

people were back in those days. My mum married out, as you know. And although I knew them, we weren't close because of me dad.'

Vi's father had been a Traveller.

'I'm looking for a family called Freedland from Stepney Green,' Mumtaz said. 'This Bernie Bennett's grandmother, Chani, was a Freedland. But when she married his grandfather it seems she lost contact with her family.'

'Well, my mum was from Stepney originally,' Vi said. 'They were called Blatt, her people. Both my grandparents was milliners. I know they lived on Globe Road and they worked from home until they got their shop in Canning Town. There used to be a synagogue on the Barking Road, but I think that'd gone by my time. There is still a synagogue in Stepney I believe, but I think it's only open on High Holy Days now. You know, you could do worse than contacting them.'

'Mmm.'

'And Jewish Care,' Vi said. 'I'm sure there's still a community centre round there. I wish I could help you more, but I don't really have contacts in the Jewish community – unless they've broken the law.'

'But you know some Jewish crims, right?'

'Some. But no one called Freedland.'

They both sat in silence for a moment and then Mumtaz said, 'And there's something else, Vi.'

'Something worrying you?'

Mumtaz pulled on the edge of her headscarf.

Fucking hell, this getting old shit was a ball-ache! Since when did he leave the front door open? And if he had, did this mark

39

a further development from trying to put the kettle in the fridge on Sunday and forgetting a dentist appointment back in May?

Bernie Bennett walked across his threshold and turned on the hall light. In retrospect that wasn't the wisest thing to do. Anyone could have got inside his house while he was at work. He approached the living room with trepidation. Knowing his luck they'd probably nicked the telly and shat on the carpet. But when he switched the light on, everything looked just the same as he'd left it. In fact, as he went from room to room, he couldn't find anything missing – which, to Bernie, seemed like some kind of miracle. Admittedly there'd been no one around on Shipman Road when he'd come home. But the area, while in some places 'gentrifying', was still known to be a bit rough round the edges from time to time.

By the time he did finally stop checking and decide to get ready for bed, Bernie had managed to convince himself that he'd probably left the door open while he'd been distracted by Rose Arnold's departure. No one was in his house nor, as far as he could tell, had they been. It was only when he was brushing his teeth in the bathroom that a doubt crossed his mind. It was a warm night and so he had the bathroom window open. As he casually scanned his back garden, had he seen something or someone move out there? Or was it just his imagination?

'I don't want to alienate people,' Mumtaz said.

'You'll only alienate them if you're not yourself,' Vi said. 'You wear hijab. It's important to you.'

'Yes, but the atmosphere now is so febrile, Vi. What with

the terror attacks in the past few years, coupled with the rise of the right in this country, Brexit . . .'

'Look,' Vi said. 'There will always be people who tar certain groups all with the same brush. They do it to Muslims, they do it to Jews, Travellers, anyone they can point at and say, "Here's the reason I've got a shit life." And yes, I know it's easy for me to say because I can "pass" very easily and you can't. And it ain't fair that it's always the minority that has to prove that they're not all terrorists, but that's the way it is – and if we start changing ourselves for these bigots we're part of the problem, in my opinion.'

'I just don't want to put people's backs up,' Mumtaz said. 'If I'm speaking to say, a rabbi, I don't want him to feel threatened by me.'

'You're a professional woman, Mumtaz. You're doing a job. Give him, or her, your card. Some Reform rabbis are women these days. These are religious people, they're supposed to play nice. They're paid to. If they won't or can't, then that's their problem not yours.'

'It will be mine if they won't talk to me!'

'Listen, love,' Vi said. 'The story of the East Ham Golem went international. It was so bloody strange, people were talking about it from here to Peru. You ain't gonna have any trouble getting some people to talk to you about it. In fact, I predict you'll probably have more bother getting certain individuals to shut up.'

'Yes, but nobody knows who Bernie Bennett is, Vi. He was kept out of the papers when the story broke. And there's no money in it, not that I can see. Not even Andy Warhol's fifteen minutes of fame. Nothing to Instagram. It's unlikely to make you famous, connection to a desecrated grave. And people these days want that, don't they?'

'Cynical but yes,' Vi said. 'But you know the legend of the golem is dark, man. It's about people being so desperate they have to build a monster to protect themselves. What's more, it's a monster they can't control. And yes I know it's not real, but even in the twenty-first century, this is weird. This is grave-robbing and the occult. This ain't no comfy woo-woo with crystals and angels. You may very well have to winkle relatives out of their shells and the rabbis may well be queasy about the golem, but I'd put money on the idea they know a lot of people who aren't. And then of course,' she smiled, 'there's also Twitter.'

FOUR

Lee Arnold didn't drink and so when he got up the following morning he didn't have a hangover. Ezra and his dad Isiah were not so lucky, and Lee had been woken early that morning by the sound of vomiting coming from the flat upstairs.

While Lee had given up the booze for the very good reason that he was an alcoholic, having to face reality head-on, especially on Saturday mornings when he was unlikely to be seeing Mumtaz, was not easy. If the football were on, he could go out to West Ham later, but it wasn't. His daughter lived down in Margate with a bloke he could cheerfully kill, so that was a no-no, and his mum, who was nearby, drove him mad with her endlessly repeated stories. Poor old Rosie hadn't been the same since Lee's older brother Roy had died during Covid. Roy had been an alcoholic too but, unlike Lee, he'd never managed to stop.

Walking into his living room, fag in one hand, cup of tea

in the other, Lee spoke to the only living being he was likely to encounter that day, his mynah bird Chronus.

'Good kip?' he asked the bird as he flopped down on his sofa.

Chronus, who had been taught a huge amount of West Ham songs and player names, had also been instructed to swear.

'Stick it up yer arse!'

'Charming,' Lee said. Then to himself, 'But I s'pose that's gonna be my level today.'

He was still pissed off from the night before. First Mumtaz had knocked him back, then he'd had to watch Ezra and Isiah Appiah get pissed and tear themselves apart yet again about the death of Kathy. They'd both blamed themselves – Isiah for taking money from his daughter for so long and apparently without thought, Ezra for not seeing Kathy often enough. Lee had told them both that they had nothing to reproach themselves for. Kathy had never told anyone she needed love, but she had and badly. Vlad had been an accident waiting to happen to Kathy.

But she was still dead and that fucking stank.

The plan was to get the Tube to Stepney Green then walk to the farmers' market at the City Farm, have a poke around there and then head for Commercial Road and the Congregation of Jacob Synagogue. Of course the building wouldn't be open, but Mumtaz wanted to see it. She also wanted to go to the farmers' market. Vi, who really didn't, tagged along for the company and because she knew where the synagogue was.

As the two women walked into the City Farm, Vi reluctantly

put her fag out and wished she hadn't worn stiletto heels. She was also a bit taken aback by the smell.

'Christ! This don't half honk!' she said as she fanned her face. 'All this muck on the floor!'

Mumtaz, smiling, said, 'It's the goats. The one time I visited Bangladesh we stayed with my grandparents and they had goats. Smelt exactly like this.'

Vi shook her head. Looking around the stalls selling organic vegetables, olive oil, honey and home-made cheese, she said, 'If I stay here too long, I'll find myself buying an air fryer.'

'Why?'

'This is middle-class land, innit?' she said. 'God Almighty, people used to queue up to leave Stepney! Now the floral-dress brigade have turned up with decking and olives!'

'You know you're a terrible classist, don't you Vi,' Mumtaz said.

'Babe, if they hadn't put the property prices up round here, I'd say come with my blessing. But for fuck's sake, some of these houses round here sell for millions. No one local stands a chance.'

'Well, look, I'm just going to buy some cheese and olives,' Mumtaz said. 'And then we can go.'

'You knock yourself out,' Vi said. 'I'll go and sit in the caff.'

Mumtaz watched Vi head off, knowing that very soon she'd discover the place she was headed to was more a cafè than a caff.

A knock on the street door brought Bernie out of a dream he'd been having about losing his keys, and into a reality that included his daughter shouting up at his bedroom window.

'Dad! Dad!'

Ever since he'd hit sixty, Kelly, had been fixated on the idea that her dad could drop dead at any moment. She might be right, but Bernie wasn't prepared to give it much time himself. So if he died, he died.

Opening his bedroom window he called down, 'It's alright, Kel! Just overslept.'

Kelly, who was a large woman in her late thirties, put a hand up to her chest and said, 'Thank God! Honestly Dad, don't frighten me like this. You'll put me in therapy!'

'You can't afford it,' Bernie said.

He let Kelly in and made them both tea. Her appearance disturbed him. His daughter watched a lot of 'reality' TV and aspired to the way many of the women looked on programmes like *Love Island*. Consequently, she had both very large lips and exceptionally dark eyebrows.

'Dad, Darren doesn't know I'm here,' Kelly said.

'Oh, why's that?'

Darren, Bernie's son-in-law, was the proprietor of a nail bar in Billericay. Darren was perma-tanned and gym-honed; Bernie called him 'Dickie' in the privacy of his own head, after Ian Dury's Essex 'hero' in his 1970s hit 'Billericay Dickie'. Neither liked nor loathed by Bernie, Darren was an uneasy mixture of metrosexual camp and far-right thuggery Bernie chose to ignore.

'I told him I was coming to see Danielle,' Kelly said. 'He's been raving.'

Danielle was one of Kelly's old friends from school.

'Oh?'

'This gollum business has got to stop, Dad.'

He'd told his daughter he was going to get a private detective involved with the desecration of his grandfather's grave, hoping she had the sense to keep it from her husband. He should've known better.

'I told Darren because we don't have secrets, Dad,' Kelly said. 'You know how all that stuff upset him at the time. Now he's beside himself.'

'I don't know why,' Bernie said. 'It's got nothing to do with him.'

'Yes, but it's me, innit, Dad. And the kids. All this Jewish business. Nobody's interested! Especially not now.'

'What do you mean, Kel?'

'Nobody wants to know about refugees,' she said. 'Coming here and taking benefits and being put up in hotels. It's disgraceful! And you know how Darren feels about all that.'

'Kel, my grandfather came here in 1938,' Bernie said. 'If he hadn't come here, he would've died in the camps.'

'What camps?' She stared straight at him as she said it. Something had changed – and not for the better.

'What's Darren got himself involved with, Kel?' Bernie asked. 'You know him and me've never seen eye to eye about politics. But I've never heard so much as a squeak about Holocaust denial and let me tell you now, I won't have that in my house.'

'Oh, don't worry Dad, Darren won't be coming here any time soon.'

'I won't have it from you neither.' Bernie said.

Kelly sat quietly for a few moments and then she said,

'Dad, Darren's hoping to become a local councillor next year.'

'Is he.'

'Yes, and if people get to know about this gollum thing, Darren thinks it may damage his campaign.'

Bernie lit a fag.

Kelly waved smoke away from her face and said, 'Dad!'

Ignoring her discomfort, Bernie said, 'So who's he planning to be a councillor for? National Front?'

'They're called the Britannia Party,' she said. 'And they're fielding councillors in Billericay and Loughton this year. Their policies make a lot of sense. Everyone can see that these people coming across the English Channel in their small boats are just take, take, take. As soon as they land, they get given a council place. And they cause trouble. Bombing and using white girls as their sex slaves. It's all over the papers, Dad. It's not just me and Darren. Britannia want to deport immediately so none of this happens. I mean, I know you're soft on these sorts of things, but what you have to understand is that if we don't get rid of them now they'll take us over, and then we'll have to have Ramadan and cover our heads—'

'Can you hear yourself?' Bernie said. 'Christ, girl, I never brought you up to be like this. Refugees don't want to leave their countries. Who in their right mind would? And anyway, if you're talking about Muslims, what's that got to do with my Jewish grandparents?'

'Darren says a Jewish connection is unhelpful.'

'Well, I'm sorry if my existence is "unhelpful" to Darren, but I'm gonna find Rudolf Baruch whether he likes it or not,' Bernie said. 'Anyway, people won't make any connection between him and me unless someone tells them.'

'That gollum thing was all over the papers, Dad,' Kelly said.

'Golem, not gollum.' Bernie put a hand up to his forehead. 'Christ! I wasn't named, Kel. Nor were you.'

'Dad! Please!'

Bernie shook his head. 'Look, Kel, I'm doing this. I have to. I'm a Bennett, you're a Ross, it's a million miles away. If you like, we don't have to see each other until all this is over. But I'm telling you now that if your husband wants to stop me finding out the truth about my family, then he can fuck right off. I don't give him advice about getting involved with a load of racist nutters, do I? So he can give me the same courtesy and leave me alone to do my own thing. And if he don't like it, you can tell him from me that I don't fucking care!'

'Doc?'

'DI Bracci, it's Saturday, my day off. What do you want?' Dr Benedict Gabor said into his phone.

'Cast your mind back to March,' Tony said. 'The golem?'

'How can I ever forget!'

'Interested to know whether you found a piece of paper in its mouth,' Tony said.

Benedict was foraging in Epping Forest. Today's mission was to gather enough elderflowers to make sweet elderflower cordial, as well as adding what would hopefully be left over to his elderberry tonic. Benedict put his collecting basket down on the forest floor and concentrated on his call.

'Paper? I don't know,' he said. 'You were there, DI Bracci, and if you access my report you'll see that once I realised the thing wasn't human, my part in what happened to it next was zero.'

'So you don't know whether it was dated?'

'As in, how old it was? No,' he said. 'It went down to Belvedere eventually.'

'Do you know whether anyone else looked at it until it was put into storage?' Tony asked.

'What, you mean like a historian?'

'Yeah.'

'I don't,' he said. 'Why so many questions about this, DI Bracci?'

'The golem's grandson, Bernie Bennett, is employing a PI I know to try and find out more about his grandfather.'

'Nothing to do with the police,' Benedict said.

'No, but if we can help, I'd like to,' Tony said. 'Bennett's obviously still traumatised and who can blame him?'

'Take your point,' Benedict said. 'I mean I don't know how these things work, but maybe consider getting permission for your PI to go down to Belvedere to see for himself.'

'Herself,' Tony corrected. 'Maybe that's not such a bad idea. Thanks, Doc.'

And then he hung up. Now Benedict needed to find some beech trees. Soon it would be Midsummer and he needed to collect a supply of beech twigs for members of the coven to write their wishes on. Buried in the ground they would gradually rot until, at some point, they would invariably come true.

Vi was earwigging on a conversation between two young women at the next table. One of them lived in a flat next door to the Congregation of Jacob Synagogue on the Commercial Road. As Mumtaz came and sat down next to her, Vi mimed what she was doing and so Mumtaz just drank her tea in silence.

In reality the 'women' were girls – both students and both twenty at the most. One blonde, one brunette. Their conversation had started with the brunette asking the blonde how she was getting on in her new flat – or 'apartment'. These were posh girls whose chatter had for a while confirmed all of Vi's prejudices about middle-class people moving into Stepney Green. Apparently the blonde's father had bought the flat for her when she became a student at nearby Queen Mary College.

'I've found this wonderful second-hand shop on Broadway Market,' the blonde had said. 'All mid-twentieth-century stuff.'

'So, like, Ercol and things like that?' the brunette asked.

'Yeah! And industrial.'

'Oh, I love industrial!'

'Metal filing cabinets and those sort of like big metal factory lamps. Honestly, it's amazing. You'll love it.'

'Sounds fab.'

'I just wish I had some outside space,' the blonde said. 'I mean I've got window boxes, you know. But I would've loved to have a little patch for herbs and things like that.'

'Mmm.' Her friend drank her coffee.

'And it's a bit weird being so near to the synagogue where Dad used to go when he was a child,' the blonde said.

It was at this point that Vi's ears had pricked up. Then Mumtaz had arrived.

The blonde continued, 'My living on the Commercial Road gives him the excuse to pop over from Gerrards Cross and wallow in nostalgia.'

'Your dad is quite old now, Pipps. I mean he must've been retired for like, years.'

'My brother took over the business when I was still at school,' Pipps said. 'Daddy's, like, eighty-five I think? Weird. He even goes to services sometimes. That's why I've got three bedrooms, so he can stay.'

The brunette laughed. 'Oh my God, what does Ronan do when your dad's in town?'

'Stays in Peckham,' Pipps said. 'If Daddy met Ronan it'd be intense!'

They both laughed. Mumtaz's phone beeped to indicate she had a text. For a moment the two girls looked over at her and then drank their drinks.

Mumtaz's text was from her father, Baharat Huq. She read it and sighed. It said, *I know it's none of my beeswax but if you love Lee and he loves you, you should be together. Allah has seen fit to bring you together and so you should be, even though your mother disagrees. I love that you wear hijab, Mumtaz – it warms my heart, which is far from my religion these days, as you know. But Lee has offered to convert for you! I mean, I don't know why you wait. I love you, your father.*

Mumtaz put her phone back in her handbag and concentrated on her coffee. Vi raised an eyebrow but said nothing.

Then Pipps came out with, 'Apparently my granddad was like a singer or whatever they call it at that synagogue.'

'Cantor,' Vi butted in.

'Excuse me?'

'They're called cantors, the singers in synagogue,' she continued. 'Sorry, love, I couldn't help overhearing. My granddad went to the Congregation of Jacob Synagogue too.'

'Oh. Amazing!'

Pipps's friend smiled.

'I've just come with my friend to show her the synagogue,' Vi continued. 'Doing a bit of family history.'

'Oh, that's brilliant,' Pipps said. 'So, like, are you Jewish?'

'Me mum was,' Vi said. 'Our family was called Blatt. Your dad might've known them.'

'Wow! My God, so we could be, like, related?'

'Dunno about that . . .'

''Cause like, my name's Richmond, but it was Reichman. My dad changed it.'

'A lot of people did.'

Pipps looked at her friend and then said, 'Hey, do you mind if we join you?'

'Knock yourself out,' Vi said.

And so Pipps and her friend Caroline pulled their chairs up to Vi and Mumtaz's table and the four women chatted. At no time did the name Freedland come up, but by the time they left, email addresses had been exchanged and Vi had rather warmed to the two posh girls.

What did you have to do to get some fucking peace?

When Kelly had gone, Bernie had made himself a bit of lunch and then fallen asleep in his chair. The first thing he did on hearing the doorbell was look at his watch. Five-fifteen.

He'd been asleep for hours.

As he pushed himself out of his chair, the doorbell rang again.

'Alright! I'm coming!' he yelled as he walked down the hallway and opened the front door.

'What?'

It was a man carrying a briefcase. Probably no more than forty, dark; he was tall and slim. Bernie didn't know him.

'Mr Bernard Bennett?'

He had a foreign accent.

'Who wants to know?' Bernie asked.

'Are you Mr Bernard Bennett?' the man repeated.

'Why?'

The man took a card out of his jacket pocket and gave it to Bernie, who looked at it and then looked up. It made no sense.

'My name is Bohuslav Kovar, I am a journalist from Czechia,' the man said. 'If you are Bernard Bennett, I may have some information for you.'

Bernie wasn't really fully awake yet. He rubbed his eyes and said, 'About what?'

'Look, Mr Bennett, it is private – may I come in? I have information.'

'About what?' Bernie reiterated. 'Try and understand, I work lates and I'm bloody shattered.'

'About your grandfather,' Bohuslav Kovar said. 'He was from Prague, I think. He was called Rudolf?'

Bernie looked the man up and down and then said, 'You weren't in my garden last night, were you?'

'Your garden? No. Why should I be in your garden?'

Someone had been and this was weird. A random foreigner turning up at his door hot on the heels of those strange shenanigans last night . . .

'I dunno,' Bernie said. 'But weird shit has been happening to me and I don't like it.'

'Look, Mr Bennett,' Kovar said, 'I can show you my ID. I am a journalist from Czechia.'

He took a copy of a newspaper out of his briefcase and held it up for Bernie to read.

Vi eventually left Mumtaz's flat just before midnight. They'd spent a nice afternoon at the farmers' market and had then gone with the two girls, Pipps and Caroline, to the synagogue on the Commercial Road. Pipps had promised Vi she'd speak to her father about 'family stuff' and get back to her.

Except when she was buying olives, Mumtaz had felt like a spare wheel almost all day. What the two girls had thought about the presence of an almost silent Muslim woman, she didn't know. But she'd not felt comfortable, especially when they'd been outside the synagogue staring at it. A lot of words like 'seder' and 'minyan' had gone right over her head, making Mumtaz feel that if she was going to help Bernie Bennett, her knowledge of Judaism had to improve. It was great having Vi around to help her, but she couldn't be with her all the time.

Now, however, she was tired. She'd done a lot of walking with Vi during the day and her legs ached. Vi herself had ended the day with her stilettos strung around her neck, walking barefoot. Much as she wanted to carry on with her research work, Mumtaz decided to get some sleep.

It was as she was pulling the curtains shut in her bedroom

that she thought she saw something move down in the garden. It was probably foxes. There were loads of them in Forest Gate and everyone knew that they roamed the graveyard next door most nights. That was what she told herself before she got into bed.

'So you're telling me that Rudolf was an undertaker?' Bernie asked.

'No. He was a . . .' He thought for a moment until the word came. 'Embalmer.'

Bernie Bennett shook his head. 'I never heard that before,' he said. 'My dad never said that.'

'Your father probably didn't know,' Bohuslav said. 'You say your father was a child when Rudolf died.'

Bohuslav Kovar seemed sincere. The story he'd written for *The Guardian* about the golem looked kosher. And he'd not known anything about someone being in Bernie's garden. He said he'd only arrived in the UK that morning.

'Any story about a golem is big news in my country,' he said. 'So when I heard there was one found here in London, I did some investigations. When Rabbi Loew created the golem in Prague in the sixteenth century, he made a legend that survives to this day. You know, in my city you can buy statues of the golem, jewellery, car stickers, anything!'

'So, you've been here to London before,' Bernie said.

'In April. I try to find you, but I fail,' he said.

When the police had asked Bernie whether he'd rather remain anonymous when the golem story had broken, he'd said yes.

'So how'd you find me this time?'

'I find this Plashet Cemetery and I speak to people there,' he said. 'Also, I don't just work on this story. I am freelance, Bernie, and so I work on many stories. But Rudolf Baruch and Levi Rozenberg have fascinated me my whole life. And, especially because I am a Jew, I have grown up with stories about the golem.'

'You know that was a name the British press made up, don't you?' Bernie said. 'I've seen it, and it's a statue. I don't even know whether it looks like Rudolf.'

'I know this is hard for you,' Bohuslav said.

'Do you? Do you really?'

Bohuslav sighed. 'No, of course I don't,' he said. 'But I think you want to know the truth about your grandfather, don't you?'

'I do.' Should he tell this man he'd hired a private detective to do just that? No.

'Rudolf Baruch was not an unusual name in my country before the Second World War,' Bohuslav said. 'Then we have the Holocaust.' He shrugged. 'No Baruch people in Prague now. All anyone knows about the name is the embalmer, because this is famous.'

'Why?'

'Because Rudolf Baruch disappeared,' he said. 'The families of both Rudolf Baruch and Levi Rozenberg all died in Auschwitz. But there are no records of Rudolf after 1938. I cannot be sure that your grandfather is the Rudolf Baruch I have spent many years looking for. But I think so. He was the right age, he was Czech from Prague.'

'So did Levi Rozenberg come here too?' Bernie asked.

'It is said he died in Theresienstadt Ghetto before his

family were taken on to Auschwitz. But I am not so sure. That I have yet to discover. But if Rudolf came here, then why not Levi too? Rudolf was apprentice to Levi.'

'So why are these men famous then?'

Bohuslav sighed. 'Because some people in my country believe they stole something. I believe this. But it is hard to prove.'

'Why?'

'Because they stole from a woman who was already dead,' Bohuslav said.

FIVE

His brother had always managed to ruin Sunday lunch. Ever since Roy and Lee Arnold's father had died, the former had taken over the old man's role as violent pisshead at the top of the table. And like his dad, Roy had always criticised Rose Arnold's cooking. Sometimes he'd even thrown his roast dinner at her. Now Roy was dead, it was just Rose and Lee, which meant that Sunday lunch was quiet and civilised. That said, Lee knew that for all his faults, Roy had been loved by his mum and she missed him. Sometimes, especially in view of the fact things were so difficult between him and Mumtaz, Lee wondered whether he might move back to Custom House to be with his mother. But then she'd nag him about something and he'd realise that was impossible.

A large part of the problem Mumtaz had with their relationship stemmed from her meeting, in a professional capacity, with a white British woman who had married a

Muslim British Asian and now chose to wear a burka. Not only was she the only woman in her husband's family to wear a burka, but she was the only woman who covered at all. And while Mumtaz could understand this woman saying that as soon as she came into contact with Muslim values she felt at home, her covering, rather than helping her to integrate into her husband's family, actually worked against it. Her mode of dress alienated her own white relatives who, she claimed, blamed her husband for 'radicalising' her. At the same time her husband's family considered her 'radical' too, and many of them wouldn't have anything to do with her. She had become, had indeed put herself at, the centre of attention for many, many people. She'd come to Hakim and Arnold because she'd thought her husband was having an affair. He wasn't. He, like the rest of his family, was distrusted by her because she believed he was not Muslim enough. In taking on something that should have been positive, this woman had lost herself entirely, throwing Mumtaz's belief in the validity of cross-cultural relationships into disarray. What if her love for Lee made her become 'someone else'? What if it made her, like this woman, an object of derision and pity?

Although Mumtaz was the one with the psychology degree, it had been Lee who had dubbed this woman a 'sociopath'. 'It's not about faith or choices or any of that stuff, but just about her,' he'd told Mumtaz. But her fear of becoming 'other' in some way, should she choose to marry him, obsessed her and he had given up trying to find a way through.

A knock at his mother's front door jerked him away from these thoughts.

'I'll get it,' Rose Arnold said when her son appeared not to want to move.

When she returned to the dinner table it was with her neighbour and his latest client, Bernie Bennett.

'I'm sorry to disturb you having your dinner,' he said.

Rose, who had cooked a very large turkey and a huge amount of vegetables, said, 'Oh, sit down and help yourself, Bernie. It's not like we're going to eat all this today.'

She often cooked 'large' so that she didn't have to switch the oven on again that week. Lee usually got a big plate of leftovers to take home.

But Bernie, although he did sit at the table with them, didn't help himself to any food. He also didn't speak and so eventually Lee said, 'Mumtaz's told me about your case, Bernie. Interesting.'

'Mmm,' he said, 'although . . .'

'Although?'

'At least have a drumstick,' his mother said. 'I ain't put nothing on it. No garlic or nothing funny.'

Which was why Lee was struggling to get through it.

'I wonder whether it's worth raking all that stuff about the golem up now it's all done and dusted,' Bernie said.

'I thought you wanted to find out more about your granddad,' Lee replied.

'I did. I do, but . . .'

'But what?'

'It all happened a long time ago. And I wonder . . .'

A lot of people had second thoughts about employing PIs. It wasn't cheap and it could reveal things that perhaps some people didn't really want to know. Sometimes an investigation resulted in a family or matrimonial rift.

'It's normal to have doubts,' Lee said. 'The past isn't something we can control, so we can become scared of it. Has anything made you feel like this?'

Rose went into the kitchen to get Bernie a plate.

'My daughter's not keen on me doing it,' Bernie said. 'All the Jewish stuff, you know.'

'She's afraid of anti-Semitism?'

Rose returned and said, 'You don't want to let them get to you, Bern. You've a right to know what all that business was about.'

'I know, but I'm . . .' He shook his head. 'What about if I find out something horrible? Something I never wanted to know?'

Lee put his knife and fork down and rested his elbows on the table while his mother filled a plate for Bernie.

'Like what?' he asked.

'Oh, I dunno . . . Like if my granddad was a murderer or if maybe he wasn't who I think he is.'

'It's a risk,' Lee said. 'It's a risk for everyone.'

Rose put a large roast dinner down in front of Bernie and said, 'Eat.'

Lee didn't know much about Bernie Bennett. He'd come to live on Shipman Road after Lee left. But he knew the look of a person who'd been 'got at' by someone who didn't necessarily have his best interests at heart and he had heard things about Bernie's son-in-law, none of them good. Darren Ross, Britannia Party candidate for a local council seat in Billericay, had been born and bred in nearby Canning Town. His family were bog-standard white locals, neither angels nor devils – except for Darren. Hard and ambitious, Darren had been introduced to far-right thuggery via the familiar old route of football hooliganism. When Lee had been a copper in the Met, he'd come across Darren a few times.

Bernie began to eat and then said, 'Lovely gravy, Rose.'

Lee's mum smiled.

Lee said, 'Bernie, I get that your daughter might not like what you're doing too much, but this is about you, not Kelly. It's also, most certainly, not about her Darren.'

Bernie put his knife and fork down on his plate while he chewed.

'Look, mate, I know I've got an interest in this because you're paying me,' Lee said. 'But before you make your final decision, talk to someone else about it. Not Kelly, not Darren, maybe a mate at work or something. I won't charge you a penny until I hear from you. But I'll also not tell Mumtaz yet because I know she's already started making enquiries. Can't say fairer than that, I don't think.'

Undertakers. Someone must have buried Rudolf Baruch. But who?

Mumtaz picked up her phone and called Tony Bracci.

'Do you know who performed Rudolf Baruch's funeral?' she asked without preamble.

'Don't you lot do weekends these days?' Tony said.

'Oh, er, oh I'm sorry, Tone,' Mumtaz said. 'Just trying to get ahead of the game before I'm back in the office tomorrow. Sorry.'

She heard him laugh. 'It's OK,' he said. 'I'm only sinning down the pub. You're right, someone must've done, but I

63

don't know who. To be honest, as soon as we discovered there wasn't a body in Rudolf's grave, we took our foot off the pedal. Enquiries were made as I remember it, but I don't think anyone come up with anything. Undertakers come and go just like other businesses, probably don't exist any more. I imagine a rabbi must've officiated. You'd do better contacting the local synagogues.'

'I've made a start with that,' she said. 'Just trying to cover as many ways into this as I can.'

'I hear ya. Look, I've not been idle myself on your behalf. I spoke to Dr Benedict, the path who unwrapped the golem's shroud. He suggested I try and get you a pass into our storage facility down in Belvedere so you can see it for yourself.'

'That'd be useful,' she said.

'So I was giving it some thought, when it occurred to me that I don't know who it officially belongs to.'

'Well, no one, I—'

'Depends whether Bennett and his family own the burial plot,' Tony said. 'I think he does, and if that's the case there may – and I mean *may* – be an argument for allowing him to see it because it's his property. So if you could persuade him to request to see it and take you with him . . .'

'Mmm. Nice,' she said. 'But hasn't he seen it already?'

'Thought you'd like it,' Tony said. 'And yes, he saw it after Dr Benedict unwrapped it. But on the basis it is his property, he should be able – theoretically – to get to it when he wants.'

Later, when Mumtaz was out in the garden, mowing her small piece of lawn, she recalled the photograph of the golem that Tony had sent her. It was impossible from that to see whether it had anything in its mouth, much less the traditional piece of paper that would allow the magician who had made the figure to control it. But if she saw the golem and saw the piece of paper in its mouth, what then? If she found the word *emet* on the paper, did that mean that, theoretically, the golem was 'active'?

The sound of a twig breaking in the privet hedge made her look around. A pair of foliage-ringed eyes observed her without amusement. A fox. The same one she'd heard the previous night? Maybe. Then it was gone. Mumtaz stopped and leant on the mower's handle.

Standing outside the Congregation of Jacob Synagogue with Vi the previous day had made her think. The size of the place had come as a shock, which had really underlined for her just how many Jews there had been in the East End before the Second World War. Probably close to or maybe even more than the Bangladeshi community that had taken their place. And like those Bangladeshis, the Jews had been abused. Still were. Vi may have missed it, but Mumtaz had noticed the swastika scrawled on a lamp post outside the synagogue. Who'd put it there? Some thick-necked white supremacist? A Muslim kid, thinking himself eager for jihad when he didn't even know what that meant?

People came and went to and from the East End of London. Always had. Brick Lane Jamme Masjid, the mosque her family attended, had been known as the Great Synagogue when Spitalfields was a majority-Jewish area. Before that, the selfsame building had been a church for the Huguenots – the Protestants fleeing religious persecution in their native France. One day some other group would come and replace her people, and what then? What would they say about the Bangladeshis who had once been there? Or would no one ever replace them? Would, as Lee believed, the country just simply slam its door shut now Brexit had been enacted with everyone stuck, static inside a land where nobody moved and nothing ever changed? It was a terrible thought, one that negated the whole history and culture of the East End, and Mumtaz turned away from it. In spite of everything, how could that happen when at every turn into a supposedly gentrified backstreet, one came upon an old inscription in Hebrew or French or Latin. Or, for that matter, when creatures of ancient magic turned up in all-but-abandoned graveyards. The Golem of East Ham had returned for a reason, and it seemed to Mumtaz that she was going to be part of its story.

'Miss Violet Blatt?'

Vi smiled. 'That was my mum's name. Not Violet, Blatt.'

'Oh.'

The voice on the other end of the call was male and posh, and sounded old. Was this possibly Pipps's Jewish dad got hold of the wrong end of the stick?

'Is that Mr Richmond?' she asked.

'Yes! You met my daughter Philippa yesterday? I'm sorry if I got your name wrong. Pipps told me that you were interested in your family, whose name was Blatt. Crossed wires. You are?'

'Violet, Vi Collins.'

'Vi, well my name is Lionel,' he said. 'I understand from Pipps that you're doing a bit of family history. Interested in the Congregation of Jacob.'

'Yeah. Although to be honest I don't know whether Mum's family actually went there, Lionel. My understanding is that a lot of the remaining congregations from all over Stepney consolidated around the Jacob in recent years.'

'That's true,' he said. 'And I have to say, I don't remember the name Blatt.'

'My mum married out,' Vi said. 'But her people did come from Stepney.'

'Do you know when your mum was there?'

'She married me dad in 1948,' Vi said. 'Then they moved to Forest Gate. A long time ago, I know.'

'I was ten in 1948,' Lionel said. 'But I can ask my brother for you if you like. Reggie is eight years older than I am, and still as sharp as a tack. He may well remember.'

'If that's OK.'

'Of course!'

'Although . . .'

Vi had always known that if she was going to be able to use Pipps's dad, she may have to push her luck.

'What?'

'Another name connected to Mum's family is Freedland. You heard of it?'

'It's a not uncommon Jewish name,' he said. 'But you mean in Stepney too, yes?'

'Yes. Sort of thirties, forties time . . .'

'Connected to your family, Vi?'

'It's possible,' she said. Should she actually mention Chani, or . . . Fuck it. 'I'm looking for a Chani Freedland. Married a foreigner about 1938 or '39.'

'A goy?'

'No, a Jew,' she said. 'Newly arrived from Prague. Escaping the Nazis.'

'Oh,' he said. 'Well, I can ask Reggie about that too. Freedland being a more common name, we might have more luck. Why do you want to know about this woman, Vi?'

'She fell out or lost contact with her family after she married this bloke,' she said. 'I want to know why. 'Course, it might've had nothing to do with him.'

'What was his name? Do you know?'

'Baruch,' she said. 'Rudolf Baruch.'

Had she heard a sharp intake of breath from the other end of the line, or had she just imagined it?

'Oh, well,' Lionel said, 'I will ask my brother and let's take it from there, Vi. I do hope that we can help you in your quest. Pipps was pleased she met you and your friend yesterday.'

'She's a nice girl,' Vi said. 'And her mate.'

Later, when she relayed this conversation to Mumtaz, Vi finally managed to articulate what Lionel's apparent intake of breath made her feel.

'It was like I'd poked him in the ribs with me elbow,' she said. 'Like I'd given him a little bit of pain.'

He usually had to stay in places like this if he was working on a speculative story, so it was no hardship. Soulless cubbyholes, generally reserved for construction workers; an ashtray on every balcony, liquid soap in a bottle bolted to the bathroom wall, white sliced toast for breakfast. The main advantage was that places like this were cheap and, in this case, close to where Bohuslav needed to be. Also, he'd stayed

68

here before, back in March/April when the golem story first broke. Although he'd not then known about Bernie Bennett, the Eastside Hotel was, like the golem, in Newham.

As he lay on his bed, trying to ignore the fact that although his sheets were clean they were also grey, he thought about Bernie Bennett and, more precisely, what Bernie might have in his possession. The golem had been put into storage by the police. Bernie had shown Bohuslav a photograph of it. Rather than just being the familiar clay lumpen male figure created by Rabbi Loew, this was a painted statue, created he imagined to look like Rudolf Baruch. Bernie thought that too. Unfortunately, the only photograph Bohuslav had ever been able to find of Rudolf Baruch was the one he'd had taken with his new employer Levi Rozenberg in 1928. It had been Rudolf's first day with Rozenberg and the image had been taken by famous Czech photographer Josef Sudek. The only reason that this photograph of two Jewish embalmers had survived at all was because of Sudek, who had been a personal friend of Rozenberg. In it, Rudolf looked very young, very thin and very dark. Very unlike the golem.

Thinking back on his conversation with Bernie, Bohuslav wondered whether it had been the right move to tell him about the Acorn. Unless Bernie had it. If he did, he'd hidden any fear hearing about it may have evoked, very well. And of course the most likely time the diamond had been stolen had to have been during the war. After all, everyone in the city had known the old woman had been buried with it and, under Nazi rule, the locals had been desperate. A lot of people also believed the jewel had been stolen by the Nazis. But it had never turned up in any of the places Hitler had used to store his booty – and also how would the Nazis, or the Czechs come to that, have got to it?

Mathilde Zimmer's mausoleum was famous. An enormous edifice, it was situated in the New Jewish Cemetery in the Olsany district of Prague. Bohuslav knew it well. Not only were many members of his family buried there, but he'd also spent a lot of time looking at Mathilde's mausoleum and trying to work out how it might have been opened, or even if that was possible. A 'monument to spite', one of the engineers he'd asked to look at it had said when he'd seen it. Mathilde Zimmer had been one of the richest women in Prague when she'd died in 1938. Those of a generous nature had positively interpreted her desire to be buried with the most costly and fabulous jewel in her considerable collection, stating she'd done so in order to deprive the Nazis of her beloved Acorn. Those of a more cynical bent said that she'd done it to spite her family.

One thing was certain: Mathilde Zimmer had been buried with something. Photographs of her funeral, her body laid out in an open coffin prior to burial, were on display for all to see at the National Library of Czechia. At her withered breast, the Acorn Diamond – or an approximation thereof. Placed there by Baruch and Rozenberg the embalmers who, the day their job had been finished, disappeared.

SIX

Mrs Igwe had a voice like a foghorn. Bernie could often hear her berating her children through the party wall they shared. A lot of it was about doing homework and going to church. But she also missed nothing and so when she knocked on Bernie's door that Monday morning, he knew that she would have something serious to say.

'Mr Bennett,' she began without preamble, 'last night I saw a man in your garden.'

Bernie invited her in and made them both tea before he quizzed her. Sitting on his three-piece suite, cradling her tea against her considerable bosom, Mrs Igwe said, 'It was about 1 a.m. Usually I am completely asleep by that time, but Roland was in a lot of pain last night and so I gave him the bed to himself.'

Roland Igwe was a tube train driver. A man of a certain age, he had arthritis in both knees and had been on the waiting list for surgery for coming up to two years. And while he rarely missed a day's work, when he was at home he was either tormented by pain or off his head on codeine.

'I went downstairs to get a glass of water and then I went outside. It was warm last night.'

'Yeah.'

'So I happen to look in your garden, Mr Bennett, which was when I saw this man.'

'Where?'

'Standing on your lawn, right at the back in front of your shed,' she said. 'An old white man, small.'

'Did he see you?' Bernie asked.

'Oh, yes,' she said. 'You think I'd leave him in my neighbour's garden without challenging him? I said, "What are you doing in Mr Bennett's garden? Tell me now or I'll call the police." He looked at me as if I was dirt and so I told him to go.'

'And he . . .'

'He climbed over your back fence and he left,' she said. 'Quite a thing for a man of his age. But I hung about in case he came back.'

'You should have knocked and told me, Mrs Igwe,' Bernie said. 'He could have been a nutter. Might've hurt you.'

'When you believe in the Lord, Mr Bennett, you don't have nothing to fear,' she said. 'I told him to go, he went, and I told myself that as soon as you were up, I would tell you.'

'Thank you.'

The man Mrs Igwe had seen clearly wasn't Bohuslav Kovar, who was neither old nor short.

'Are you in any sort of trouble, Mr Bennett?' Mrs Igwe

cut across his thoughts. 'I could not help but notice you had a foreign guest yesterday.'

'Yes,' he said. 'A friend of the family.' Bohuslav was going to come back and so calling him a family friend seemed like a good idea. 'I'm not in trouble that I know of, Mrs Igwe.'

'Maybe the man in your garden was "casing the joint" preparatory to robbing you, Mr Bennett.'

Maybe he was, but Bernie doubted it. Ever since he'd come home to find his front door open, he'd had the distinct feeling that someone had been inside his house. But nothing had been taken. Bernie didn't have much to take.

On Sunday, Lee Arnold had finally succeeded in persuading Bernie to let the Arnold Agency carry on with their investigations into the golem and his grandfather Rudolf. Bernie hadn't told Lee that someone had been in his house, and maybe he should have. Now this. He'd have to come clean and stop this now. When Mrs Igwe left, he called their office on Green Street and told them he was coming over to talk.

The Met had security-teched the shit out of that place and yet here we are, Tony Bracci thought to himself as he read the bulletin on his computer screen. The police evidence security facility at Belvedere had been breached on Sunday night. All the cameras had failed and the skeleton staff who had been on-site had been quickly overwhelmed by a gang of armed raiders. Fucking personnel cuts. All about saving money – like everything.

The Belvedere warehouse was a treasure trove of evidential material relating to some of the most notorious criminals and crime syndicates in the capital. Bloody useless to anyone else, these documents and items had either been used in the successful prosecution of criminals or had failed to secure a conviction. Either way, Tony couldn't see how breaking into Belvedere benefitted even the most significant criminals in the country. Unless of course they knew something about said material no one else did.

As yet, it was not known what had been taken, which was understandable given that, although none of the night staff had been shot, one had been pistol-whipped and was currently unconscious. It was a massive site and so it could easily take a few days, if not weeks, for investigators to work out what was missing. One thing was for sure, however, and that was that there was no way he could ask permission for Mumtaz Hakim and Bernard Bennett to visit the golem in the foreseeable future. For the moment, the whole place would be locked shut like a clam.

On the basis that he'd rather tell Mumtaz about Belvedere himself than have her find out online or via the TV, Tony phoned her. He also, thankfully, had a bit of information he knew she wanted.

'The undertakers who buried Rudolf Bennett were called Jaggers,' he told her. 'They were on the Barking Road, just before the Green Gate.'

The Green Gate was an area of Plaistow situated around a building that used to be a pub of the same name. Now a Tesco Metro, the old pub still presided over a poor district, characterised by battered early twentieth-century housing and small shops.

'Do you know what Jaggers is now?' Mumtaz asked.

'Greggs,' he said. 'So if you fancy a sausage roll . . .'

'How did you find out?'

'Buried, if you'll excuse the pun, in my DS's notes on the original golem investigation,' he said. 'We didn't pursue it because, well, nobody died and we had three stabbings that week. Don't think you've met Kamran Shah. He's on leave today, but I can ask him to call you when he gets back tomorrow.'

'That'd be helpful,' Mumtaz said. 'I doubt there's anyone left alive who can remember Bennett's burial, but maybe the family still have some old records.'

'Maybe. Anyway, sorry about Belvedere.'

'Can you let me know whether the golem or anything related to it has been stolen?' Mumtaz asked.

'That did cross my mind,' Tony said. It hadn't, but now Mumtaz had said it, he wondered. The question, if that had happened, was why.

When he finally put the phone down, Tony pondered on this. He knew that as soon as more serious work had come along, he'd dropped the case of the buried statue like a hot bollock. Either it had been put there as a joke or someone had removed Rudolf Bennett's corpse, replaced it with the golem and done . . . what? And assuming that Bennett had been dead at the time, for what bloody reason?

But what, a small voice at the back of Tony's head said now, if Bennett and the golem were a much bigger story than the rash of stabbings that had swept across the borough in recent months?

'I know you'd never try to mug me off, Lee.'

The look on Ronnie O'Mara's weathered old face as he

looked at the pictures on Lee's phone were enough to break the hardest heart. He'd been with his wife, Philomena, for forty years and now here she was cuddling up to another bloke in The Duke of Wellington in Epping. Who he was, Ronnie didn't know – even if Phil, as he called her, being in Epping was not that hard to understand.

'Her mam's buried over there,' Ronnie told Lee. 'She goes to put flowers on her grave, or so I thought.'

The O'Maras were Travellers and had lived on their current site just off the Leyton Road for the past eleven years. Before that they'd lived on what was now the Olympic Park at Stratford, until they'd been evicted to make way for the Games in 2012.

'I've been with that woman since I was fifteen,' Ronnie said.

It wasn't usual for Travellers to appeal for help from settled people like Lee. But infidelity was very much taboo in the community, and also Lee had been to school with Ronnie's younger brother, Paddy. The O'Maras knew and trusted him.

To be truthful, Lee hadn't wanted this job. Phil O'Mara had been one of Lee's many unofficial aunties in his youth and he'd felt disloyal following her about like a stalker. However, in spite of the tale, the photographs he'd taken of her and this unknown man were not all they seemed.

'She met him at Epping Cemetery,' Lee said.

'Fucking—'

'Hold on, Ronnie,' Lee said. 'He was there at Phil's mum's graveside when she arrived. They hugged each other and then, and this was where I started to think that things might not be what they seemed, both Phil and this bloke laid flowers on the grave.'

'Trying to get in with her,' Ronnie said. 'Bastard.'

'They walked to the pub then and had a fish and chip lunch. He had a pint of lager and she had an Aperol Spritz.'

'She's partial to an Aperol.'

'Not once did they kiss on the lips, but they both clung to each other at the cemetery and there was crying both in the pub and by the graveside,' Lee said. 'I couldn't get too close in case Phil clocked me, but I did hear her call this man "Kevin". Now I know that you wanted this to be just between us, Ron . . .'

'Oh, Christ Almighty! Who did you tell? Jesus, Lee, I trusted you.'

'The geezer looked familiar,' Lee said. 'I didn't know where from until I fell on who he looked like. So I talked to Paddy—'

'Fuck!'

By the look of him, Ronnie didn't know whether to punch Lee or cry.

'Hear me out.' Lee said. 'I had a theory by this time which I ran past Paddy, who confirmed it. Kevin isn't this bloke's real name. His real name's Micheal, Paddy told me, and the reason I recognised him is because he looks like Phil.'

Ronnie blinked, frowned and then said, 'Micheal Ryan? God Almighty! Really? Christ, he left his family when he wasn't much more'n a kid! I don't remember meeting him more'n once. Paddy can't have known him at all. How does he know this bloke's Micheal Ryan if he calls himself Kevin?'

'Because they were in Pentonville together back in the eighties.'

Paddy O'Mara had experienced a wild youth which had eventually landed him in prison. While banged up in

Pentonville, he'd met a man called Micheal Ryan, whom he'd worked out was related to his sister-in-law Philomena. At first he'd been delighted to have found Phil's long-lost brother but then when he'd finally persuaded Micheal to acknowledge the connection, the older man had sworn him to secrecy.

'Micheal Ryan was involved in a pub brawl in south London in 1980,' Lee said. 'A man died and Micheal was done for manslaughter. And because he couldn't behave himself in prison, he ended up serving fifteen years. Long story short, he never wanted his family to know what he'd done. So why he's suddenly popped up in Phil's life now, neither me nor Paddy know.'

'Phil's mam died in 2005,' Ronnie said. 'But she's only been visiting the grave every week since Christmas.'

'Maybe that was when she met Micheal.'

'Maybe.' He shook his head. Then he smiled. 'But she's not having an affair then, Lee?'

'No, she isn't.'

Ronnie let out a breath and said, 'Ah, well, so that's a relief. Thank you, Lee.'

'Of course, it does mean that you have a brother-in-law who's killed a man.'

Ronnie put a hand on Lee's shoulder and said, 'He must've had a good reason, Lee. And anyway, now I know this man Phil's meeting is actually Micheal Ryan, it'll save me from committing murder meself.'

Ronnie, as was his custom, paid Lee in cash. When he got back to the office, Lee knew that Mumtaz would want it to be recorded in the books and banked. She was so straight. Left to his own devices Lee would have trousered a third of it and, the way he was feeling, gone for a drink. Not a good idea for an alcoholic.

When he'd joined the Met, Lee had been addicted to both booze and painkillers. Legacies of his military service in Iraq. It had been Vi Collins who had got him clean by providing him with someone to live for, his Mynah bird Chronus. Later, he'd met Mumtaz and fallen in love. He was still in love, even though she'd ultimately rejected him. But lately the burden of that had been hard to bear and he'd found himself thinking more and more about drink. In his fifties now, Lee knew he was still attractive to women; it wasn't too late for him to 'find' someone. Except that he knew that he had found her, and the knowledge of that cut deep and bloodily into his soul.

'I think you should tell the police,' Mumtaz said to Bernie Bennett when he told her both he and his neighbour had seen a man in his garden.

'Yeah, but I might've left my front door open myself. I probably did,' he said.

'So? Bernie, your neighbour saw this man too, so whether or not you left your door open is irrelevant. Someone was in your garden who shouldn't have been. There's nothing for you to be embarrassed about.'

'Yeah, but . . . Look, I saw Lee yesterday and I told him I'm thinking of jacking the whole thing in anyway.'

'Why?'

He told her about his daughter and her husband and how the 'Jewish thing' could make things difficult for Darren.

'Lee said I shouldn't worry about that,' he said.

'He's right! This is important to you,' she said. 'Nothing

to do with Darren as far as I can see.'

'I know.'

'So?'

And there was that foreigner too, Bohuslav Kovar. What if his grandfather had stolen that diamond from that rich dead woman back in Prague? What if the thing was still knocking around somewhere? Bernie had no illusions that were it to be found now, he would be entitled to it. But that didn't stop him wanting to know what had happened to it.

'I was visited by this journalist from Prague on Saturday,' he blurted.

'Where your grandfather came from?'

'Yeah. A Mr Kovar,' Bernie said. 'Bohuslav Kovar. He said he'd worked for some English newspapers in the past. I looked him up and he wasn't lying.'

He relayed what had been told to him – about Rudolf being an embalmer and the legend surrounding him that still persisted in Prague.

'This diamond is called the Acorn,' he said. 'Bohuslav has been fascinated by the stories around it for years.'

Mumtaz said, 'So if there's a question mark over whether this Mathilde Zimmer was buried with the diamond or not, couldn't the Czech government order an exhumation?'

'Bohuslav reckons the old woman's tomb is too heavy to be lifted off her.'

'Mmm.' Mumtaz wondered, assuming Mathilde Zimmer's family had died in the camps, who the Acorn would belong to now. Maybe the Czech state? Surely were that the case, they would have found some way to lift the mausoleum by now?

'The embalmers, my grandfather and his boss Levi

Rozenberg, prepared the old woman for burial, including putting the Acorn round her neck,' Bernie said. 'Bohuslav says there are pictures of her, dead, with the jewel lying on her chest. He believes they took it off her just before they nailed her coffin down.'

'Do you know why he thinks this?' Mumtaz asked.

'There've been rumours about it for years over there,' Bernie said. 'The Germans were starting all sorts of trouble for the Jews in Prague by 1938 and a lot of people were skint, so it's unlikely Rudolf and Levi could have got out of the country unless they got some money from somewhere.'

'It's all speculative though, isn't it?' Mumtaz said. 'They could have got some money from almost any friendly source.'

'Yeah, but Bohuslav says that the pair of them disappeared directly after they nailed the coffin down,' Bernie said.

'Bernie, did you know that Rudolf was an embalmer until this Bohuslav told you?'

'No.'

'So maybe your grandfather was a different Rudolf Baruch.'

'Maybe.'

'Also, assuming that the embalmer and your grandfather are one and the same, why did he leave his family behind in Prague? Surely if the two men did steal that diamond, they did so in order to free their loved ones too?'

'You'd think so,' Bernie said. 'But maybe they couldn't. Maybe they could only get themselves out.'

'Mmm. But whatever may or may not have been going on, this is really interesting,' Mumtaz said. 'And I sense that you're very intrigued by this too, Bernie.'

'I am, but I'm scared.'

'Because of the man in the garden?'

'And because I don't want to fall out with my Kelly,' he said.

She nodded. Then she said, 'I shouldn't say this, I know, but Bernie, you could tell her you're no longer pursuing it when you are. I mean she doesn't exactly live around the corner, does she?'

'No . . .'

'And we are making progress,' Mumtaz said. 'I've just been given the name of the firm of undertakers who buried your granddad, or rather the golem. Jaggers on the Barking Road.'

'I remember them,' Bernie said.

'Did any of your family use their services?'

'Not as far as I know,' he said. 'Just remember their shop. Had gold lettering on the window and thick black curtains. They had stables round the back for their horses.'

'It's a Greggs now, apparently,' Mumtaz said. 'But look, I'm going to speak to the police officer who tracked down Jaggers tomorrow and see if I can find out something more.'

Bernie didn't say anything, just looked down at the floor. Would what Mumtaz had to say next galvanise him or simply freak him out? Eventually she decided to err on the side of danger and tell him.

'Also, Bernie, I have to tell you that the Met Police's storage facility in Belvedere was attacked last night. There's been some damage and they think that some items may have been stolen.'

'The golem?'

'They don't know yet,' she said. 'It might have nothing to do with the burglary but until we can be sure it's still there, we won't know.'

SEVEN

Lionel lit another oil lamp so that he could actually see his brother.

'So spend my money, why don't you?' Reggie Richmond said. 'What do I care?'

As his ninety-three-year-old brother's yellowing face came into view, Lionel rolled his eyes.

'You do know you've got some sort of tree growing out of your doorstep, don't you?' Lionel said.

Reggie had always been strange. When Lionel first became fully aware of his brother, Reggie had been thirteen. Thirteen, quoting Baudelaire and living in the old air-raid shelter their father had dug into the ground at the back of their flat in Stepney. He'd only finally left the Anderson shelter when he'd gone to work at Mr Silver's sweatshop in Spitalfields. From then on, even when he'd started his own business in the sixties, he'd lived in a basement flat on Brick Lane. Then he'd bought this place from Transport for London.

Referring to what was essentially a wooden shed with a garden, Reggie always said that his 'gaff' was 'handy for Archway Road'. And as it was part of the old long-derelict Highgate Station site, he wasn't wrong. It was next to the Archway Road, if you were prepared to cut your way through urban jungle to get out.

Reggie ignored him. 'So if you don't like being here, why are you?' he said.

'For your benefit, not mine,' Lionel said. He sat down. 'Your toilet working this time, is it?'

'As far as I know.'

Reggie, in spite of his age, tended to go to the toilet al fresco. 'God!'

'So, Lionel, what is it?' Reggie asked. 'It'll be dark soon and you could fall over a tree root or something.'

'Years ago,' Lionel said, 'you asked me to tell you if I ever came across the name Rudolf Baruch. So that's happened.'

'Has it.'

Reggie, bald, age-spotted and yellowing, looked androgynous in the pale light from the oil lamps. God only knew what sexual activity he'd indulged in when young; Lionel shuddered to think. He'd certainly never married.

'Tell me in what context,' Reggie said. 'You read about him, did you? Or you met someone who knew him?'

'A woman called Violet Collins asked me whether I'd heard of him. I said I hadn't. Also interested in a woman she reckoned was Rudolf's wife, Chani Freedland.'

Reggie knitted his gnarled arthritic fingers underneath his chin.

'I told this woman I'd ask you about these people and so I'm asking,' Lionel continued. 'I've never asked you about this Baruch man before, but now I am. What's this about, Reg?'

'You don't want to know.'

'So why do I have to tell you?' he said. 'What's the big mystery about?'

'I will deal with it,' his brother said.

'Deal with what?'

'Something you don't have to worry about.'

'Oh, so we're back as per, are we?' Lionel said. 'Christ, Reg, if I thought you'd had a good time being Mr Mystery all your life, I wouldn't mind. But you've been nothing but miserable, hiding yourself away . . .'

'Have you finished?' Reggie said.

'Have I finished what?'

'Have you finished tearing my character apart? For God's sake, Lionel, let me get on with it! Go back to Gerrards Cross, make yourself a gin and tonic and forget about it. I appreciate your telling me, you did absolutely the right thing. But now go away and forget all about it. As I said, I will take it from here. And don't ask "take what" either. Go, forget. Live your life with my blessing, but don't come back here again. As your only brother, who loves you, do this for me and for yourself.'

She'd let him into the flat and now the pair of them were dancing around each other, trying not to invade each other's personal space.

'Do you want a cup of tea?' Mumtaz asked.

'No. No thank you,' Lee said. 'Just er, because I've been

out all day, wondered what's happening with Bernie Bennett.'

He sat down on her sofa. Mumtaz sat in the chair opposite.

'Oh, he was in the office today,' she said. 'Actually I was going to ring you about it.'

'Did he want to stop the investigation?'

'Yes, although I think I've persuaded him not to,' she said. 'He's really worried about upsetting his son-in-law, Darren, who wants to be a councillor for that awful Britannia Party.'

'Darren Ross was always a twat,' Lee said. 'Whole Ross family were proper Canning Town scrotes. Violent, racist, dodgy as hell. How'd you persuade Bernie to carry on?'

'I simply pointed out how things were heating up around the golem,' she said. Then she went on to tell Lee about the break-in at Belvedere, the appearance in Bernie's life of a journalist from Prague and the presence of an unknown man in his garden.

All news to Lee. 'He never said a word to me about this man in his garden when I saw him yesterday. He sure that wasn't the Czech journalist?'

'Positive. Apparently this Bohuslav Kovar has been following the story of Rudolf Baruch and Levi Rozenberg for years. The whereabouts of this diamond, the Acorn, is a big story in Czechia. Bernie's going to try and set up a meeting between this journalist, him and me, or us.'

'I finally cleared Ronnie O'Mara's case up today,' Lee said.

'How did it go?' she asked.

He shrugged. 'Ecstatic his Phil's not doing the dirty on him, not bothered that his long-lost brother-in-law's a murderer. The more I do this job, the less I understand people.'

She smiled. Mumtaz felt like that herself at times. You

never knew how clients were going to react when you either confirmed or denied their suspicions.

'What you got booked for tomorrow?' Lee said.

He'd looked a bit what Mumtaz called 'sleepy-eyed' when he'd arrived at her door. It was a polite term she usually reserved for people who'd had a drink or two. Not that she'd been able to smell booze on him when he came in. But if he was drinking again, that didn't bode well. Although she'd never experienced him drinking herself, Mumtaz had heard stories, none of them pretty. But it wasn't her business, not now. She said, 'Kamran Shah, Tony Bracci's DS, is going to give me a call at about ten tomorrow morning. It was Shah who found out who the firm of undertakers who buried Rudolf Baruch were back in March. Called Jaggers on the Barking Road.'

'Mmm.' Lee frowned. 'I think they did my dad's funeral.'

'It's a Greggs now, but Tony reckons that Shah spoke to someone in the Jaggers family and so I'm going to pick his brains. Now we know that Rudolf was an embalmer . . .'

'We think . . .'

'We think he was . . .'

'Bernie's no idea what Rudolf did for a living,' Lee said. 'Seemed to think he lived off his wife.'

'Yes, but if for a moment we assume that Rudolf was the Rudolf Baruch this journalist is tracing and if we also give some credence to his story about the Acorn, then was he still with or in contact with Levi Rozenberg at the time of his death?'

Lee sighed. Mumtaz loved a mystery – sometimes a bit too much.

He said, 'Look, before you get carried away, I can't imagine anyone working around the jewellery of rich people, living or dead, would be allowed to leave without being searched. If those blokes did steal the Acorn, then how?'

'I don't know.'

'Prague was taken by the Nazis in 1939. And like everywhere they went, they stripped the place of its art and culture,' he said. 'Hitler liked nothing more than a bit of looted art, and a whacking great diamond would have been right up his street. If that Acorn isn't in that old woman's grave then it's because Hitler and his boys dug her up.'

'This journalist thinks the mausoleum she's in is too big to be dug up.'

'Look, Mumtaz,' Lee said. 'We're talking about the Nazis here. Say what you like about them, when they wanted something they took it – and if Hitler himself ordered it got, then it got got. These weren't a bunch of blokes working on a building site in Hackney. There are thousands of artefacts stolen by the Nazis that are still missing. I'll come with you to meet this bloke, but I have me suspicions. There are nuts all over the world looking for fucking sacred spears, lost gold and God knows what else. Conspiracy nuts most of them – as if we didn't already have enough of those!'

It was still open. Eight-thirty and Greggs on the Barking Road was open. Who knew?

Not Tony Bracci, who'd been going to drive straight past on his way home, until he'd seen that the lights were on and the door was open. He parked up.

Outside, a mixed group of white and British Asian lads

stood about rapping and chomping down on all sorts of baked goods, drinking coffee from cardboard cups. As Tony passed them, one of the boys muttered, 'Looks like you don't need a sausage roll, bro.'

Tony ignored him and went inside. Behind the counter a young woman with long red hair asked him, 'What can I get you?'

And Tony, to be truthful, could have done with a couple of sausage rolls and a cup of coffee, but he also knew he really was carrying too much weight – and also, he'd not come to Greggs for food and drink. Holding up his badge for the girl to see, he said, 'Police.'

'Oh.'

A boy who had just come out from the back of the shop with a tray of cakes turned his head away.

'Er . . .'

'No problem, love,' Tony said to the girl. 'Just want to have a look out the back of the shop.'

'Why would you . . .'

'Just let me look, eh love?' he said. 'It's nothing to do with you or this shop. I'm a police officer and I just want to have a butcher's out back. OK?'

She nodded, nervously.

He'd had a quick look at Kamran's notes about Jaggers the undertaker's. According to Kam, all that remained of the business was the old chapel of rest behind what was now Greggs. The boy who'd come in with the cakes took him out to the yard, which was full of rubbish sacks but also included a ramshackle brick building with its windows boarded up.

After the kid left him to his own devices, Tony tried the

door, which was clearly locked. Not only the chapel of rest, this building had also contained a room where embalming was performed. Clearly long-forgotten, this small structure was now used as somewhere to stack things against – bicycles, planks of wood, empty pallets. Although there were CCTV cameras and security lights on the back wall of the shop, none of them pointed in the direction of this dark building. Tony shuddered. Then he had a word with himself. It was just an empty building.

When he didn't pick up, Bohuslav Kovar left a message for Bernie Bennett. Much as he'd like to stay on in London, he told him he had to get home and so he asked Bernie whether they could meet, together with his PIs, on Wednesday. That would give him Tuesday to follow the other lead he needed to look at. Then he phoned New York.

'How you doing?'

Adam Sachs had the kind of New York drawl a lot of people, Bohuslav included, associated with gangsters. He certainly didn't sound like the scion of a once super-rich middle European Jewish dynasty. But he was Mathilde Zimmer's great-great-grandson, descended from the old woman's only relative to escape the Holocaust, her youngest son Franz. He was also obsessed with the diamond called the Acorn.

Bohuslav exchanged pleasantries with Adam, but then the latter got down to business.

'So what about the Acorn?' he asked. 'And the golem? You think it could be somewhere inside the thing?'

'I don't know,' Bohuslav said. 'When the British police

found the golem in March, I don't know how much they searched inside it. Bernard Bennett saw it. He has a photograph.'

'Send it to me.'

'I can ask,' he said.

'Make him,' the American said. 'Tell him you need to send the picture to some expert.'

Bernie Bennett was still suspicious of him, and so Bohuslav wondered whether Adam Sachs's can do approach was going to work. What remained of the Zimmer dynasty had lived in America for three generations now, and it was clear they had taken on American values.

'I have asked to meet with Bernie and his private investigators on Wednesday,' Bohuslav said.

'Why Wednesday? Why not tomorrow?'

'Bernie is on day shifts at work this week. His one day off is Wednesday.'

He heard Adam sigh.

'Look, man,' Adam said, 'you know the provenance of the Acorn. You know how important it is. I think you should tell this Bernie just what it is—'

'Adam, if we reveal the true nature of the Acorn it will attract treasure hunters. Anything to do with monarchy does. I am here, I am European, I understand this continent, let me do my job.'

The first time Bohuslav Kovar had ever heard about the Acorn having a royal connection was when he'd met Adam Sachs in Prague the previous year. Well known for his long quest to find the Acorn, Bohuslav had been tracked down by Adam, who had regaled him with a story about how his great-great-grandmother Mathilde had received the Acorn as a gift from her friend Austro-Hungarian Empress Elisabeth in 1895 in Vienna. The Acorn had belonged to her son, Crown Prince Rudolf, who had given it to his lover, Maria Vetsera, a girl from a minor aristocratic family. The prince had subsequently committed suicide with Maria in the Hapsburgs' hunting lodge, Mayerling, in 1889. The Acorn had been retrieved from the hunting lodge after the incident. Anything to do with the incident was of huge international interest, and any 'relics' associated with either Prince Rudolf or Maria could be worth a fortune. Bohuslav's personal opinion was that Adam's story was bullshit. But since the American was paying his expenses now, who was he to argue?

'Listen,' Bohuslav said, 'I can tell Bernie and these private investigators, but I truly believe it would be unwise for this information to go any further.'

Adam didn't answer immediately. Then he said, 'OK. But when we do find it, when I have it in my hands, I want blanket press coverage. When you've got a great story, you need to share it, *capisce?*'

Lee Arnold had waited until he'd got home from Ronnie's site and then gone to the pub. The Holly Tree was a short walk from his flat and so he'd gone there, bought an alcoholic drink and then sat in the beer garden looking at it for an hour.

He'd chosen something he thought he wouldn't like, which had turned out to be a relatively new drink called an Aperol Spritz. Made from some aperitif, which was violent orange in colour, it was topped up with sparkling wine and soda water. Over the years he'd observed that a lot of young women drank this concoction and so he imagined it to be overly sweet. However, when he did finally take a sip, he discovered that it wasn't. Taking a second sip, he also found out that he liked it – so he immediately poured the rest of it onto the ground.

Although he'd been to Alcoholics Anonymous a few times when he'd finally decided to give up booze, he'd never stuck with them and so he had no sponsor he could call up at times like this for advice. He did however have Vi Collins, the person who had actually got him off the drink. So he'd called her.

'This is all to do with this situation with Mumtaz, is it?' Vi had asked him.

It was and so he admitted it.

'You know, Lee, the one good thing that came out of my divorce was the realisation that you can't make your happiness dependent on another person,' she said.

'I'm divorced,' Lee muttered.

'Yeah, but you ain't learnt that have you?' she said. 'When my old man sodded off, I promised myself I'd always put meself first, and that includes when I was with you.'

They'd had a 'fuck-buddy' arrangement for years before Lee had become serious about Mumtaz. Vi had been clear right from the start that it was in no way a 'romance'.

'Mumtaz'll either get over these fears she has about losing her identity or she won't,' Vi continued. 'You can't do nothing to make up her mind either way. But whatever happens, it's not worth going back to the booze for. Today it'll be one Aperol, tomorrow twelve pints and half a bottle of vodka. You know how it goes. You don't have an off switch, Lee.'

She was right. In his time, Lee had been addicted to pills and drink, and he still smoked like a chimney.

'I had two sips before I poured it away,' Lee said.

'Well, good for you for doing that,' she said. 'How much did it cost?'

'Eleven quid.'

'Fuck me! See, that's another reason to stop it.'

She'd persuaded him. Although before he'd gone round to Mumtaz's flat, he'd eaten half a packet of mints just in case she noticed. Now, on his way home from her place, he felt a slight pull towards The Holly Tree but ignored it. Vi had been right about him not having an off button when it came to booze – and also it was dark now. If he sat inside the pub and looked at his drink for over an hour, the barman would have him sectioned.

EIGHT

'You know I can't give you his details, Mumtaz. Let me ring him and see whether he's up for it.'

Kam Shah was right. He couldn't give out anything related to Mr Jaggers's identity or whereabouts without his permission.

Eventually, she said, 'OK.'

'You know I'm right,' Kam said.

'Yeah.'

'And I'll get back to you ASAP.'

She smiled. Kamran Shah was a bright officer in his twenties, and if Mumtaz's stepdaughter Shazia hadn't been living with her lovely Sikh boyfriend, Mumtaz could have seen herself doing some matchmaking.

'OK, Kam,' she said, 'and thanks.'

'What I can tell you though is that what looks like a random selection of items were taken during the Belvedere break-in,' he said.

'Not associated with any particular case or crime syndicate?'

'They don't think so,' Kam said. 'But whoever did it did take your golem.'

Not having a telephone was wonderful, most of the time. Back in the day, when Reggie had been in the rag trade, he'd had to have one. The insistent clanging of that bastard was one of the things that had turned him into a recluse. Even if you went out, the telephone would always get you in the end. Just the thought of owning a mobile phone made Reggie want to vomit.

However, if and when you wanted to contact someone, the lack of a telephone was annoying. Reggie Richmond slipped his arthritic arms into his tattered Barbour jacket and then reached down to put on his shoes. Mercifully someone had invented Velcro, meaning he didn't have to faff about with laces – but he still had to physically go out, which was a pain. Going out meant carrying keys and money and even sometimes using public transport. He could stand on the side of the road and hail a black cab, but that would cost him a fortune, so he wasn't going to do that.

For a moment, Reggie considered not going, but then dismissed that from his mind. What his brother had told him the previous night could not be ignored, and just as Lionel had an obligation to him, so he had an obligation to his dead father.

'If you ever hear anyone use the name Rudolf Baruch, you go here,' Menachim Reichman had told his eldest son when he'd handed Reg that sealed envelope all those years ago. 'Someone will meet you. Tell them what you know and then leave.'

He'd opened the envelope the previous night. He knew where he had to go. And so, armed with a heavily soiled copy of the *A to Z of London*, he pushed his way through bushes and trees out onto the Archway Road and began to walk towards Highgate Tube Station.

It had been 'one of those mornings' on A&E at Newham General Hospital. A fight had broken out between two addicts just after Bernie had come on shift, which had resulted in blood all over the floor. Then some poor old girl who'd been waiting to be triaged since midnight had shat herself. So while one of the nurses took care of the lady, Bernie had cleaned shit off the plastic chair she'd been sitting on, and the floor. Now on a well-earned fag break, he was outside the hospital when his phone beeped.

It was a message from Lee Arnold to let him know that he and Mrs Hakim could meet him and Bohuslav Kovar at his place at 11 a.m. tomorrow. He sent this on to the Czech and then put his phone back in his pocket. To be truthful, Bernie was still in shock over the theft of the golem. Mumtaz Hakim had sent him a message just after he'd come on shift and he was still digesting the information. No fool, Bernie knew that he was nevertheless out of his depth with all this family history bollocks. Even the fact that Rudolf Baruch, his grandfather, had been an embalmer baffled him. Bernie's dad, Morris, had been such a nothing. And yet Rudolf had moved in intellectual circles, he'd had money, and he'd also mixed with people like his boss Levi Rozenberg. And this was where Bernie felt really at sea.

According to Bohuslav, Rozenberg had been some kind

of wizard. At first, pictures of Harry Potter had slipped into Bernie's mind and he'd dismissed the whole thing as shite. But then the Czech had explained a bit more, and he thought he now had a slightly better idea about what Rozenberg had been. 'A cross between a rabbi and an astrologer' was how Bohuslav had described him. 'A holy man who understands occult forces.' Bernie had imagined the TV astrologer Russell Grant wearing a kippah. It made him want to laugh and if what was happening around him weren't so serious, he would have. But Mrs Igwe had buttonholed him again on his doorstep just that morning, to tell him she'd seen a man standing outside his front door in the middle of the night. All of it was doing Bernie's head in.

Kam had been true to his word – just after Lee arrived at the office, Mumtaz found herself talking to a man called Robin Jaggers, grandson of Henry Jaggers, the Barking Road undertaker's last owner. Robin, probably unlike his grandfather, sounded very posh. He also, it turned out, lived somewhere relatively posh too: High Ongar, just outside London, in Essex.

'I do remember DS Shah coming to see me back in March,' he told Mumtaz over the phone. 'When the golem was discovered. I told him what I'll tell you, which is that I personally know nothing about Granddad's business.'

'I don't expect you do after all this time,' Mumtaz said.

'I used to be taken there by my father when I was a child,' Robin said. 'But that was back in the eighties and my dad's dead now.'

'I understand.'

'But, as I told DS Shah back then, we do still own Granddad's house. He died in the nineties and Dad could never bring himself to clear the place, much less sell it.'

'Where is it?' Mumtaz asked.

'Plaistow. Jedburgh Road.'

'I know it.'

'Shah never did follow up on it, but if you think looking through Granddad's stuff might be useful to you, then I can meet you there.'

'That would be helpful.'

'I'm at work at the moment,' Robin said. 'But I could meet you there this evening. About seven?'

Mumtaz hadn't expected Robin Jaggers to act so quickly. She was pleased. 'That would be great,' she said. 'I'll come with my business partner, Mr Arnold, if that's OK.'

'Fine,' he said. 'It's number 134.'

When she'd finished the call, Mumtaz looked at Lee and said, 'OK with you?'

'Yeah.' He sat down at his desk. 'Do you know whether Bernie's reported this geezer hanging around his place to Plod yet?'

'Not as far as I know.'

He shook his head. Then he said, 'You know that even though we've managed to keep him onside with this investigation, I think he's still not fully on board.'

'It's a lot for him to absorb,' Mumtaz said.

'What do you mean?'

'The story about his grandfather,' she said. 'Bernie's like thousands of other white, working-class Londoners – hard-working, not much money, some Jewish heritage. Then, this

Prague connection, which I hope we'll find out more about when we meet this Czech journalist. Since March there have been odd things he barely understands in his life.'

'And his son-in-law's Darren Ross,' Lee said. He shook his head. 'Might've guessed someone in that family'd get themselves involved in the Britannia Party. Back in the day they were all members of the Custom House Firm, who were basically football hooligans. Don't get me wrong, that lot haven't gone anywhere – but they have got old now and some of them are part of this movement to make fascism respectable, which is what Britannia is all about.'

'What does Darren do?' Mumtaz asked.

'Owns a nail bar in Billericay. He and Kelly, Bernie's daughter, live in a massive great house out towards Wickford,' he said. 'He drives a Range Rover, blah, blah, blah. Personally I suspect the nail bar's a front for something – you're not going to get his lifestyle from painting nails – but I can't prove anything.'

'And now Darren wants to become a councillor for Britannia.'

'Yes,' Lee said.

'Bernie's got a lot on his plate.'

Lee stood up and put his jacket on. 'Which is why I'm going to keep a discreet watch on his place,' he said.

'What now?'

'Why not?' he said.

'Because whoever this man is turns up at night,' Mumtaz said.

'Or in the day when everyone's out,' Lee countered. 'Bernie told me he came home the other night to find his front door open. If this man opened the door, then he did that when Bernie was at work. And while he reckoned nothing had been taken from his gaff, who's to say what this bloke might have done in there that we don't know about?'

It was difficult for Reggie to remember whether or not he'd ever been inside a church. A lot of the younger members of the Richmond family had married 'out', and so he knew that some of them would have almost certainly married in church. But because he didn't ever go to any sort of family celebration, people had mercifully stopped inviting 'Uncle' Reg years ago.

This iteration of the Church of St Magnus the Martyr had been built by Sir Christopher Wren in the wake of the Great Fire of London in 1666. Firmly in the City's square mile, it stood on Lower Thames Street, opposite the Monument and at what used to be the northern end of the original London Bridge. Now separated from the modern bridge, it was nevertheless still associated with it, mainly because Charles Dickens had placed the church right beside the bridge in his novel *Oliver Twist*.

When Reggie entered the church and once he'd become accustomed to the smell of incense, he looked around at the many statues of biblical figures that stood on altars and around the walls, some of them in niches. These together with all the paintings and fresh flowers made for a crowded space. And while Reggie had come to St Magnus with instructions to head for a particular place, he couldn't yet work out where that might be – and so he allowed himself the luxury of perusing an amazingly intricate model of the original London Bridge in a glass case at the back of the nave.

Like the actual Old London Bridge, the model was made from wood, and it very clearly demonstrated how the structure had looked until it had been pulled down in the 1820s. A hive of activity, the Bridge had been its own self-contained borough, with shops, its own water supply, houses, workshops and even latrines. Because so many lived there and crossed the Thames at this point, it was always crowded with people. Reggie saw little wooden women carrying baskets, workmen sawing wood and hammering nails, as well as members of the clergy and some very obvious drunks. And as well as being fascinated, looking at this model allowed Reg to put off the dreaded moment when he had to try to find the cupola, which he assumed had to be in the church's bell tower. The door into that was, as far as he could tell, locked.

Breaking away from looking at the model for a moment, he stared at the yellowing piece of paper his father had given him all those decades ago and thought, not for the first time, that this whole venture was bollocks. What the hell did Rudolf Baruch have to do with a church in the City of London?

When she'd retired from the police, Vi Collins had moved out of London to Waltham Abbey. Not only was it cheaper to buy property there, but it was also nearer to her two sons and grandchildren. On her own since her divorce, she lived in a two-bedroom flat above an occult supplies shop in Sun Street. She got on well with the owner of the shop, a woman called Mandy, and in the summer the two of them would often sit out on Vi's balcony in the evenings overlooking the mediaeval Abbey Church, drinking wine. It wasn't a bad retirement, except for days like this. Today she missed 'The Job' and she knew exactly why.

Pipps Richmond's dad had done as his daughter had asked and contacted Vi about the Freedland family. He'd told her he'd get back to her, but Vi knew that he wouldn't. That sharp intake of breath he'd given when she mentioned Rudolf Baruch had sparked off her copper's sixth sense, and she just couldn't put it from her mind. Lionel Richmond had known something and Vi was niggled by it. Were she still on the job, maybe she could have pursued it, but as things stood she couldn't – because if Lionel did know something about the golem, maybe he was involved in some way and her getting in touch would simply put him on his guard.

Now Tony Bracci had told her that the golem had been stolen from the Met's storage facility in south London. Whoever had done that job – a lot of other things had been nicked too – had used violence and so it was serious. Why half-inch the golem?

Some people who used the shop downstairs, called Tree of Life, assumed that the owner Mandy was a witch or a pagan, but she wasn't. Although she sold books about 'magick' and tarot and ghosts, Mandy was in reality a dabbler who was more into aromatherapy, candles and incense than anything else. She was also a great proponent of mindfulness and most definitely against anything she deemed 'negative'. In Mandy's opinion, in order for Vi to really enjoy her retirement, she had to get rid of any vestigial negativity she may have carried over from her time as a police detective. This seemed, to Vi, to involve more meditation than she felt she could handle – which was none – plus involvement in things she considered to be distraction activities, like embroidery. Mandy was very nice to have a glass of wine with every so often, but Vi felt as if she wanted to do a few more exciting things before she died – and so she called Mumtaz.

'I think you want the cupola, don't you? Shall I take you?'

Reg hadn't seen the man, who was small and of indeterminate age, creep up on him and look at the paper in his hand.

'How do you know?' Reg asked.

'Says so on that paper in your hand,' the man said. Then he turned back to look at the model of Old London Bridge again.

'You know, back in the eighteenth century, after the bridge had been damaged, when it was commercially a shadow of its former self, a man called Chaim Falk lived at this end,' he said. 'An alchemist by trade. Some say he created a golem out of Thames mud. Called, unsurprisingly, the London Golem, this figure is supposed to still be in the river somewhere, buried in the silt.'

This had to be significant, Reggie Richmond thought. This man, whom he now noticed was a cleric of some sort, had mentioned the golem and had offered to take him to the cupola. He didn't know what to say.

The man took him by the elbow and began to walk him towards the exit. As he guided Reg outside he said, 'That said, no one can be entirely sure the golem is still intact. Maybe it's even melted back into the mud from whence it came?'

The clock tower rose above the large entrance to the church, balanced on four substantial piers. In one was a small black door, which the cleric unlocked with a key. Inside was a spiral staircase. Reggie hated spiral staircases – they made him feel sick. He looked at the man.

'Up you go,' he said.

He didn't want to. His legs felt like jelly, but he made the first six steps before he had to stop to breathe. Noticing that the man was still behind him, he said, 'I think I have to meet someone there.'

The man smiled and then said, 'Yes. That'll be me.'

'Um. Can't we talk down here?' Reg asked.

'What do your instructions say?' the man asked.

'I'm to go to the cupola.'

'Exactly,' he said. 'So go to the cupola.'

'But . . .'

'We're neither of us young, Mr Richmond,' the man said. 'The climb will be just as difficult for me as it will be for you. There's no getting around it. Sacrifices do have to be made.'

NINE

Number 134 Jedburgh Road was a house lost in time. While all of those around it had been altered in some way, if only by a fresh lick of paint, this house was significant for its crumbling, Edwardian facade as well as for the bags of rubbish in its small front garden.

When Mumtaz and Lee arrived, Robin Jaggers was already there, moving some of the bags onto the pavement.

'Some people round here seem to think that just because the house is empty, they can use the garden as a dumping ground for their rubbish,' he said.

Mumtaz introduced Lee while locals, probably returning from work, peered at them and a small group of Asian kids played in the street.

Robin Jaggers was about forty, tall and smartly dressed in a dark suit. He looked and spoke like someone who worked in the City. He took a bunch of keys out of his pocket and opened the front door. He said, 'It's chaos in here, which probably accounts for why it's been left to its own devices for so long. Dad couldn't face clearing it after Granddad died and neither can I.'

The hallway, which was dominated by an uncarpeted staircase, was gloomy even when Jaggers put on the light.

'Granddad's office is upstairs,' Jaggers said. 'But when he became infirm, he moved downstairs – so basically his bedroom is on the left here, the living room at the end of the hall which leads into the scullery—'

'Scullery?' Mumtaz asked.

'Kitchen,' Lee translated.

'It's very small,' Jaggers said. 'Just a sink, some cupboards and an old gas cooker really. The toilet's out in the back yard.' He laughed. 'Must be one of the only outside lavatories left in the country.'

Lee, who probably knew the poor side of life rather better than this man, said, 'You'd be surprised.'

'Really? Oh, well anyway there are three bedrooms upstairs, one of which is Granddad's office where, as far as I know, all his records pertaining to the business are kept. I've no idea how far they go back. I'll take you up there.'

At least the hall floor was covered in, admittedly damaged, black and white ceramic tiles, typical of many Edwardian houses, while upstairs it was bare floorboards. Jaggers, apologising profusely for the terrible smell of damp that pervaded the whole building, opened a door to his right, with some difficulty. Pushing against a tsunami of paper and cardboard, he revealed a room that looked like the scene of a particularly destructive burglary. An unknown number of collapsed paper skyscrapers had fallen onto each other, creating a waterfall effect in the middle of which was a large, dark-wood bureau, its surface covered in the corpses of pens, ink bottles and typewriter parts.

Jaggers grimaced. 'If there's still anything remaining to do with the Bennett burial in 1940, it will be here and only here,' he said.

'How do you know?' Lee asked.

'Dad told me that all of the records from the Barking Road, except the very old ones, were brought here when Granddad retired.'

'When you say "very old" records, what do you mean?' Mumtaz asked.

'I don't know, to be honest,' he said. 'I imagine that all the late nineteenth-century stuff would have been destroyed – maybe that even went in the war, I don't know.'

'Was the premises bombed then?' Lee asked.

'No. But being so close to the docks, this area sustained enormous damage. I know the roof of the business came off at some point. One of the reasons this house is so damp is because the foundations were damaged by bomb blast. Granddad could never abide the idea of workmen coming in here to fix it, said it was too much upheaval.'

Lee and Mumtaz looked into the 'office', which was large and had probably been designed to be the main bedroom. Looking for details of a burial performed so long ago amid such chaos was going to be a nightmare. And even if they did find something, would that information tell them anything more about the golem or Rudolf Bennett?

Eventually, Mumtaz said, 'I'll be honest with you, Mr

Jaggers – looking through all this may or may not be worth our while.'

Lee, who had been thinking along similar lines, said, 'In order to do anything with this we'd have to employ casuals, and I'm not sure our client can run to that.'

Jaggers shrugged.

'We're grateful for your time,' Mumtaz said.

'No problem.' Then he frowned. 'When DS Shah came to see me I was taken aback and, I'll be honest, a little disturbed by the whole golem story. Granddad would have been the one to organise that funeral, alongside his father – and I was shocked, frankly.'

'Why?'

'Because whichever way you swing it, that whole thing was dodgy, wasn't it? And Granddad was, to me, a very straight-up guy. He was proud of his business, honest as the day is long, so Dad always used to say.'

'No one's saying your grandfather necessarily did anything dodgy,' Lee said.

'No, but if he and his father didn't, then who did?' Jaggers replied.

The cupola turned out to be a wooden room, right at the top of the clock tower. Mercifully, to Reggie's way of thinking, the lighting was better up there than it had been on the fucking spiral fucking staircase. In spite of many, many stops along the way, he'd really struggled with that and could now hardly breathe. If he didn't die of a coronary, Reg would be amazed. His companion, by contrast, hadn't even broken a sweat. He was also, or so it seemed to Reg, completely oblivious to his life-threatening condition.

'Give me the paper,' the man said as he stretched a hand out to him.

Reg complied. He was too exhausted not to, even though this was exactly the sort of thing that had made him retreat from other people – they were rude and wanted things.

Looking at the paper, the man continued, 'Is this all your father gave you?'

How did he know his father had given it to him? Still unable to speak, Reg nodded.

'So what happened? Did your father tell you to open this envelope if you ever heard the name Rudolf Baruch?'

Again Reg nodded.

'You even know who Rudolf Baruch is?'

Reg shook his head.

'Mmm.'

Finally capable of speech, Reg croaked, 'Who are you?'

'Terry.'

'Terry?'

'That's right. Where did you hear the name Rudolf Baruch and from whom?'

There was a platform around the edge of the curved room and Reg, without asking whether he could, sat down. Terry didn't object.

'From my brother,' Reg said. 'Although why I should tell you anything when I don't know who you are, I don't know.'

Terry sat down beside him.

'Did your father really only tell you to open this envelope if you ever heard the name Rudolf Baruch? Didn't he tell you anything else?'

'No.'

'But didn't you question what that might be about?'

'My father wasn't a man you questioned,' Reg said. 'Anyway, he was dying when he did this. Lost any ability he'd ever had to speak English, and so I had to make out what I could from the Yiddish I'd all but forgotten by that time. I wrote the name Rudolf Baruch, in my notebook. I've always carried a notebook, all my life, and have always written that name in the latest one so I don't forget.'

'Did you ever question why?'

'Well of course I did!' Reg spluttered. 'But why am I talking to you anyway? Who are you?'

Terry ignored him. 'In what context did you hear the name Rudolf Baruch?'

Reg sighed. 'My brother heard the name.'

'Who from?'

'Some woman trying to trace her family. Her relatives may have gone to my father's synagogue. My brother knows nothing about this, by the way.'

'Who is this woman?'

'I don't know!'

He did, she was called Violet Collins, but he wasn't going to tell Terry that. He didn't know who he was! Reg got to his feet. As far as he was concerned, he'd discharged his duty to his dead father and it was now time to go home. But Terry, it seemed, had one more trick up his sleeve. He said, 'Well then we'll have to ask your brother Lionel, won't we?'

Mumtaz put the key Jaggers had given her in her handbag.

Sitting beside her in the driving seat of his car, Lee said,

'Christ, this is impossible. Bernie's a hospital cleaner, Mumtaz, he won't be able to pay for a casual.'

'Maybe not, but we have to try,' she said. 'I think Mr Jaggers would like to know more about the golem too.'

'Then let him pay! He's obviously got money.'

'He may,' she said. 'If we find something.'

'Find something! Are you proposing we put someone in there and pay for their time ourselves?'

'We could try that, see what comes of it,' Mumtaz said. 'Lee, there's something here. We both know it and now that the golem has gone missing . . .'

'There's a lot of possible reasons why Belvedere was broken into,' Lee said. 'A lot of those involve organised crime. Tony Bracci told me there's a county lines case coming up next week. Could be evidence related to that that's gone missing.'

'Maybe. But why take the golem?' Mumtaz asked.

'For a laugh?'

She pulled a face. Lee said, 'Oh come on. You know county lines operations are more often than not fronted by kids. If you're sixteen, some great big dolly'll make you laugh. P'raps they thought it was a sex toy.'

County lines were drug routes usually operating out of cities into often deprived parts of rural Britain. Although frequently organised and run by adults, they famously used kids to move the merchandise around.

'Did you see anyone lurking around Bernie's place this afternoon?' Mumtaz asked. He'd spent a few hours in Custom House, watching the comings and goings on Shipman Road.

'No,' he said. 'But Bernie needs to tell Plod. That's the only bit of this I'm worried about, to be honest. I'm up to my neck in matrimonial work, we've got Malcolm on cyberstalking in Manor Park, if Bernie's paying us to find out about his family, fine. But the golem thing is a dead duck, as evidenced by the fact that Plod gave up on it. They don't have time to track down corpses and neither do we. Tell Bernie about Jedburgh Road and ask him what he wants us to do. Amanda's good at all that paperwork business and I'm sure she could do with a bit more cash.'

Amanda Flynn was an ex-copper who sometimes did some work for the Agency; ditto Malcolm Shaw, who had worked in cybersecurity before he retired.

'Forget about missing diamonds and all that lot,' Lee continued. 'Mumtaz, I know this is the part of the job you like, the mysteries. But most of our work is pretty mundane and it's that what pays our wages.'

He was right on both counts, but sometimes Mumtaz looked back on some of the cases they'd been involved in pre-pandemic and craved some of that old excitement. The business had suffered terribly during Covid-19 and of course the 'bread and butter' work was what was slowly digging it out of its financial hole. Pre-2019 the two of them had also been a couple, and now that was over, everything felt very flat. Then again, she knew she wasn't wrong about feeling that something was about to happen to Bernie. Maybe when they met this journalist from Prague, Lee would change his mind?

They drove back to Forest Gate in silence. Once inside her flat, Mumtaz took off her headscarf and flopped down on the sofa. It was then that she remembered the phone conversation she'd had earlier in the afternoon with Vi Collins.

* * *

There was a remote control on the carpet in the middle of the hall. That never left the lounge. Then there was the smell – like toilets. If the fucking downstairs bog had flooded again, Bernie'd go mad. He blamed all the building work going on around the manor – shoving up yet more glass and steel towers for rich people put a big strain on existing sewers. Well, that was what Greg the plumber had told him when he'd come to fix it last year.

Bernie walked into his lounge, or rather as far in as the mess in there allowed. Everything was upended, scattered, smashed. His flat-screen TV, the coffee table, cutlery and crockery dragged out of the sideboard and broken up on the floor. He went back into the hall and then entered the kitchen. Ditto. The microwave hung off the wall, work surfaces had been cracked by something, the fridge door was open and milk had been splashed around the walls; tins of beans and stewed steak lay dented on the floor. Upstairs was a nightmare. On his bed the duvet was wet – with piss by the stink of it – and in the bathroom the sink was smashed to pieces and the contents of the medicine cabinet had been hurled into the toilet. For a couple of seconds he blanked it all out by closing his eyes, but when he opened them again, it was all still there. And this time there was no question of not calling the police. Whether or not this had anything to do with the man hanging about round his house or not, now he had no choice.

Bernie took his phone out of his pocket and dialled 999.

'I've no idea who she is! Pippa met her at that city farm she goes to,' Lionel yelled into the phone at his brother. 'Why?'

'Just interested,' Reggie said.

Considering his brother didn't have a phone of any sort and was currently speaking from one of the last payphones in the country, whatever he was talking about had to be serious.

'You're not just interested though, are you Reg,' Lionel said. 'Ever since my twenty-first birthday I've had that name Rudolf Baruch in my diary, now on my phone. And in all that time I've never asked you why. So now I'm asking.'

'I don't know,' Reggie said. 'I promised Father . . .'

'Well, he must've told you something!'

'He didn't!'

'He must have!'

'He was dying!'

Lionel became quiet. He'd always felt sorry for Reggie when he'd been a child. Unlike him, Reg hadn't been able to go to the grammar school because he'd had to help keep the family afloat by working. Their father Menachim had always been harder on Reg than Lionel. Even their mother had joined in the shouting whenever Reg screwed up. And working in Menachim's schmutter sweatshop had been no life for anyone. Lionel was grateful every day that he'd been too young to get involved in all that. Then his education had pulled him out of there. He'd been lucky.

Now calmer, he said, 'Reg, look, I know you say you know nothing about this thing, but I can tell you're rattled. I'm not going to ask why, but as your brother who loves you, I want to help. I'll ask Pipps what she knows about this Violet Collins, and if necessary I'll speak to her again myself.'

There was a pause and then Reggie, breathing out a sigh of relief, said, 'Thank you.'

'If I find out anything, I'll come round to your place. I

know I'm speaking to myself, but if you'd just get a phone—'

'I'm indebted to you, Lionel,' Reggie said and then he cut the connection.

God, he was hard work! Lionel poured himself a brandy and soda from his bar and then sat down in his chair. He'd speak to Pippa, but after he'd had a drink. In her own way she was just as difficult to talk to as his brother. But at least she had a phone.

'A man has been hanging about around Mr Bennett's house for some days,' Mrs Igwe told Constable Popescu when he asked her about the break-in at the house next door. 'Old white man, outside the front door, in the back garden. He was wearing a dark coat like it was winter. Is Mr Bennett alright?'

'Bit shaken up, but he's not hurt,' Popescu said.

The police had arrived an hour after Bernie had called them. Time was they'd have attended within minutes, but a break-in with no casualties was pretty low down on the Met's list of priorities. With fewer officers than ever, a backed-up judicial system and rock-bottom morale, they were struggling just to stand still.

'You hear anything from Mr Bennett's property this afternoon or early evening?' Popescu asked.

'I was out until six,' Mrs Igwe said. 'Then I was cooking the children's tea. They would have been home from school by then. You want to speak to them?'

'Please. And your husband?'

'Oh, he's working. Went on shift at two.' She walked out of the living room and yelled up the stairs, 'Ronnie! Andi! Get down here!'

When she returned, she smiled at Popescu and then said, 'I think maybe they're on their phones. Day and night children on those things these days! You even see them with the things in church! Not my two, I should say, but you see others!'

Then when her children didn't appear, she went out into the hall again and yelled a second time, 'Ronnie! Andi! You get down here and come speak to this officer!'

Bernie wanted to weep. Everything he valued was in bits and whoever had done him over had even pissed on his bed.

'You got anywhere you can stay tonight, Bernie?' Sergeant Rogers asked him. 'Kids or siblings?'

'My daughter lives in Billericay but I'd rather stick a pole up me arse than stay there,' Bernie said.

'You insured?'

'Yeah.'

'Well, I'll give you a crime number,' Rogers said. 'You know what the score is.'

He did. Very few break-ins got much police attention these days. The thinly stretched Metropolitan Police didn't have either the time or the resources to give an incident where no one got hurt too much attention.

'Your door locked when you got home?' Roger continued.

'Yeah.'

'Windows?'

'None broken,' Bernie said. 'Although I've got one of them old-fashioned louvre windows in the kitchen which can just be lifted out.'

'Don't tell the insurance company that,' Rogers said. 'We'll dust for prints with particular attention to the kitchen.

117

Anything missing as far as you can tell?'

'No.'

The constable who had been next door to Mrs Igwe's arrived and took Rogers aside to speak to him while Bernie, not for the first time, wondered why whoever had done this had chucked his diabetes meds into the toilet.

When Rogers came back to him, he said, 'Bernie, Constable Popescu has been talking to the lady next door. She says she's seen some bloke hanging round here in the past few days. Old, white. She says she told you about him.'

'Yeah, well . . .' Bernie hadn't wanted to get into this, even though Mrs Hakim had told him he had to. 'People often hang about . . .'

'In your garden? Really?'

He shrugged.

'Is someone hassling you, Bernie? Because if they are, we need to know about it.'

He took a breath. 'Yeah. There has been someone,' he said. 'I dunno who. Look, I don't know whether or not you recognise my name, but I was the victim of what could have been an anti-Semitic attack on my property back in March.'

'Were you?' Rogers nodded. 'And you didn't see fit to tell—'

'It was me grandfather's grave up in Plashet Cemetery,' Bernie said. 'Desecrated.'

Rogers narrowed his eyes. 'You're that golem bloke, aren't you.'

He nodded. 'Yeah. Dealt with DI Bracci. But the case was closed.'

'I see.'

'Thing is that it's been bothering me,' Bernie said. 'So I got some private investigators involved. It's not right me granddad's body being out there somewhere. And also I want to know why that thing was in his grave. Last week or so, they've been looking into it for me. Hakim and Arnold, up Green Street.'

Rogers smiled. 'I know Lee Arnold. He's a *mensch*.'

The sergeant looked as if he was only probably in his forties, and yet he still casually used old Yiddish words like *mensch* that Bernie remembered people, both Jewish and non-Jewish, had used in his childhood.

'Granddad came here from Prague as a refugee in 1938,' Bernie said. 'Seems he left a bit of a mystery behind when he went.'

Then he told Rogers about the Czech journalist.

TEN

Vi Collins had been waiting on the office doorstep when Mumtaz arrived for work.

'You're keen!' Mumtaz said as she unlocked the door and let them both inside.

'I'm bored,' Vi said. 'There's only so much *Homes Under the Hammer* one woman can watch without losing her mind.'

Mumtaz remembered the popular property daytime TV show from the long months she had spent locked inside her flat during the pandemic, and she smiled.

'Well, 134 Jedburgh Road will top anything you're ever likely to see on *Homes*,' Mumtaz said. 'It's actually like one of those shows about hoarders that used to be on.'

'Look, I know paperwork was never exactly my strong point,' Vi said. 'But let's face it, it's gonna be different and if your client can't afford a casual then at least I can kid myself I'm doing it to help him.'

'You are.'

'Yeah, but I'm also helping meself by warding off Alzheimer's,' Vi said.

'It's going to be long-winded and laborious,' Mumtaz said. 'If I were you, I'd get myself a coffee and take some water. There are a couple of nice little cafès in Plaistow where you can pick those up. You're going to be dealing with a lot of old paperwork and even more dust, so it's not going to be pleasant.'

'I don't suppose I can smoke?'

Mumtaz gave her a look and then said, 'I'd go out in the back garden.'

'Gotcha.'

A knock on the still-open door made them both look round. Tony Bracci's large body filled the void. Smiling he said, 'Hello, Mumtaz.' Then spotting Vi he added, 'Hello, guv! What you doing down here?'

Bernie had managed to get hold of four reasonably undamaged chairs, which he set up around an old pouffe that he'd use for a table in the lounge. Mrs Igwe had offered to make tea and coffee and was also baking a cake for Bernie to give to his guests when they arrived at eleven. She was one of the loudest women he'd ever met, but she was one of the kindest. He'd also, since the break-in, managed to get her to call him 'Bernie' instead of 'Mr Bennett'. She was Rosalind, apparently.

The rest of the house would just have to do until the insurance assessor had visited – whenever that was going to be. Bernie had managed to cobble a bed together for himself in the box room and he'd treat himself to takeaways for the rest of the week, and so he'd survive. He'd still not discovered whether anything was missing. He'd looked in the old bureau where he kept all his family paperwork but that was still intact and still locked. What the hell did all this mean?

DI Bracci had turned up at the house that morning at around seven. Bernie had just spent what had remained of that night snoozing on the makeshift bed in the box room. He hadn't managed to even wash his face and knew he looked like shit. He'd subsequently done it in the sink with washing-up liquid and still looked rough.

Bracci had told him he was going to tell Hakim and Arnold what had happened and then he was going to come with them to the meeting with Bohuslav Kovar. No argument. The only way this was going to get sorted out was if all parties concerned were in the loop. The golem had disappeared but, at this point in time, the coppers were working on the assumption it had been taken for shits and giggles. A big county lines case was coming up at Snaresbrook Crown Court next week and Bracci, looking at what had been taken, was now of the opinion that someone connected to that had broken into the police store in south London.

Bernie wasn't so sure.

It had been nice seeing Tony Bracci again after all this time. But it had been hard too. His rotund form turning up at the Hakim and Arnold offices had reminded Vi how much she missed 'The Job'. It had been good that she'd had to come here to Jedburgh Road immediately after Tony had left. Of course, the real meat of this job was going to happen when they all met up at Bernie Bennett's place in Custom House – without her.

Vi looked at Robin Jaggers's grandfather's chaotic spare room and took a sip from her coffee cup. Mumtaz had been right: this was utter chaos. There was so much paperwork, she'd have to be careful that she didn't mix up documents she'd looked at with those she hadn't. She went downstairs to the kitchen to look for some black dustbin bags she could put papers she had seen into. There was a large roll of bags underneath the sink; she grabbed it and then went back upstairs. She was just about to sit down on the chair she'd dragged into the box room and make a start when her phone rang. It was Lionel Richmond. What did he want? Had he spoken to his brother already? She greeted him cordially and then said, 'So what can I do you for then, Lionel?'

'I spoke to my brother about your relative Chani Freedland,' he said. 'But he has no memory of such a person. What relative is or was this lady to you, Violet?'

That put her on the spot. She said, 'Well, it's to do with her husband really . . .'

'My brother does remember a family called Blatt but not Freedland,' Lionel said. 'Are you sure you're related to this woman?'

'Well, not directly no. Her husband—'

'Rudolf Baruch, you're related to him?'

It was all beginning to sound a bit suss now. Vi panicked.

'Yeah,' she said. 'He come from abroad so only, like, distantly . . .'

'He married into your family?'

'Um, yeah. Look, I—'

'We want to help you,' Lionel said, 'but we need to know a bit more. Rudolf Baruch married into that branch of the

Freedland family who were related to the Blatts, or . . . You said you were related to Rudolf Baruch, implying by blood.'

Finally taking hold of herself, Vi said, 'Lionel, look, I'm in the middle of something here and can't really talk at the moment.'

'Oh. I'm sorry . . .'

'No, I should be sorry,' she said. 'You're kind enough to ring me and . . . Look, if your brother don't know anything, that's OK. I'll try and . . . I'll get in touch with the rabbi. I shouldn't have bothered you or your daughter. I just overheard her conversation, me and my mate . . .'

'Mumtaz, my daughter said her name was. Muslim lady.'

'Yes, Mumtaz Hakim,' she said. 'But look, you can't find anything so no worries. But thank you.'

And then she ended the call, sweating. Vi breathed in deeply for a few seconds and then went out into the garden to have a cigarette. She'd lost it completely! She knew why. When she'd had that first phone call from Lionel Richmond, there'd been a strange catch in his throat when she'd mentioned Rudolf Baruch. This time, although he'd had no information for her, it felt to Vi as if he'd been trying to get information *from* her. Why?

She knew all too well why she'd offered to help Mumtaz with this Baruch thing right from the word go. She hated retirement. Hated it! When she'd seen Tony Bracci, she'd just wanted to go back to the nick with him and carry on as if nothing had changed. Instead she was in this strange mausoleum of a house looking for paperwork pertaining to this same Rudolf Baruch everyone wanted to know about. Yes, it was a mystery and yes, it was weird and disturbing and she really wanted to know the truth behind it – but it was also nothing to do with her and now, when she looked back on the call she'd just taken from Lionel Richmond, she could see it was turning her into a blithering idiot too. Why? Because she was afraid. Of what or who Vi couldn't say, but she was.

Lee was the first to arrive at Bernie's house. Luckily Mumtaz had called him about the break-in, but it still came as a shock. Whoever had done this had done a thorough job. The place was a shithole. But in spite of that, Bernie was ready with tea and a very nice cake that tasted of lime.

Mumtaz and Tony Bracci were next and then, finally, a tall dark man from Czechia who was called Bohuslav Kovar. The first thing he said when Bernie told him what had happened was, 'I think you must move out for a while, Bernie.'

Once they had all been introduced and been given tea and lime cake, Bernie, who was up to his molars in Mrs Igwe's creation, spluttered, 'I ain't got nowhere to go. Anyway, why should I?'

They all looked at Bohuslav, who looked down at the floor. Eventually he spoke.

At first he repeated what he'd already told Bernie, which Mumtaz and Lee already knew about. Rudolf Baruch's escape from Prague and his involvement, or not, with the diamond known as the Acorn. But then when Bernie told him that the golem had been stolen, he began to speak about things nobody else in Bernie's lounge could really understand.

Looking at Tony Bracci, the Czech said, 'You have to get it back!'

'We aim to get everything that was stolen from Belvedere back, sir,' Tony said. 'We've got to go through the inventory first. The only reason anyone knew that the golem had gone is because it's so big.'

'You have to get it back!' he reiterated. 'You must!'

'Yeah, but my granddad's body's the real priority,' Bernie said.

Kovar turned on him. 'Rudolf Baruch's body and the golem, they are equal.' he said. Then he looked at all the others. 'Baruch's body may or may not hold the key to where the diamond is, I don't know. But the golem . . .' He shook his head. 'The golem was not put in that place by accident.'

'Where?' Mumtaz asked. 'The cemetery?'

'Yes.'

'Why?'

'So it would be safe,' Kovar said.

'Safe from whom?'

He looked at the floor again.

Tony Bracci said, 'Considering it was 1940, I s'pose safe from the Nazis?'

'Exactly.'

'But the Nazis never did invade, did they,' Mumtaz said. 'That's what the Battle of Britain was all about.'

Kovar stared at her. 'The threat has not gone away. Look around you. Jewish people are not safe in Europe.'

'Yeah, but Mr Kovar, what does the golem have to do with that?' Tony said. 'It was put in Rudolf Baruch's grave to cover up that he was elsewhere, as far as the police are concerned.'

'That's part of it,' Kovar said. 'But it was also hidden for protection.'

'Mr Kovar, are you saying that the golem was buried with a view to activating it?' Mumtaz asked.

'You know about the camps,' he said. 'Our people were trying to protect themselves in every way they could. Of course it was designed to be activated. For those who believe such things are possible . . .'

'Do you . . . believe?'

'Do you think I would be here if I did not?' he said.

Lee frowned. 'Activated?'

'Brought to life,' Mumtaz said. 'With the right prayers and spells, the golem may be activated in order to protect the Jews. That's right isn't it, Mr Kovar?'

'Yes. I can see you don't believe me, Mr Arnold.'

'I can't,' Lee said. 'It's a fairy story.'

'What's it got to do with my granddad?' Bernie said. 'Bohuslav, you said you come here to find out about Rudolf.'

'I did, Bernie. I do,' he said. 'To solve the mystery of Mathilde Zimmer's Acorn diamond will make my career. But the golem . . .'

'You think you can bring that thing to life?' Tony said.

Bohuslav shook his head. 'No. But there are those who can.'

'Who are?'

'All I know is that such people exist in this country,' the Czech said. 'I don't know who they are. But I do know that if we do not find them, and the golem, terrible damage may be done here.'

'By an activated golem,' Mumtaz said.

'Yes. I know you won't believe it, but it is true.'

Mumtaz could see that none of the other men believed

him, but she did. Or rather she believed that Bohuslav Kovar believed with every fibre of his soul that the golem could live. Looking at Tony Bracci, Bohuslav said, 'Now the golem has gone from your store, anything can happen. While it was with you, it was safe, but now . . .'

'What do you think will happen if these people activate the golem, Bohuslav?' Mumtaz asked. 'Do you think it might be dangerous?'

'I do,' he said. 'Anyone who acts against Jews, it is bound to kill.'

Tony Bracci leant forward in his chair and said, 'Mr Kovar, with respect, you must know that while we can and will look for the golem, we can't take what you've just told us seriously. Your beliefs are your beliefs, but I can't in all good conscience make finding the golem my priority. I've a gang-related case coming up in court next week which may be related to the break-in at Belvedere, and if that is so, we the police could be in a world of shit. That said, if you have even the slightest idea about who may have stolen the golem then you must tell me. Without a lead I can't do a damn thing. Do you understand?'

There were invoices, thousands of them. Some looked as if they'd been typed on the old typewriter in front of her, some had been written by hand. Then there were orders of service, letters – from bereaved relatives, priests, rabbis; bills from coffin-makers and even one dated 11th November 1910 from 'Mutes'. Mutes, as Vi recalled, were professional mourners who used to walk behind funeral processions carrying staffs covered in black crêpe, looking sad.

Looking up from the latest pile of paper in front of her, Vi Collins glanced at the bag into which she'd put documents she'd already perused. It wasn't even half full and she was suffering from 'death indigestion'. So much misery, so much grim reality, to be honest. Did she need to know how much a cremation had cost in 1975? And what about when the cremator had malfunctioned in 1978? That was something it was best not to ponder on. What had happened to those lined up for the fire during that one presumably difficult week in April that year?

Vi went out into the tiny back yard for a fag. Still disturbed by the call she'd had from Lionel Richmond, she knew she'd have to tell Mumtaz about it when she returned to the Green Street office. But what was she going to actually say? That Lionel's brother wanted to know more about her was natural, wasn't it? If he really was looking into the whereabouts of Chani Freedland's family, he'd want to know he wasn't doing this for some random nutter. Lionel himself may well be secular, but his brother might be religious and thus protective of his fellow Jews. Vi understood that. Even though her mother's family had rejected her after she had married Vi's dad, she'd still never been able to hear a bad word about Jews without losing her shit. Small communities banded together for protection even when a member or members had left.

Vi's cover story had been vague and woolly, and she felt like a fool for not having prepared something better. So yeah, what had happened had been partly her fault. Partly but not completely. Putting aside the idea that Lionel's brother might quite rightly want to know more about her before he gave her any information about his fellow Jews, there was an edge to this that made her feel afraid. And this feeling only increased when she came across a familiar name on a funeral invoice.

As a child in Stepney, Lionel Richmond had, like the rest of his family and neighbours, been obliged to use the toilet out in the back yard of the house they rented. With two families upstairs and another – one his father had always called the 'tribe of Irish' – in the basement, the old lavvy had taken a bashing for years. Cracked and leaking, it had been a dark little cabin, often encrusted with spiders and not unlike his brother Reggie's grim privy now. As he returned to Reggie's shack from the wilds of his garden, Lionel shuddered.

'You know you've got sewerage bubbling up down your bog,' he said to his brother as he tried and failed to find something with which to clean his hands.

Reg shrugged. 'I'll go to the council about it,' he said. 'Now you were saying about this Mumtaz Hakim woman . . .'

Just before he'd gone to the toilet, Lionel had been telling Reggie what he'd found out about a certain Newham woman.

'Now look, I've not had sight of the electoral register for Newham. I love you as my brother, Reg, but I'm not going to spend days on end in Newham Council Offices for anyone,' Lionel said. 'So I Googled it.'

Reg looked blank.

'The internet,' Lionel said. 'Mumtaz Hakim, Newham. There were a lot of results. A school parent-teacher rep, the owner of a dress shop on the Barking Road, the wife of a man who was mugged in February – I could go on. But one entry did catch my eye and that was a Mumtaz Hakim who is a partner in a private detective agency in Green Street, Upton Park.'

'Mmm.'

'And while not wishing to know anything more about this Rudolf Baruch situation, it seemed to me that PIs are the sort of people who sometimes concern themselves with the mysteries and secrets of others.'

He put a piece of paper down in front of his brother. 'There's the details,' he said. 'But that's it now, Reggie. Every time I do something for you I have to schlepp over here, because you don't have the good manners to get a phone.'

'I find phones intrusive.'

'And I find driving halfway across London a pain in the arse,' Lionel said. 'Christ, Reg, it's not as if you can't afford a phone! If you wanted, you could have a real house! You could have staff if you felt like it.'

'I think you overestimate my financial situation, Lionel.'

'Do I?' He sat down. 'I don't. Father bought you that dive on Brick Lane where you lived and worked in Dickensian poverty, despite charging eye-watering sums for your tailoring.'

'I think you're confusing me with Savile Row.'

'I'm not!' Lionel said. Then he leant forward and continued, 'What's it all been about, Reg? All those years, you hidden away in a basement sewing *schmutter* for goys? Titled, some of them. But you just crouched in the background, wearing your fifty-year-old suit and drinking Heinz chicken soup. You know what I asked myself the other day? I asked where Rudolf Baruch features in all this. And our father. I remember all those old men who used to come to our flat, because I remember how much I cried when my own father shut me in my bedroom.'

'I don't know anything about that,' Reg said.

'Oh, yes, because you'd moved out by that time, hadn't you?' Lionel said.

'I had.'

'And so why do I get the feeling that in spite of being in your own gaff by that time, you knew exactly what he was up to.'

'I didn't and don't, and I don't know what you're talking about.'

Lionel shrugged. 'I've never understood you, Reg. But that's OK, provided it doesn't do me or mine any harm. I don't know what this Baruch business is about and I don't want to know. But I've a feeling whatever it is, you're being pulled in. So with that in mind, when I leave now I won't be back, Reg. You do you and I'll do me, but I don't want to come here again.' He stood. 'So Mumtaz Hakim, private investigator. Give her a call, see if you can find out more about this Violet woman through her. Goodbye.'

Tony Bracci didn't get the chance to find out if Bohuslav Kovar knew who might have stolen the golem. When Kam Shah interrupted him with a phone call, that diverted his attention completely.

As he put his phone back in his pocket and prepared to leave Bernie Bennett's house, he said to Lee Arnold, 'Kam's been called by Belvedere. Two fucking great bags of evidence in the Cyprus House case can't be found. I fucking knew it! I've gotta get over to Kent.'

'That your county lines job?' Lee asked.

'Yeah.' He opened the front door and began to walk down the garden path. 'Makes your golem a bit redundant, don't it?'

It did. The county lines case known as Cyprus House – because it originated in a part of south Newham known as Cyprus Place – involved the coming together of two local, mainly teenage gangs, under the tutelage of one older, very experienced gangster and his small, tight-knit group of henchmen. This man, Gabriel 'Gabe' York, had started his career as a teenage Yardie back in the 1980s in Peckham. A clever boy, Gabe had always managed to evade arrest and had matured into a canny drug dealer and now an apparently respectable businessman. When Tony Bracci and his colleagues had managed to infiltrate the Cyprus Place county lines operation, they had been thrilled to discover that all those particular roads led to Gabe York. Putting him away had been a dream which now looked as if it might turn into a nightmare.

Lee joined the others in Bernie's living room. He heard Mumtaz ask the Czech journalist, 'Bohuslav, do you have any idea who might activate the golem? And why now?'

'Because people seem to have forgotten the crimes of the past,' he said. 'In my country we now have right-wing parties who seem to want to use policies the Nazis used when they occupied Czechoslovakia in the 1940s. Anti-Semitic, anti-Roma, anti-immigrant. Such a government is now in power in Hungary. How long before we all have to face those horrors again?'

Bernie began, 'I think we've all noticed a drift to the right, but—'

133

'There are people who were given the job to stop this,' Bohuslav said. 'Many, many years ago.'

'Who?'

The Czech didn't answer.

'Who?' Lee reiterated.

Bohuslav shook his head. 'I don't know,' he said.

'Then how—'

'There have been rumours, stories.'

'From?'

'From our history and also from those who wish harm to Prague's Jews,' he said. 'The Prague golem was created at a time of great repression. Rabbi Judah Loew ben Bezalel made it from clay. It was meant to act as a protector for the community. But it went wrong, it became violent, and so he deactivated it and put it in the attic of the Old New Synagogue in Prague. Some say it still lies there, waiting for a descendant of Rabbi Loew to activate it again. He and his family were Kabbalists – Jewish magicians some say, others say simply learned men. I don't know. But this idea that Jews have magical powers is destructive in these days.'

'What do you mean?' Mumtaz asked.

'You see on the internet stories about Jews taking over the world? About how we own all the banks and governments? We do this by evil magic, they say. By sacrificing Christian children.'

Lee could feel his hackles rise. 'I've seen some of that stuff,' he said, 'it's bullshit.'

'Of course it is!' Bohuslav shook his head. 'But Mr Arnold, while there are those who believe it, there will always be danger for us. Those who guard the golem do so to prevent it from hurting anyone.'

'But if the golem is in a synagogue in Prague, how can it also be here?' Mumtaz asked.

The Czech smiled. 'There have been many golems, Mrs Hakim,' he said. 'Some just clay figures, some made with ritual and purpose. Like the Prague golem, it is said that this one here was made to be used. Your country was being bombed by the Nazis at the time, and you will find people who believe that this golem was part of why Britain was spared from the Nazis. Of course, we will never know. But whether you believe in magic or not, a golem in the wrong hands can be a dangerous weapon. Imagine how a far-right politician would parade one as proof that his Jewish conspiracies are true. Imagine how he would be if he made it talk!'

'You can't believe that, Mr Kovar!' Lee said.

'Of course not,' the Czech replied. 'But there are magic tricks that can make something inert appear to speak, are there not? People see what they want to see, believe what they want to believe. And I have to say that you in the West have been complacent. Democracy is a fine thing. Letting people express their point of view, whatever that may be, should be a right. But we live in an imperfect world and some people exploit this freedom for their own purposes, to undermine democracy.'

'So why are you here?' Mumtaz asked. 'Apart from as a journalist following the story of the East Ham Golem?'

'If I can find it and it is in safe hands, I will leave it where it is,' he said. 'If the golem is in danger of being used for bad purposes, I will destroy it.'

* * *

135

Rosalind Igwe had worked hard to be promoted to Sister on the maternity ward at Newham General Hospital. But when she'd become pregnant herself, with her son Ronnie, she'd opted to become a stay-at-home mum. Roland, her husband, was by that time earning enough money for the family to support themselves – and so when their daughter Andi came along, Rosalind continued to stay at home.

Unlike a lot of teenagers, Andi still liked to come home to eat at lunchtime. Rosalind liked to make food from her native Ghana and today was no exception. When Andi walked through the front door, she called out, 'Fufu and groundnut soup, baby!'

Andi dropped her backpack in the hall and wandered into the kitchen. 'Cool.'

'How is your day?' Rosalind asked as she stirred the soup on the hob while Andi sat down at the breakfast bar.

'OK,' Andi said. But then she frowned.

'What's the matter?' her mother asked. 'Tell me.'

Andi shrugged. 'I don't know whether it's anything, but when me and Ronnie left for school this morning, there was a man sitting in his car outside the flats.'

Some new, expensive flats had been built at the top of Shipman Road on the site of the old Working Men's Club.

'So?' Rosalind scooped some plantain fufu into a bowl and then poured groundnut soup over the top.

'He was still there just now,' Andi said. 'Old white man just sitting and staring at this house.'

Rosalind put the soup down in front of her daughter and took off her apron.

'One minute, Andi,' she said. 'Must go and tell Bernie.'

ELEVEN

Chani Freedland. Not Chani Baruch or even Bennett. The invoice from Jaggers Undertakers had been made out to Chani Freedland. In fact as Vi Collins looked at that faint, delicate piece of paper from the something of October 1940, she couldn't see the deceased's name anywhere on it. Services listed included coffin, transportation to Plashet Jewish Cemetery, grave-digging, printing and embalming, but some of the fees and the final total cost were indecipherable.

Takeaways from this were that Chani Freedland had existed, and there was an address: 8 Coburg Dwellings, Hardinge Street, Stepney. In October 1940 she had paid for the burial of someone in Plashet Jewish Cemetery, East Ham. But firstly, if Chani lived in Stepney, why had this unnamed person been buried in East Ham? Then Vi remembered that her mother had been buried in East Ham too. Jews were moving out of Tower Hamlets by that time. But that didn't solve the mystery of Chani's surname. Why wasn't she Mrs Baruch or Bennett? Had Chani and Rudolf actually married? Maybe they hadn't. But then Vi recalled that when the golem had been found, Chani Bennett's coffin had lain beside Rudolf Bennett's. Could the different surname be an error on the part of the undertaker? Had he, Jaggers senior, maybe known the Freedlands prior to Chani's marriage?

Vi put the invoice inside one of the sandwich bags she'd brought with her in lieu of actual police evidence bags, and resumed her search. It didn't take long for her to come across a mourning card for Rudolf Bennett.

This example of the small card used by many to announce the death of a loved one, usually made of good-quality paper, had clearly been printed in a hurry on very inferior card. Bombs must have been raining down on the East End when this had been made. In light of that, whoever had printed it had done his best. All it said was *Rudolf Bennett, RIP* and then what was probably the same in Hebrew underneath. It was sad. Vi looked for more evidence.

Reg didn't know anything about computers. If asked about them, his standard reply was to say that they were 'after my time'. However, he did know that Highgate Library had computers and people who could help others use them. A nice young man called Kenton came to his aid. Nothing was too much trouble and so Reg's search for private investigation agencies in Newham very soon bore fruit.

'So, if I want to look at say this one, Hakim and Arnold, what do I do?' Reg said when he saw those names come up on a seemingly endless list.

'You can go to their website,' Kenton said. 'That'll include all their contact details.'

Kenton pointed something he had told Reg was a 'mouse' at the word *Website* on the screen, and what the young man called the welcome page appeared. Reg had to admit it was really quite marvellous – or rather it would be if people didn't use these things to seek out those, like himself, who didn't want to be found.

'If you use the mouse to navigate your way around the site, you can see what services they offer, who they are and where to contact them.'

Reg was heavy-handed when he started whizzing the mouse around the screen. Jabbing at the button, he made the whole site apparently shoot off to one side. But Kenton just smiled and brought it all back again.

'Gently,' he told Reg as he put the mouse in his hand again. 'You don't need much pressure. Just tap, like this.'

And eventually Reg did get it, sort of. Also, while struggling with the mouse he'd noticed a category labelled *Press*. He assumed this was press coverage of cases Hakim and Arnold had solved. Or maybe it was just ads?

With Kenton's help he found out it was the former. Stories from the local press, mainly the *Newham Recorder*, as well as a few very small pieces in the national press, singing Hakim and Arnold's praises. One of the big stories from the *Recorder* had a picture of a middle-aged white man and a young Asian woman wearing a headscarf. The caption indicated that he was called Lee Arnold, while she was Mumtaz Hakim. Was this the woman his niece had seen with the mysterious Violet Collins up at the City Farm?

Kenton was called away by one of the librarians, leaving Reg alone with the Hakim and Arnold press page. By this time he had just about mastered the art of scrolling down, which he very gingerly did now.

From the *Newham Recorder* dated December 2019, the article told how Hakim and Arnold had helped the Metropolitan Police expose a far-right terror plot centred around St Paul's Cathedral. Arnold it seemed was an ex-policeman while Hakim had trained in psychology. Several of the police officers who'd worked alongside them on this case chipped their two penn'orth in at the end of the article, including a DI Violet Collins, a senior officer based at Forest Gate nick at the time.

When Kenton returned to help the old man who'd been looking for a private investigator, he discovered that he'd gone.

The American liked using WhatsApp; Bohuslav did not and so he called him.

'I could not get Bernard Bennett and the private investigators alone without the police,' he told a weary Adam Sachs in New York. It was the early hours of the morning over there.

'So they don't know the real story of the Acorn?'

'We agreed no police and so we have no police,' Bohuslav said. 'Anyway, the golem is missing again.'

'What!'

'From a police storage facility across the Thames. Stolen they think.'

'God!'

'But listen, it may be nothing to do with the golem,' Bohuslav said. 'The police here are working on a big drugs case and much of the evidence connected with that is missing too.'

'You mean drug dealers may have taken the golem?'

'The police say they sometimes take things that mean nothing to divert attention away from what they really want.'

'Mmm.'

He didn't buy it and Bohuslav could understand why. Apart from Adam Sachs there were two, maybe more, groups of people who also wanted the golem. Adam Sachs was fixated on the idea that the diamond was somehow hidden inside it. And while Bohuslav didn't believe this himself, because the Mathilde Zimmer/Rudolf Baruch case had obsessed him since he was a child, he was prepared to go along with it. The American was paying him, which was more than any newspaper was doing. The golem was old news now. The world was obsessed with the war in Ukraine – quite rightly. The horrors perpetuated by Putin's Russia sent a cold wind across Eastern Europe – even if some in the old Soviet empire, and this American, appeared to applaud the Russian dictator.

'Look, if I could get over to Europe, I would,' Sachs said. 'Just stay on it, Bohuslav. Use the British PIs, they're on the ground and they know more about UK crime than you do. The Bennett guy too.'

'Bernie just wants to find his grandfather's body.'

'So he says . . .'

'I think he is sincere,' Bohuslav said.

'You think? Look, the Acorn is worth in excess of twenty million dollars at today's prices,' Sachs said. 'And that tends to knock sincerity, honesty and decency to one side in my experience. This is a war, Bohuslav, and we have to win.'

Bohuslav was being paid well to do this job. All his expenses were being covered and he was being given an unrivalled chance to pursue his personal interests. But that didn't stop him from distrusting Adam Sachs. Although Sachs was apparently a well-respected Broadway show producer with money to burn, Bohuslav wondered whether he was all he purported to be. And in the absence of any evidence whatsoever, he also wondered why he got the impression Adam needed the money the diamond would bring him so much.

Although the afternoon was bright, the stained-glass windows clean and beautiful, there was something leaden about the church of St Magnus the Martyr. Maybe it had something to do with all the statues and dark paintings around the walls. Or maybe it was just simply that the church was empty and silent.

Reggie Richmond sat on a pew at the back of the church, near the glass case containing the model of Old London Bridge. Had an alchemist really lived on the old bridge? Had he really created a golem? In a dark place, down a well in his soul, Reg knew that his father would have known. Menachim Reichman had been a man who knew things. He had surrounded himself with other men who knew things too. But it had never been talked about. Years before his brother had been locked in his room when these men appeared, Reg had suffered the same fate. Whether Lionel remembered the noises they made, Reg didn't know. Because of the age difference between them, they'd not talked much. They'd had little in common.

A priest walked up to the altar, bowed and then disappeared through a doorway to the side of it. This was ridiculous! Reg had been sitting here for over an hour and still no one had come. What was he supposed to do now? Follow the priest and ask him where 'Terry' might be? Who was 'Terry' anyway? Did he even work at the church? He'd worn one of those collars they all had, but that didn't mean a lot. He could have pinched that.

'Reg.'

And there he was, suddenly beside him on the pew. Not one to clutch his chest when he was surprised, Reg nevertheless felt his heart jolt.

'Christ!' he said, then looking upwards, 'Sorry. How did you know I was here?'

'How did you know that I'd be here?' Terry asked.

'I didn't know how else to contact you,' Reg said.

'Same way your brother contacts you,' he replied. 'You and me, Reg, we insist on the in-person approach. What have you got for me? Have you spoken to Lionel?'

He was about to launch into what he'd discovered about Vi Collins when he suddenly lost his nerve and said, 'Who exactly are you?'

Terry stared, right into Reg's eyes, but he said nothing. He was never going to. Reg reasoned that he'd lived as long as he had partly via knowing when he was beaten. He sighed and then said, 'The woman who spoke to my niece about Rudolf Baruch is called Violet Collins. The woman who was with her is called Mumtaz Hakim and she's a private detective. She didn't ask about Baruch, she was just there when my niece met Violet.'

'Good work,' Terry said.

'So you'll leave my brother out of this, whatever it is?' Reg asked.

'I'm a man of my word.'

'Yes, but will you?'

'Of course!' he said. 'And from now on, and I'm sure to your relief Reg, this now concludes our business too.'

Reg was relieved. But that didn't mean he didn't want to know what this was about.

'Er . . .'

'Listen,' Terry said, 'you know there's an old saying that goes "If I tell you, I'll have to kill you". That.'

'Yes, but . . . At least can you tell me whether we are the good guys?'

Terry smiled. 'Depends how you define "good".'

And then he walked away.

The hat didn't suit him and anyway, who wore a homburg these days?

Mumtaz had left to go back to the office, the Czech had gone back to his hotel, and Bernie was now waiting for his insurance company assessor to arrive. Lee, meanwhile, was acting on what Mrs Igwe had told them. Investigating some fella sitting in his car looking at the houses from outside the new flats.

Because whoever was in the car was looking at the houses, Lee made use of the weed- and rubbish-filled back lane behind Shipman Road, which eventually led him to a small close of council houses just before Prince Regent Lane. This meant that he came upon the car, a battered red Ford Focus, from behind. And while he couldn't get a very good view from that vantage point, as soon as he saw the bloke's profile, he knew. No one had a nose like Stuart Zell.

Walking towards the car in what he reckoned was probably Zell's blind spot, Lee opened the creaking passenger door, lowered himself down onto the seat and then closed the door in one smooth movement.

'So, Stu,' he said to his slightly shocked, much older companion, 'what's the story?'

Zell had been around the PI circuit in Newham for decades. Now in his early seventies, he was a thin, sallow-skinned man with a nose one didn't forget in a hurry. Broken, it was alleged, on three separate occasions, it looked like a staircase as it roamed down his face in three distinct steps.

'Fucking hell, Arnold.' Stuart Zell said. 'What the shit are you doing here?'

'You've been watching me, mate. You tell me.'

'I'm not watching you.' Zell said.

'So . . .'

'Mate, I'm on a job, alright? Nothing to do with you. You've got your clients, I've got mine.'

'Your clients? Who?'

Zell pulled a face. It made him look a bit like 1970s comedian Bernie Winters. 'I'm not telling you that!' he said. 'Imagine if I asked you who your clients were? You'd tell me to fuck off.'

'Stu, if you think you can hide behind that ridiculous hat, then think again,' Lee said. 'You've been seen lurking round number twenty-one and I want to know why.'

'Seen?'

'In the garden, on the doorstep,' Lee said. 'Now if you're the Stuart Zell I remember from my youth, you'll know that that house has recently had a break-in. You'll have seen the police turn up in the early hours and you'll know who that house belongs to. And while I have to say that the homburg did throw me for a moment or two just now, the description I got of you – old white guy in a long black coat – was and is you to a tee. What's it all about, Stu?'

The older man said nothing. Lee lit a cigarette and then rolled down his window.

'It's like this,' he said, 'you either tell me or you tell the Old Bill. Number twenty-one is an ongoing investigation for the police. And as I'm sure you no doubt know, DI Tony Bracci is on it. Not some kid with a bum-fluff moustache, Tony Bracci – great mind trapped in a body that's mostly doughnuts.'

'Fuck off, Arnold!' Zell said. 'Bracci's on a big county lines case.'

'And now he's got himself a little Shipman Road gig on the side,' Lee said. He pointed to Bernie's house. 'The man who lives there is having his life turned upside down at the moment. Nice ordinary hospital cleaner, as I'm sure you know.'

'Is he?' Zell said. 'You sure about that?'

'What do you mean?'

Zell suddenly looked frightened and then said, 'Nothing.'

'If you're recceing Bernie Bennett's gaff then the police will want to know about it,' Lee said.

'No they won't.'

'I'm telling you they will.'

'It's domestic,' Zell said. 'I don't know why you're involved but for me, it's domestic.'

Domestic could mean many things, including family disputes and neighbour issues, but it was usually something to do with matrimony or, more crudely, sex.

'So your client trashed Bennett's place?' Lee asked. 'Revenge, was it?'

'I don't know who trashed the gaff.' Zell said. 'It wasn't me. But if it was my client, then he must've had help.'

'Why?'

'Never mind.'

'Stu, we can do this the easy way, or the hard way. I don't really give a shit which it is.'

Coburg Dwellings on Hardinge Street, Stepney still existed. Mumtaz was a bit surprised if she was honest. That area had been all but bombed back to the Stone Age during the Second World War. But thanks to Google Maps, she was looking at an early twentieth-century block of flats in what was now called Shadwell. Further investigation on property sites told her that, according to the size of flat and its state of decoration, owners could now get between five hundred and eight hundred pounds a week in rent from properties in the Coburg. A week!

But that wasn't the point. The point was that Vi had found out where Chani Freedland and, presumably, Rudolf Baruch had lived. And it still existed, even though the chances of any resident who might remember the couple still being in situ was zero. Maybe their children still lived in the area? Although at those sort of prices it was unlikely. She needed to know whether Tower Hamlets Council, or a housing association, still had any flats rented out in the block. That was easy enough to find out, and she was just about to pick up her phone in order to do so when the thing rang. Looking at the screen, she didn't recognise the number. But she took the call.

'Hakim and Arnold Private Investigators. How may I help?'

The voice was young, male and had a very slight foreign accent.

'Hi,' he said. 'My name's Milton Dreyfus. I understand you've been trying to get hold of me?'

'No. I think you must have the wrong number,' Mumtaz said. 'We're a private investigation office.'

'Yes.' He laughed a little and then said, 'Sorry, I should explain. I'm calling from the Congregation of Jacob Synagogue in Stepney Green. I'm one of the rabbis here. I understand you and a friend wanted to see the place?'

How had he known? When she'd gone along with Vi, all they'd done was stand outside the synagogue. And why did he do that rising questioning thing at the end of his sentences?

Once again he laughed a little into the silence between them and said, 'I believe you met Philippa Richmond?'

'Oh, er, yes.'

Posh 'Pipps'. That made sense. She'd told Vi her grandfather was Jewish and sometimes attended the synagogue. However, Vi was in contact with said grandfather, Lionel Richmond, so why was this rabbi on the phone to her? Vi must have given Lionel Richmond her number.

'So, would you and your friend still like to come and see our synagogue?'

'Yes,' she said. Should she mention Chani Freedland? The original idea had been for her to make contact with a rabbi at the synagogue, on the basis that he may have access to records pertaining to Chani and maybe even Rudolf.

'Well, I'm going to be in Stepney Green tomorrow if you and – Violet, isn't it? If you and Violet would like to come along?'

Mumtaz reached for her diary. Lee was forever telling her to put all her appointments in the online calendar, but she only did that when she remembered. There was something about paper that gave her confidence.

'That's very kind of you,' Mumtaz said. 'Did you have a particular time in mind?'

'No. Whatever suits you?'

They settled on 3 p.m., which would give Vi the chance to do some more work at Jedburgh Road. Mumtaz was hoping to catch up with Tony Bracci in the morning, although now that Lee had discovered who Bernie Bennett's mysterious stalker was, that might have to take precedence. This case was turning into one where they were working very much alongside the police, and it wasn't entirely comfortable. But then, as she ended her call with the rabbi, Mumtaz realised she felt uneasy about that too.

Lee had told her that Stuart Zell had been employed by someone to follow Bernie Bennett because of a relationship he was in with a woman connected to Zell's client. This was news to Mumtaz and to Lee. Bernie came across as a classic example of a lonely widower. Zell's answer to this was that the relationship was happening at work – and, true, neither Lee nor Mumtaz knew who he interacted with at the hospital. However, Mumtaz felt it was safe to assume that were Bernie in a relationship with a woman, he would bring her to his place at some point – unless they had sex in A&E. Bernie was too old for such stunts, surely! But then his nosy neighbour, Mrs Igwe, had told Lee that Bernie hadn't been with anyone at home, apart from his daughter, Lee's mum and the Czech journalist, for months if not years. Zell hadn't told Lee who his client was, but he was going to tell the police – or so he said. Zell, as far as Mumtaz was concerned, was one of those low-rent PIs who picked up clients no one else would touch. A lot of thugs checking up on their 'missus', a lot of slum landlords.

But in the meantime she had work to do, and so she telephoned Tower Hamlets Council.

TWELVE

Superintendent Ross wasn't interested in the golem. All he cared about was the Cyprus Place case. He was right to do so. If that fell apart now due to lack of evidence, then the police were going to lose their chance of shutting down a massive county lines operation as well as getting their hands on Gabe York. So far the raid on Belvedere had produced no leads. Whoever had done it was tech- and forensic-savvy, and the raiders had all been covered up in what looked like black Lycra. Tony had told Ross they'd looked like a load of serious cyclists with guns.

No evidence so far notwithstanding, Belvedere was now a massive crime scene and CID technical were damaging their eyesight combing the internet for anything that might point towards some dickhead who'd taken video of himself on the job. It never ceased to amaze how many people did this. It was almost as if they didn't believe that the internet was real.

But then in a way, it wasn't.

'Forget about the golem,' Ross said, waking Tony from a small moment of inattention. 'It's probably just a pile of dust now anyway.'

'No sign of it in the warehouse,' Tony said.

'They took it for a laugh, Tony.'

Ross knew very little about the East Ham Golem case. He'd only just come into post in May. Unlike Tony, he hadn't seen how big the thing was or, considering it was made of clay, how robust. Dr Gabor, the pathologist, had almost dropped it because it was so heavy. Why take something that big away 'for a laugh'. Also, it had been in a completely different part of the complex from the evidence relating to Cyprus Place.

'Sir, I think they took the golem for a reason,' Tony said.

But what reason? That Czech journalist, Kovar, believed it was possible to 'activate' the golem so it would go on the rampage and murder people opposed to Jews. But that was nonsense. He couldn't tell Ross about that. Ditto Kovar's other belief that the golem could also be used by presumably far-right activists against the Jews. All sounded like mad conspiracy bollocks to Tony.

He said, 'The golem's a, like a sort of cultural thing . . .'

'So maybe one of the raiders was Jewish,' Ross said. 'It's all irrelevant, DI Bracci. What we need to do now is put our shoulders to the wheel, get out into the criminal community and see what intel we can beg, borrow or steal. What about your snouts?'

Informers. No one had informed against York. Old Bill in Exeter had picked up a kid from Cyprus Place coming out of the railway station and it had gone from there. Random. A lot of the most successful cases were.

'I've put the word out,' Tony said.

'So do it again.'

'Yeah.' And then a thought came into Tony's head. It had the same texture as those few thoughts that had stood him in good stead in the past and so he went with it.

'Sir,' he said, 'what if the thieves' target was both the Cyprus Place evidence and the golem?'

'What?'

'What if both those things were wanted?' Tony said. 'Nicking to order. What I'm saying is maybe if we look for the golem, then we'll find the Cyprus Place stuff.'

'We don't know where the golem is, DI Bracci,' Ross said. 'And unless you do, for some reason—'

'I think I know where it might be,' Tony said. 'I mean it's a leap of faith, but . . .'

Until recently, he'd only ever once asked his brother about the name. He'd been about thirty at the time. He'd been visiting Reg at his workshop in Brick Lane. The only other person who'd been there had been Mrs Siddiqi, Reg's pattern cutter, whose English had remained basic to the end of her life.

'This Rudolf Baruch,' he'd said to Reg, 'what's it about?'

'Don't ask.'

Reg had been using his sewing machine at the time. Only when Lionel had persisted with his questioning had he stopped.

'If I don't know what it's about, how do I know that you're not involved in something hooky? I mean letting you know that I've heard that name, Rudolf Baruch, could mean I put him or someone else in danger. I know you make suits for those dodgy Kray brothers—'

'You do as you're fucking told!' Reg had said. 'Not because I tell you, but because that came from Father. And you can keep my business with the Kray boys to yourself as well.'

Ronnie and Reggie Kray had been the most successful and brutal London gang bosses in the 1960s. They were eventually arrested and their firm taken down in 1968.

Lionel had given up. Even when the internet had come along and people began to Google every damn thing, he'd never thought to look up Rudolf Baruch. Now that had changed. There weren't many. One in Germany, a couple of Americans – one an architect aged thirty-five, the other a car showroom owner from Texas. It was only when he added his father's birthplace – Prague – into the search that things changed. After all, if Menachim had known this man then it was possible he'd come across him in Czechia.

Helpfully, most of the search results related to one Rudolf Baruch of Prague who, it seemed, had been variously an embalmer, a magician, a con-man and a Nazi agent. Apparently he'd been involved in embalming a rich widow called Mathilde Zimmer together with his superior, a man called Levi Rozenberg. After that, Baruch had disappeared and there was a conspiracy theory that he'd stolen a massive diamond that was supposed to be buried with the Zimmer corpse. Rozenberg had died in a concentration camp.

Had he been able to phone Reg, Lionel would have asked him whether this subterfuge was about this diamond – called the Acorn. It would be typical if it were. Though he might not spend much, Reg had always been acquisitive about money. But not so their father. And this instruction regarding Rudolf Baruch had come from Menachim.

Lionel sat back in his chair and finished his gin and tonic. Rudolf Baruch was a warning of some sort. But a warning about what and to whom?

Mandy had been angling to come up for some wine for a while now and so Vi decided to invite her when she got home from Plaistow that evening. She was good company, even if she could drone on about 'manifesting' things a bit too much at times. Vi opened a bottle of Chardonnay, grabbed two glasses from the kitchen and joined her guest out on her balcony. It felt good to be out in the open air, looking at the evening sunshine, after being locked in a house lost to time all day long.

Mandy, who also smoked, offered Vi a cigarette and they both lit up.

'So how was your day, honey?' Mandy asked. Considerably younger than Vi, Mandy, in spite of her green credentials, had been heavily influenced by reality television culture and consequently had disarmingly heavy eyelashes and eyebrows. She also had a lot of hair extensions which she pushed back over her shoulders from time to time.

'Helping out a couple of old mates,' Vi said. 'Sorting out an old house in Plaistow.'

She didn't want to say anything more than that. But Mandy was interested.

'Oh, bereavement?' she said.

'No, just neglect,' Vi replied.

'Mmm. Can get negative energy off old stuff, Vi. Thought you looked a bit pale.'

'Probably dust,' Vi said.

'A lot of it?'

'Over everything.'

'Oooh!' Mandy frowned. 'That's not good, babe.'

'I had a shower when I got home,' Vi said.

''Course you did,' Mandy said. 'But I'm actually more worried about psychic negativity. So destructive! You have to let me know if you want me to come and cleanse this house, Vi. You know I do spiritual house cleansing, right?'

She did. One of the first things Mandy had done when Vi had moved into the flat was cleanse it. Vi said she'd let Mandy know. She didn't really know what she felt about what she called 'New Age woo-woo'. On the one hand, as a pragmatic ex-copper, Vi thought it was all bollocks, but she was also the daughter of a Traveller and so she was aware of at least some vestigial belief in 'unseen forces'. And she enjoyed chatting to Mandy and felt a bit bereft when she finally left. It was getting dark by that time and, although it was still warm, Vi felt the need to go indoors and settle down for the night. So she gathered up the empty wine bottle, glasses and ashtray and was just about to leave the balcony when she saw a figure in the car park behind Mandy's shop, looking up at her.

'I wondered when you'd show up,' Rose Arnold said to her son as he stepped across her threshold. 'What were you doing chatting to some bloke in his car?'

They both went into the kitchen and Rose put the kettle on for tea.

'I know him,' Lee said.

'So what's all this with Bernie Bennett's house being broken into?' Rose asked.

'Bernie's house was broken into.'

She gave him a look. 'Clever bugger,' she said. 'Come on, I want details. Florrie told me it was some gang.'

Lee knew his mother's sister, Florrie, used the word 'gang' as shorthand for 'black' and so he ignored it.

'We don't know yet,' he said.

She gave him an ashtray and Lee lit up.

'You staying for a bite?' she asked. 'I'm doing ham, egg and chips.'

'Yeah, that'd be nice. Mum. I know you've told me but what was Grandpa Lincoln's real name?'

'Vladimir Litvak,' she said as she took out her frying pan. 'But he never used it. Dad was always Jack Lincoln. Wanted to blend in.'

'So did his father change it then?'

'No,' she said. 'They come through the immigration centre at Tower Hill. The immigration people give it to them.' She put the oven on.

'How old was Grandpa when he came here?'

'About two he always reckoned,' Rose said. ''Course, he remembered nothing before that. I think they come from Poland, but I don't know.'

Lee frowned. 'So did the immigration officers give all the Jews new names when they came here?'

'Dunno. Dad always used to say that they only done it when they couldn't understand what the people were saying.'

'Litvak's not hard,' Lee said.

'No, but back in the 1900s people weren't as educated as they are now. The immigration officers were just ordinary people. So if they couldn't make it out they put down words of cities and colours, things they could understand. Why so many Jews have the name Green. Why do you want to know?'

''Cause Bernie's Jewish. I want to understand him a bit better.'

'So what do you know about his break-in?'

She wasn't going to let it go. Rose didn't.

'I told you, nothing yet,' Lee said. 'Mum, have you ever heard about the golem?'

Rose poured a load of frozen oven chips onto a metal tray and put them in the oven.

'Mum?'

She turned and looked at him. 'Lee, I know the papers called that thing they found in Bernie's granddad's grave a golem, but that was just to get readers. How would someone from India know what a golem is?'

'From India?'

'The reporter,' she said. 'That chief editor or whatever he is comes from Delhi or somewhere.'

'Really?'

'Got an Indian name. Krishna.'

Lee rolled his eyes. 'Mum, he's a British Asian, about as Indian as I am!'

'Oh, well . . .' She sat down opposite him at the breakfast bar. 'Listen Lee, I know almost sod all about Judaism. My grandpa, David, could barely speak English and me and my brothers and sisters had not a lot of Yiddish.'

'You use Yiddish words,' Lee said.

'Yeah, but I don't speak it,' Rose said. 'But we were told some of the old folk stories, you know. About ghosts and golems.'

'You know about golems?'

'Mud men, yes,' she said. 'Load of old pony! Mind you, I wouldn't want to get on the wrong side of one. These old things can have a habit of coming back and biting you on the arse.'

It was going to be an early start. But Tony Bracci had no one to blame but himself. It had been him who had persuaded Superintendent Ross to call the Burial Society and arrange for access at bloody dawn. The thinking behind it was so that the local residents weren't too disturbed by coppers poking about in the cemetery – again. He got it. Also, there was no concrete reason for thinking that the golem was back at Plashet Cemetery, much less the Cyprus Place evidence.

But it had been the sheer unlikelihood of that happening that had brought it to Tony's mind. Vi Collins had always said that in order to catch criminals you had to be able to think like them. She'd always been good at that on account, she'd said, of 'being proper dodgy' herself. She had been. It had been well known that Vi could get you almost anything your heart desired by judicious use of her 'contacts'. It had also been well known that if you killed, defrauded or used violence she was going to rip your head off and shit down your neck. Tony missed her.

On his way home he stopped at the Greggs on the Barking Road and bought a steak bake, which he sat and ate in his car outside. This shop was where Rudolf Baruch's body had been taken after his death in 1940. During the first investigation into the golem, the police had obtained a copy of Baruch's death certificate which stated he'd died from 'bomb blast'. These had been common during the Blitz. People died because the blast from a bomb, usually nearby, stopped their hearts. Often victims wouldn't have a mark on them. There were many stories about rescuers going into houses and flats and finding groups of people, stone dead, still sitting around dinner tables, killed by bomb blast. They'd looked, some accounts stated, like statues.

Had it been here, at what had been Jaggers the undertaker's, that Rudolf Baruch's body had been switched with that of the golem? If so, what had happened to Rudolf? That small building that still remained at the back of Greggs had been both the Jaggers' chapel of rest and their embalming laboratory. Tony had read somewhere that during the embalming process, the blood of the deceased was pumped out of the body and replaced by formaldehyde. This meant that the embalmer would be left with a load of blood. What happened to that? Was it just poured away and if so, where? And how, if at all, did this relate to Rudolf Baruch's body?

Could it be that Baruch's corpse was still somewhere inside, underneath or beside that building at the back of Greggs?

Mumtaz Hakim's heart hammered. She looked at her bedside clock – it was 3 a.m. – and then picked up her ringing phone. Whoever was calling at this time of night had to be in trouble and it was probably someone close. Her stepdaughter? Her parents? Lee?

'Mumtaz here,' she slurred.

'I know this is a fucking ungodly hour to be calling, but I don't know what to do,' a dry, husky voice said.

Vi Collins.

'What is it?' Mumtaz asked.

'Just before I went to bed, I noticed some bloke looking at me from the car park out the back here,' she said. 'As you know, I live above a spooky shop so we get weirdos. Anyway, I went to bed, then because I'm as old as time I had to get up to go to the bog and I happened to look out the living room window. This time no one was there. So, phew, back to bed. Then I heard what sounded like someone trying the front door. So, I checked again – no one, the street outside quiet as the grave. So back to bed, maybe an hour's kip? So then my brain keeps churning over what's happened and so I go and look out of the living room window again and suddenly there's this face pressed up against the glass outside. I swear to God I nearly died! Big, grey face, squashed-up nose . . . Christ, it was like something out of a horror film! I jumped backwards and crashed into the coffee table and fell on my arse. I thought if he tries the living room door or smashes the window, I'm toast. But when I looked up again, he'd gone. Took me a minute to get up again, I think I've fucked my knee, so I hobbled to the door onto the balcony, opened it and went out.'

'You shouldn't have done, Vi.'

'I know! But anyway, it was all quiet on the Western Front and so I came back in, made myself a cup of tea, had a fag and shoved an ice pack on my knee.'

'Do you want me to come?' Mumtaz asked.

'No. It's the middle of the fucking night. Also, if this geezer wanted to kill me he'd've already done it by now. I was an open goal sprawled on the floor in my jim-jams. I just wanted someone else to know in case of a repeat performance and I wanted to talk about why. Look, I'm not blaming you, sweetheart, and I wouldn't have it any other way, but it occurs to me that before I started giving you a hand, the only man with any interest in me was Mandy's French Bulldog, Claude. Now I appear to have a stalker. What is this? And is it just me?'

Mumtaz took a deep breath in and then said, 'No Vi, it's not just you. Look, if you don't want me to come to you, do you want to come here?'

THIRTEEN

There was nothing. Rudolf's grave was still covered by the same tarpaulin that had been put there back in March, his headstone on its back to one side, his wife's plot beside his, untouched. Tony Bracci, smoking into the cool early morning air, felt like a prat. Why, even if those who had stolen the Cyprus Place evidence had also stolen the golem, would they come back to Plashet Cemetery? In one sense Tony had been right about it being the last place you'd expect the stuff to be, but that also included the thieves themselves.

Kam Shah walked over to him with the bloke from the burial society, Gerry Gomes.

'Not your fault, guv,' Kam said. 'I can see why you felt it was worth a shot.'

'People get in and out all the time,' Mr Gomes said. 'This place is like a magnet! Anyway, we got better security after March. Cameras front and back. We keep disks for two weeks. I've got the latest ones here.'

He put some disks into Tony's hands.

'Thanks, Mr Gomes.'

'Guv?'

One of the uniforms was walking towards him.

'What?'

'Looks like some disturbed earth over by the back wall.'

Tony looked at Gomes. 'Anyone been here lately?'

'Not that I know of,' Gomes said. 'Mind you, if it's over by any of the walls, it's most likely to be kids.'

'It wasn't Stuart Zell,' Vi said. 'I'd know that nose anywhere.'

'And whoever was in my garden was most certainly not a man on the edge of old age,' Mumtaz said. 'For one thing he was wearing a hoodie, and for another he jumped over the back fence like a hare.'

Lee Arnold sighed. Mumtaz had called him early and now he was sitting with her and Vi Collins in her living room. Both women had apparently picked up 'tails' – men following or stalking them. This made three including Bernie Bennett.

'Zell aside, we're being watched,' Mumtaz said. 'It first happened to me just after Bernie engaged our services. Then Vi had her little experience last night after being at Jedburgh Road for most of the day. Someone's trying to frighten us off.'

'I've not seen anyone tailing me,' Lee said.

'With respect, you're a big, strong man,' Vi said.

'And you're an ex-DI with weapons experience,' Lee said.

'Yeah, but they don't know that!' Vi said.

'They might.'

'And now we're on Tony Bracci's territory, because

whoever stole the Cyprus Place evidence may also have stolen the golem,' Mumtaz said.

'Following the golem won't necessarily get us any further forward in our search for Bernie's grandfather,' Lee said. 'We were hired first to try and find out as much about Bernie's granddad as we could and secondly to find his body, if possible. The golem is—'

'The golem is key!' Mumtaz said. 'You heard what that Czech journalist said about that diamond.'

Lee looked at Vi and said, 'You know about this?'

'Mumtaz filled me in during the early hours,' she said.

'Mumtaz, that diamond is either underneath a big lump of marble in a graveyard in Prague, or Hitler took it and it's now in some rich bloke's private collection,' Lee said. 'Look, how's it going with tracking down Bernie's family?'

'Not very far,' Mumtaz said. 'I've tracked down where Rudolf and Chani lived – amazingly their block of flats survives. But most of the property is in private hands now. I doubt anyone remembers them. That said, I'm going to visit a local community centre this morning and see what I can find out. Maybe when Zell tells Tony who his client is, something will fall into place.'

'Tony's not obliged to tell us who that is,' Lee said.

'He shouldn't,' Vi added.

'Unless you work your charm on him, Vi . . .'

She smiled at him. Lee and Vi had been lovers once, long ago, and they retained huge affection for each other. She put a hand on his knee. 'I'll do my best.'

Mumtaz looked away and then said, 'Vi, have you managed to get any sense of documents having been filed at some time in Jedburgh Road?'

'No,' she said. 'The fact that I found the invoice and a mourning card in the same pile was, I think, just luck. I'll be honest with you – that house, and particularly that room, is a nightmare. When I first saw that bloke outside my place yesterday evening I thought I was seeing things. Spooked doesn't cover it. But I'll go back, if you want me to. Got the bit between me teeth now and I'll speak to Tony.'

Lee smiled.

'Well, I'd like you to come with me to Stepney, or rather Shadwell, to scope out the Coburg flats this morning,' Mumtaz said.

'OK.'

'Oh, and I've got an appointment in Stepney Green at three to meet a Rabbi Dreyfus at the Congregation of Jacob Synagogue,' she continued. 'He rang me yesterday. Said he got my number from Lionel Richmond. Did you give it to him, Vi?'

'No,' she said. 'Why would I? He's got my number. Not sure I even mentioned your name.'

'Oh, well,' Mumtaz said. 'Be good to have you along for that too. Then, depending upon what happens, we can both crack back on with Jedburgh Road tomorrow.'

'I think I'll have recovered by then!' Vi said.

But Lee Arnold was thoughtful during this exchange – or so it seemed.

Now the insurance assessor had been, Bernie could begin the job of tidying up. Whoever had trashed his house had smashed up a lot of stuff. Vases broken, crockery pulled out of cupboards and flung on the floor, upholstery ripped, mattresses cut open. As he'd told the insurance assessor, it was as if whoever had done this had been looking for something. That bloody diamond Bohuslav Kovar had told them about, the one Rudolf might have stolen.

As he swept up a load of broken ornaments, Bernie wondered how seriously Tony Bracci had taken all that stuff about the Acorn. Lee Arnold was, he knew, a sceptical type and so he probably thought that it was just a story, like Bernie did himself. But then if whoever had done this believed it was true . . .

The Czech had talked about how the golem could be used by both Jews and those who opposed Jews to further their respective causes. Gary, a security guard at work, talked about 'deepfakes' and how pieces of video could be doctored to look like something they weren't. Crystal, another guard whom he knew rather better, said that Gary was a fantasist and full of shit. It was difficult to know who to believe, although Bernie did fancy Crystal a bit and so that tipped it rather more in her favour.

He'd spoken to his manager first thing and had been given the night off to finish clearing up. The main thing he had to do was go out and buy a new bed. He could get one off the internet but it was important, Bernie felt, to try out a mattress before buying one. Also, if he went to one of the little independent shops up in East Ham, he could probably get them to deliver almost immediately. After flinging his old mattress into the garden and breaking up the already broken bed frame, Bernie got ready to go out and get the bus. The coppers reckoned that whoever had done him over got in via that louvre window in the kitchen. Just lifted it out and then put it back again when they'd finished, it seemed. Now he'd nailed it shut, but he still didn't really feel secure about leaving the house. But there was no choice, and also Mrs Igwe said she'd keep an eye on the place if he wanted to leave. And so he did, feeling his neighbour's eyes on him as he passed her front gate.

'I remember him when he used to drink,' front desk sergeant Rory McManus said. 'He was never any bother, except when he threw up and that was because of his tipple.'

'Snowballs,' Lee Arnold said. 'Stuart Zell and his sodding snowballs.'

'I think he used to drink them with his mum when she was alive,' Rory said. 'All the old girls used to drink them back in the day. Snowballs or Cherry B. Or if they were a bit rough, Mackeson.'

Lee laughed. McManus's catalogue of drinks from the 1970s engulfed him in a wave of nostalgia, albeit for a time that had been pretty grim for him. He'd come to Forest Gate Police Station to make sure that Stuart Zell turned up to see Tony Bracci, as he'd promised Lee he would. And Zell had been true to his word, although Bracci hadn't been in when he'd arrived and so Lee had waited with him until Tony turned up. Now he was tapping up McManus, a notoriously loose-lipped old desk sergeant.

Lee moved close up to the sergeant and said, 'Know where Bracci was this morning, Rory?'

He pulled a face. Rory McManus, with his red scrubbed-looking skin and faded ginger hair, looked how

Lee imagined Ed Sheeran would in old age.

'Plashet Cemetery,' Rory said.

'Why?'

There was only one punter in the waiting area and the office behind Rory was empty. But he still whispered. 'Connected to Cyprus Place,' he said.

'Cyprus Place?'

Lee knew that as well as the golem, evidence related to the Cyprus Place county lines gang had also been robbed from Belvedere. But that didn't mean they'd both turn up in the golem's old burial plot.

'Yeah,' Rory said. 'And word is, they found something.'

'What?'

'Dunno.'

Lee went and sat down near to, but not beside, the one and only punter. Although he'd always hoped he might have a word with Tony Bracci once Zell had done his stuff, in light of what McManus had told him, that had become even more urgent. When Mumtaz had told him about how Rabbi Dreyfus from the Congregation of Jacob Synagogue had contacted her, it had bothered him. Vi had refuted any suggestion she'd told this Lionel Richmond bloke, the source for Rabbi Dreyfus, anything about Mumtaz. And yet the rabbi had phoned Mumtaz.

Was he becoming paranoid? Probably. But then Vi and Mumtaz were not the sort of people to make stuff up and if they were being stalked, it was concerning. This golem case was expanding in ways he couldn't have imagined, and he was keen to share this with Tony.

* * *

169

Gladys had moved into the Coburg in 1954, according to Zonaira the community centre worker. Gladys herself, however, could only say, 'Oh my good God!' which she did repeatedly. Pushed to the centre in a wheelchair by her neighbour, a Mrs Badar, Gladys was very far along the dementia spectrum and really annoyed another old lady called Milly.

Although not resident in the Coburg, Milly lived on Hardinge Street in a house with her son. Whenever Gladys came out with 'Oh my good God!' Milly would yell, 'Oh shut up for fuck's sake, you silly old cow!' And while Zonaira always asked her, politely, to keep her observations to herself, Milly wouldn't be told.

So while Mumtaz attempted to communicate with a Mrs Causland who had lived in the Coburg since 1960, but had then moved to a care home one year ago, Vi went and sat beside Milly.

Tipping her head in the direction of Gladys, Vi said, 'She get on your wick?'

'Off her head,' Milly said. 'Should be in a home. My son makes me come here every week, and every week I tell him it'll just be that silly mare *oh good Godding* all over the place. What's the point?'

'To get out and see other people?' Vi said.

Milly looked at her with total disdain. 'What do I wanna do that for?' she said. 'I've met everyone who interests me. All people do these days is talk bloody nonsense.'

Vi smiled.

'Oh, you can laugh if you like, mate, but I mean it,' Milly continued. 'Everyone my age has got dementia and all of you younger ones treat us like we're kids.'

'No one could accuse you of being either demented or a kid,' Vi said. 'How long you lived round here, Milly?'

'Me? I was born here,' she said. '1930 in the same house I live in now. My dad was a docker, my mum took in washing. What you wanna know for? Why you here anyway? You don't come from round here.'

'No, but me and my friend are trying to find out whether anyone remembers a family who used to live here until, we think, just after the war.'

'What family?'

Her eyes half closed now, Milly was deeply suspicious. She was 'proper East End', Vi thought.

'Called Freedland,' Vi said. 'We only know one of their first names. Chani, a woman, and then there was her husband, Rudolf. His surname was Baruch. Lived in the Coburg and had a little boy, Morris.'

For a long time it was as if Milly hadn't heard her, but Vi waited. She was a sharp old girl this one, and either she did know something or she was playing at being deaf for a laugh.

'He was sick, that foreigner Chani Freedland married. The Nazis tortured him, my dad said. Then he died in a raid. Poor bastard.'

'Did you know the family then, Milly?'

'A bit,' she said. 'Me and my brothers used to play in the street with the Freedlands. Not Chani, she was a lot older. But her and her sisters had three young brothers.'

'You played with the brothers?'

'Yes.'

'Do you know what happened to the family after the war?'

'Not really. Chani and her mum stayed on in the Coburg

for a bit, I think. The three boys was evacuated. My brother Ernie was mates with their boy Saul. But Ernie died back in the eighties.' Her hard shell softened for a moment and then she said, 'Ernie and Saul was gay, you know. Ernie never married and neither did Saul.'

'How do you know that Saul never married?' Vi asked. 'Did Ernie tell you?'

'He must've,' Milly said. 'I never saw Saul or none of the boys after the war. A lot of people lost each other then. We lost our mum. She hated going down the shelters. Made us all go. When the raid was over we found her sat up in her chair with a cup in her hand, a piece of guttering clean through her chest. She looked surprised . . .'

Milly began to cry.

Cynthia was Lionel Richmond's second wife. Twenty years his junior, she'd been a flight attendant for British Airways and then Emirates when she'd met Lionel on a business flight to Dubai in 2015. His first wife, Hazel, had only been dead for just over a year at the time and so Cynthia had been obliged to endure a frosty reception from her husband's two sons and their children for quite a while. Now fully integrated into the family, Cynthia was loved and trusted by everyone and it was universally acknowledged that she was good for Lionel. Consequently they did most things together, although Lionel drew the line at shopping trips – especially to those vast American-style malls, like Westfield in Shepherd's Bush. Planting a kiss on her husband's forehead, Cynthia was off to Westfield with her sister.

'I'll be back around five,' she told him as she picked up her handbag and began to walk toward the front hall.

'Take your time,' Lionel called out after her. 'Have fun.'

Alone now, Lionel spent half an hour with the *Financial Times* and then went to the kitchen to make himself a sandwich. He'd been a barrister all his working life and, while he knew several colleagues who had carried on working into their nineties, it hadn't been for him. He'd been retired for six years now and enjoyed it. With his much younger, very active wife, this enormous house in up-market Gerrards Cross and his sons and grandchildren living locally, he was never hard up for things to do. It was nice therefore to have a lazy day on his own for a change.

As he carried his lunch back to his study, he wondered whether he might watch a bit of horse racing on the telly after the news at one. His father Menachim had always had a weakness for the horses. Lionel liked it too, but without the betting that had sometimes cost his father the family's rent money. Lionel had never really got used to how far he'd come from his impoverished childhood. He'd worked hard for it, of course. No one had ever given him anything. But what drive he'd had back then!

He sat down in his chair, put the TV on and began to eat. It was only a cheese-and-tomato sandwich, but it was like a banquet compared to what he'd eaten as a child. Boiled cabbage with soggy latkas. His mother had been no cook, and if his dad had lost money on the horses the fare was basic to say the least. Beetroot. He still couldn't bear it. Reg probably still ate beetroot, mainly because it was cheap.

Thinking about his brother made Lionel frown. Because he was so much younger, he couldn't imagine what horrors

Reg had endured. When Reg had been little the family had been really poor. He'd sometimes gone to school with no shoes on and any sort of food had been scarce. Although that hadn't been the worst of it. No. That had been the fear about what his father was doing when he filled the flat with those men. They made sounds, even now, Lionel couldn't describe. What had they been doing and why had he, like Reg before him, been locked in his room while they did it?

When Reg had been young this had happened all the time. Lionel had been lucky he'd experienced it so infrequently. But it still baffled him, and he suspected it was at least in part to blame for his brother's strange life. Even though he and his father had talked about lots of things, Lionel had never found out anything about his life before he came to England. Maybe it had been too painful for him to talk about it?

The racing had just started on the telly when Lionel heard his front door open. It was probably his eldest boy. He was often in and out.

'Alex? Is that you?' Lionel called out.

'It goes no further,' Tony Bracci told Lee Arnold.

''Course.'

They were outside Forest Gate Police Station, in the car park, smoking.

'Smack,' Tony said.

'What? Buried in the . . .'

'By the back wall,' Tony said. 'All bagged up and ready for its court appearance.'

'So definitely from Cyprus Place?'

'Oh yeah. But nothing else,' Tony said. 'No statements, no

forensic evidence. Elsewhere or destroyed. Probably destroyed.'

'What now?'

'Back to the flat in Cyprus Place. It's still empty. I've requested a warrant to search Gabe York's gaff in Wapping. Much good that'll do me. But belt and braces, you know.'

'I do.'

Tony leant against the back wall of the station. 'He'll have the most cast-iron alibi for the Belvedere break-in known to humanity. Ditto his heavies. All the kids are on remand and so it can't have been them. Anyway, the Belvedere job was professional, way beyond the pay grade of an amateur rapper from Beckton.'

The unspoken name of the cemetery where the heroin had been found sat between them.

It was Tony who eventually broke the silence. He said, 'We never found the golem.'

Lee looked up. 'You think there's a connection between Cyprus Place and the golem?'

'Whoever raided Belvedere took the Cyprus Place evidence and the golem. Why?' Tony said. 'There has to be a connection on some level. You must see that.'

'Course I do!' Lee smiled. 'Just waiting for you to say it first.'

'Why?'

'Why? Because you're the Filth, man,' he said. 'I'm just a PI. I can't affect nothing. You can ask me to work with you while I . . .' He shrugged.

'I can't ask you to work with me, Lee, you know that,' Tony said. 'But—'

'Let's leave it at "but", shall we?' Lee said. 'Let's go with

175

but and . . . Look, Tone, Mumtaz and Vi are being shadowed by someone.'

'What do you mean?'

He told him what the women had said to him, and Tony frowned. Lee continued, 'It's since we started working for Bernie Bennett. So it's something to do with the golem is my guess.'

Tony nodded. 'Does this lurking outside their places happen mostly at night?'

'Yeah.'

'Well, I can try and get a patrol or two to swing by Mumtaz's place and I can have a word with Waltham Abbey for Vi,' Tony said. 'But you know how stretched we are. Thinner on the ground every fucking day. Accepting this is about the golem, I wonder why now? We found the thing back in March. It was all over the papers. If it means so much to someone, why wait until now to nick it? And what they gonna do with it, eh? And how's it connected to Cyprus Place? Makes my fucking head hurt.'

Lee smiled. He knew that feeling. He said, 'Did you find out who Zell's been working for?'

Tony gave a short, bark-like laugh. 'You ever hear of an old variety star called Ramesses? Otherwise known as the High Priest of Thebes?'

'What?' Lee stubbed his fag out and then lit another. 'What's that?'

'A mentalist act,' Tony said. 'Mind-reading. Zell's been working for Ramesses, keeping an eye on Bernie Bennett because the High Priest reckons his daughter's been having an affair with him.'

'So Ramesses can't read his own daughter's mind, then? Don't give you much confidence in his act,' Lee said.

Tony shook his head. 'Clever bugger.'

'I aim to please.'

'So the old man's got Zell obboing Bernie and this daughter, who also apparently works at Newham General. She's married and so the Pharaoh Ramesses doesn't approve of her fling with Bernie. Doesn't want his grandkids upset.'

'And this is the only kind of job poor old Zell can get?'

Tony shrugged.

'Anyway, that's why Stuart Zell was on Shipman Road, staking out Bennett.'

'So is Bernie having an affair?' Lee asked.

'Zell said he can find no evidence to suggest he is,' Tony said. 'But then you have to ask yourself why the Pharaoh's daughter, Rosamund, would have it off with a hospital cleaner. I mean let's face it, Bernie's pretty good for his age, but he's no George Clooney.'

'No, but he's a nice enough bloke,' Lee said. 'And what's wrong with dating a cleaner anyway?'

'Nothing,' Tony said, 'unless you're a consultant gynaecologist.'

'What, you mean this Pharaoh's daughter's—'

'A consultant gynaecologist at Newham General,' Tony said. 'A Dr Rosamund Black.'

He was a nice man, Milly Atkins's son. Somewhere in his sixties, divorced – which was why he'd come to live back with his mum – and a long-time Labour Party activist, he was also embarrassed.

177

'I'm sorry about Mum,' he said to Mumtaz. 'Honest to God, I don't know what to do with her sometimes. She means well . . .'

Mumtaz put a hand on Philip Atkins's wrist. 'It's alright, Mr Atkins,' she said. 'I can assure you that I've been called much worse than "the Asian girl" in my time.'

He led Vi and Mumtaz into his mother's dingy, mainly brown lounge and asked them to sit down. He'd already made tea, which he'd set out on a low coffee table – teapot, cups, milk jug, sugar. Milly herself had gone for a lie-down after her exertions at the community centre. But she'd invited Vi and Mumtaz back to speak to Philip because he remembered his Uncle Ernie and Saul well. And he was gay.

Once they all had drinks, Philip said, 'Uncle Ernie worked in a kennels out in Essex. He was always much happier around animals. He had a flat near the kennels.'

'Where?'

'Rainham,' he said. 'But that was also where Saul lived. They never lived together, you understand. That generation were so damaged by anti-LGBTQ+ legislation I don't think it would have occurred to them. They'd've been too frightened.'

'Things have come a long way,' Vi said.

'After a struggle and a half,' Philip said. 'Whenever I hear about how so many lives of the older generation were ruined, I always think of them. But in old age, Uncle Ernie got bolder. He really supported me when I came out in the early eighties. Saul was dead by then. I mean, Mum and Dad were fine, but some members of the family weren't. Some cousins still don't talk to me.'

'That's terrible,' Mumtaz said.

'Oh, I'm used to it.' He smiled. 'But anyway, Mum said you wanted to talk about Ernie and Saul – and Chani.'

'Yes. We're trying to trace whoever we can from the Freedland family,' Vi said.

'Well, I'll tell you what I know,' Philip said. 'It's not much, but . . . Saul, as I said, lived in Rainham. He had a seafood stall down there outside a pub called The Phoenix. When I was little, Uncle Ernie used to take us there to buy cockles. Then we'd have them for our tea with bread and marge. Sometimes Saul'd have a brother with him, can't remember his name. When me and my sister used to go down and stay with Uncle Ernie in the school holidays, we weren't really interested in anything except Ernie's dogs. When we grew up we didn't go much, but then when Ernie got ill in 1980, I went and stayed with him – which was when he told me things. He had cancer.'

'I'm sorry,' Vi said.

Philip smiled. 'That's when he told me about him and Saul,' he said. 'I suppose he wanted to get things off his chest before he died. Also I think he'd always suspected about me. He died in 1985. Anyway, Saul. He was evacuated with his brothers to Devon during the war. They went to a farm, which they loved, which was why Saul moved to the country after the war. Sometimes their mum would go down there to see them with their sister Chani, and later on with their nephew who was a baby. They came down just after Chani's husband was killed in a raid in 1940, and it had a huge impact on Saul.'

'In what way?'

'Chani's husband was a foreigner. He'd escaped from the Nazis and arrived in Britain in 1938. But he'd been tortured before he left his country and was in a bad way when he got here. Then he was killed and Chani was in bits. They'd been really in love, apparently. But there was more to it as well. Chani told Saul that her husband had some sort of secret. He always feared he'd be murdered, she'd said. Something he'd done back in his own country meant that someone wanted him dead. She didn't know who. But she did tell Saul that if the war was ever over and we had peace again, she was going to leave London and take Morris with her. She said she didn't think that the baby was safe. Saul told Ernie she'd sounded like a nutter, talking about curses and secret societies and all sorts of conspiracy rubbish.'

'Philip, do you know anything about Chani's husband's funeral?' Vi asked.

'No,' he said. 'I wasn't born then.'

'I know, but maybe you heard something?'

'Not that I can remember,' he said. 'Mum was only a kid when he died and so I don't think she would've gone.'

It was at this moment that Milly appeared.

'I can't sleep with all you lot down here, gassing away,' she said. 'Phil, love, can you pour me a cuppa.'

As she sat down, Vi took the old woman's hand and said, 'Sorry, Milly.'

'When you get to my age, you never really know when you can sleep and when you can't,' Milly said. 'You can feel knackered and it won't come, wide awake and then you'll be spark out for ten hours. You was asking about Chani's husband's funeral . . .'

'Yeah.'

'No one went,' she said. 'The Freedlands had a plot up

180

Plashet Cemetery and he went in there, but no one saw him off. Only Jaggers the undertaker and the rabbi. It was at the height of the Blitz and people never knew what was coming next. They stayed close to home if they could, especially if they had a shelter. A lot of sad little funerals with no one at them back in them days. My brother Ernie had this idea Chani's husband had been murdered, he probably got that off her. Nobody knew him when he come here, and he was always too sick to do anyone any harm. Why would anyone murder someone like that?'

FOURTEEN

Something black, like a slug, slowly succumbed to the force of gravity and fell to the floor. There was a short slapping noise as it hit the parquet, which nobody heard. The living, upstairs and other lounge and reception rooms were far too busy for such gruesome stunts. The dead didn't care.

'You know the drill, Gabe.'

He did. Gabriel York was a veteran of police searches. He was also an intelligent man who never brought his work home and had never been addicted to anything in his life. Tony Bracci knew it, as did his search team, but procedure had to be observed.

'All I ask, DI Bracci, is that your guys be respectful of my property,' Gabe said.

He was a good-looking man. At sixty-five he was gym-honed and smart. He wore Savile Row suits; his wife, Imelda, was pure understated chic with not a plastic surgery scar in sight and the bearing of an aristocrat. Their son, Timothy, was a respected academic specialising in computer science. He'd always been kept well away from his father's business and appeared on television from time to time talking about the internet and cybersecurity. Gabe had done well for a poor boy from the arse end of Jamaica. He was also, to Tony's eternal chagrin, likeable too. Gabe York was a drug dealer. As a young man he'd been involved in people being beaten up, terrorised and maybe even killed. Now he had other people to do that for him. It was those people who recruited kids for his many county lines operations.

'Of course, Gabe,' Tony said. Then to his team, 'You heard what Mr York said – gentle, no breakages.'

'Would you like a cup of coffee, DI Bracci?' Imelda York asked.

She was so beautiful.

'Thank you, Mrs York,' Tony said. 'That would be great.'

'Do sit down, DI Bracci.'

Gabe and Imelda's furniture was extraordinary. Art Deco, probably original, it too was understated and beautiful and it fitted into Gabe's cool Wapping warehouse conversion as if it had been made for the place. This man was clever, wealthy, cultured, and Tony wanted to bring him down so badly it hurt.

'So tell me what this is about?' Gabe asked as he sat opposite Tony, lifting his elegant trousers just a little as he settled into his chair.

'Well, Gabe, as you know, our evidence store over the water was broken into and a lot of stuff pertaining to your case was stolen,' Tony said.

'My case?' Gabe smiled. 'Not mine, DI Bracci. However much you may wish to believe that it is. I understand what you are referring to is the "Cyprus Place" case.'

'Whatever.' Tony also smiled.

'I know that certain delusional allegations have been made about me,' Gabe said. 'It pains me that an intelligent man like yourself is now here on the basis of those allegations – which I have addressed, as you know, DI Bracci.'

'Oh, I know you're gonna come up clean, Gabe,' Tony said. 'But we have to go through the motions, don't we?'

'We do.'

Imelda York returned carrying a cup and saucer, which she placed down in front of Tony. Then she left. A few worrying sounds floated down from upstairs and Tony yelled, 'Careful up there! You break it, you fucking pay for it! And Mr York don't have no rubbish!'

'Thank you, DI Bracci.'

'I also know how much your lawyers cost, Gabe,' Tony said. 'Hate for my lot to force you to have to employ them over a perfectly avoidable breakage.' His eyes glittered. 'So why the golem, Gabe? Why take a worthless clay figure? I've seen it. It's not even pretty.'

For a moment Gabriel York said nothing and then he smiled. But this time the smile didn't reach his eyes.

'I've no idea what you're talking about, DI Bracci.'

'Life-size clay model of a man,' Tony said. 'Taken from Belvedere along with five kilos of smack, some pretty scary, for you, paperwork and some of your DNA. Now I don't know why someone kindly gave us back two kilos of smack very badly hidden in Plashet Cemetery this morning. I know they didn't mean to do that, and I also know that gift was not made to us by you. So considering all that, I would suggest, Gabe, that you have a good long look at who you're working with, or who's working for you – because they're putting your profit margins in danger, mate.'

'Nothing to do with me.' Still he smiled, but still it didn't reach his eyes. And as anyone who was even slightly acquainted with Gabe York knew, he was a human masterclass in covering up his emotions, body language and tells. He was rattled.

The Congregation of Jacob Synagogue was beautiful inside. The walls, painted white and light blue, enhanced the natural daylight pouring in from high arched windows. Built in 1921 it nevertheless had a Georgian feel to it. Dark wood pews, rather than capturing light, served to enhance the slightly otherworldly feel of the building.

Rabbi Dreyfus was a good-looking, apparently easy-going man, probably in his forties. Vi had to remind herself that he was actually an Orthodox Jew and so his views, as well as those of his congregants, would be religiously conservative. This, oddly, made him more like Mumtaz than her – but, she assumed, without Mumtaz's strong streak of feminism. He was also, seemingly without instruction – Mumtaz had told Vi she'd told the rabbi nothing about the real reason for their visit – well prepared with information about the Freedlands.

'I've done some digging for you,' the rabbi said. 'And the family you're interested in, the Freedlands, were not congregants here but at the East London Synagogue on Rectory Square. That doesn't exist any more, and so most of the remaining Jews in the East End now come here. But we keep the old records, which was why I was able to trace your family.'

He had a sheaf of papers with him which, the women noticed, were handwritten. Much of it was in Hebrew. Clearly Lionel Richmond had clued him in.

'We're looking specifically for a Chani Freedland,' Vi said. 'Also known as Chani Baruch or Chani Bennett. She died in 1970. Had a brother called Saul.'

'Mmm.' The rabbi looked through his papers. 'Ah, yes – here, Chani, daughter of Israel Freedland. They lived in the Coburg buildings.'

'Yes,' Mumtaz said. 'Rabbi, do you know whether Chani had any other siblings besides Saul?'

'I think she did . . .' He looked through his paperwork again. 'Yes: Reuben, Nathan and of course Saul. Then, older than Chani, Aaron and a girl, Bina.'

'We know Saul's dead,' Mumtaz said. 'But I wonder whether you'd know if any of the others are still alive. We know that Chani is buried with her husband in Plashet Cemetery, East Ham. But she may be an outlier. Her husband was a foreigner and he died during the war, when things must have been chaotic.'

'Indeed.'

Then she said, 'Rabbi, do you know anything about Chani's husband, Rudolf Baruch?'

For a moment he was quite impassive and then he said, 'You mean the Golem of East Ham?'

Mumtaz felt herself flush. 'Well, um . . .'

'That's him,' Vi cut in. 'Know about it, do you?'

'Of course,' he said. 'It's not every day a golem is discovered in an apparently ordinary city graveyard.'

'So what do you think?' Vi asked.

'Think? Miss Collins, the story of the golem is an old Jewish tale. My understanding is that the figure found in the Plashet graveyard was just that, a figure. A reporter called it the golem. It's nothing of the sort. Golems don't exist. It's a fairy story.'

'Someone's stolen it,' Vi said.

Did he pale because he hadn't known?

'From the Met storage facility in Kent,' Vi continued. 'Look, Rabbi, I'll level with you. I'm not related to the Freedlands. What me and my colleague here are doing is trying to find the body of Rudolf Baruch. His grandson needs to have a bit of peace. But he never knew his grandfather, he didn't know Chani as an adult, and she lost contact with her family decades ago. The golem, or whatever it is that replaced Rudolf in his coffin, isn't our concern – except to say it seems someone wanted it, because someone nicked it. We've made contact with the grandson of the undertaker who buried Rudolf and he's let us go through his records, but this hasn't helped us locate any relatives. We've yet to get hold of the Burial Society but we thought that maybe we could shortcut that via you.'

'Rabbi, we're working for a man whose grandfather's grave has been desecrated,' Mumtaz said. 'The same grandfather who was denied a decent burial. A man some think may even have been murdered.'

Rabbi Dreyfus looked down at the papers beside him on the pew and said, 'You know that for a small number of people these old legends, like the golem, are very real? And powerful. They can also play into the hands of people who hate Jews too.'

'I've heard that,' Mumtaz said.

'I thought you said it was a fairy tale,' Vi added.

'It is, on one level. Of course it is. But if some people, even only a small number, do believe it – then it does have a sort of life of its own,' he said. 'The attic of the Old New Synagogue in Prague, where the most famous golem of all is supposed to lie, still exerts a powerful influence over people. It's a symbol of resistance. And as such a symbol, it's also an object of hate amongst those who oppose that resistance. Whatever the rational, Western parts of our brains might think, the ancient structures, beneath our consciousness, still respond to things like the golem. I knew why you were coming here today . . .'

'Via Lionel Richmond?'

The rabbi didn't answer. But then he said, 'My job is not just to minister to my congregants here in London. My job is also, in as much as I can, to protect all people, regardless of race or religion. I know you mean well, ladies, but you must stop this now. My advice to you is to tell Bernard Bennett you can go no further. Disappointing for him, but look, things are in hand. I can't say any more than this.'

Mumtaz felt she could trust this man and so she said, 'Rabbi Dreyfus, Violet and I have noticed unknown men following us.'

'Oh God.' He shook his head. 'Tell the police if you haven't already done so. Please.'

The Nazis had murdered his grandparents and so when it came to anything to do with the Holocaust, Bohuslav Kovar

188

had skin in the game. The American, Adam Sachs, might be after the Acorn for its monetary value, but he wanted to find it because if the Nazis did have it, he had to take it from them. Also, he wanted to be right. Mathilde Zimmer had not been buried with the Acorn round her neck. He'd always believed it. He'd also always believed that somehow Rudolf Baruch and Levi Rozenberg had taken it. But how? Rozenberg had died in Theresienstadt just before his family were taken to Auschwitz. But Baruch had escaped to England, which was why he was here now.

Assuming he'd smuggled the Acorn out of Prague and across the Channel to England, then where was it now? Bernie Bennett claimed to know nothing about it. But someone had been looking for something when they'd broken into his house. Bohuslav was a journalist and so he picked up rumours like other people picked up colds. Even when they were uncomfortable or completely deranged, there was always, he felt, a tiny viral core of truth in there somewhere. Bohuslav knew to his bones that, as well as Adam Sachs, there were two other groups of people who were actively looking for the diamond. Those who had created the golem, and those who wished to control the ancient symbol for their own ends whilst using the Acorn to help fund their activities. What the first group would do with the jewel if they found it, Bohuslav didn't know; money meant little to people like them. But that didn't mean they wouldn't kill to obtain the golem, because they would. They had.

Bohuslav had called Bernie that morning, who had told him that whatever was going on he had to replace his ruined bed today and try to bring some order back to his house.

Unlike Prague, London didn't have a huge history of Jewish mysticism, but Bohuslav had read that a Kabbalist had once lived on Old London Bridge. He'd created a golem, it was said, back in the eighteenth century. Old London Bridge no longer existed but Bohuslav had gone to look at its new incarnation that morning. He'd watched, mesmerised for hours as the tidal Thames rose and fell, revealing the mud underneath the river. Anecdotally this was the mud that had been used to make the London golem all those centuries ago. Had the mud used to create Rudolf Baruch's golem also been taken from the river? Was there any significance to this river?

His phone pinged to tell him he had a message. It was confirmation of his meeting on the other bridge, Tower Bridge, at two. Maybe after this he would know more.

The Czech journalist was staying in what some people called 'a workman's hotel'. It wasn't bad, in Lee's opinion. It wasn't a front for a brothel, like some of them. But it was definitely downmarket from a Travelodge.

Kovar had left his digs just after nine and had headed into the City on the Docklands Light Railway. From there he'd walked to London Bridge where he'd stood looking at the Thames for two hours, occasionally checking his phone, but mostly staring into space. What was his deal? He'd told them he'd come to England to follow up on the Rudolf Baruch story. It had fascinated him all his life. But was that true?

Lee was unable to shake the conviction that there was more than met the eye here. Even though he was staying in cheap accommodation, London was an expensive city and if, as he'd said, Bohuslav was doing all this as a speculative investigation, he had to be paying for it himself. But was he? According to the Czech, this diamond, the Acorn, was worth twenty million dollars, which was a lot of dosh. But even if he found the diamond, Bohuslav had no claim on it himself. Was there, Lee wondered, something else about the Acorn that made it so desirable? Clearly the government of Czechia didn't think so, or they would have exhumed Mathilde Zimmer's body in spite of the physical difficulties. All he'd managed to find out about it online was that the Acorn had gone missing during the Second World War, that it had belonged to the Zimmer family of Prague after being given to them by the Empress Elisabeth of Austria-Hungary. Nothing about why the Empress had given it to her.

Now the Czech was on the move, finally. Lee made sure that he wasn't being followed and moved off after him. Then his phone rang – it was Mumtaz. As he walked, following Kovar walking east along Lower Thames Street, he listened to what she had to say about meeting Rabbi Dreyfus.

'I believe he was genuinely worried for our safety,' she said. 'Although it all came over a bit conspiracy theory for my liking.'

'I told Tony Bracci about you and Vi's shadows,' Lee said. 'Something's going on.'

'Yes, and I've been giving that some more thought too,' Mumtaz said. 'So look, the golem was stolen alongside evidence in the Cyprus Place case, which is coming to court. Why? I know we've already asked this question, but hear me out. What if all this has nothing to do with the golem? What if us being followed, Bernie's break-in, is actually a sleight of hand, a distraction?'

He sighed. Then he told her about the heroin Tony Bracci had found in Plashet Cemetery.

'Seized during the Cyprus Place investigation,' he said. 'Of course there's a connection, but whether the chicken comes before the egg or vice versa is the question we all have to ask ourselves now.'

'I know it's irrational and, as you can imagine, Vi is straining every nerve not to believe this, but I can feel something really evil here, Lee. If I could put that better and not use the "e" word I would, but I can't. In fact the more I think about Rudolf Baruch, the old lady he maybe stole from, the golem, the sicker I feel. Accepting that someone connected to Cyprus Place and/or Gabe York hid the drugs from the Belvedere break-in at Plashet Cemetery, we have to at least ask why. I mean, I get that if they're pinching evidence it makes sense to take it all. It also makes sense to keep the smack separate so they can sell it. But the cemetery? Whoever took the Cyprus Place evidence also took the golem and, I think, they took it for someone, to order.'

'These people your rabbi is so afraid of.'

'Looks like it,' she said. 'Anyway, I'm going to Plaistow now. Spend a few hours helping Vi at Jedburgh Road.'

'I'm going to find out what Kovar's up to if I can,' Lee said. 'At the moment it looks as if he's headed for Tower Bridge.'

Predictably, the police found nothing of note either in or around Gabriel York's Wapping warehouse. Tony Bracci was unsurprised. What did surprise him however was that Gabe, who was usually openly exultant when things like this happened, looked unusually thoughtful.

Prior to Tony joining his officers down in the street, Gabe took him to one side.

'What is all this about the golem?' he asked him.

'What's what?' Tony said.

Gabe frowned. 'What does it mean?'

'Mean? It's a religious thing, is my understanding,' he said. 'Jewish. I can't tell you about the ins and outs, but basically golems were created to protect Jews back when they were being persecuted.'

'How?'

'I don't know. Legend is that it could be brought to life somehow. Not possible, I know – but while some people believe it is, the thing has meaning. Why do you want to know? You got it, have you?'

'Of course not!'

'Because if you have, you may have got more than you bargained for.'

Gabe frowned again.

Tony moved in close to him and said, 'We live in a world where symbols from the past have been making a comeback. And while some people who rally around flags and statues and golems do so for comfort and reassurance, there are other people who use stuff like that to prop up, or enforce, their prejudices. And they're not the sort of people you want poking around in your Neff kitchen or knowing where your wife shops. Know what I mean?'

Gabriel didn't say anything. But as he left, Tony Bracci smiled. Gabe York was a ruthless drug dealer who had possibly even killed, but he was also a bright man who would know real wrong'uns if he met them, and Tony was now convinced that he had. He'd let Gabe stew overnight and then see where they were the following day.

'Until the Convert or Exile Decree of 1290, some Jews actually lived in the Tower of London,' Cooper told him. 'The whole convert-or-get-out thing was, of course, in response to accusations made against Jews for the best part of a century.'

'The Blood Libel,' Bohuslav said.

As well as economic decline, the other main predictor of an outbreak of anti-Semitism in Europe had always been the contention some Christians put about that Jews drank the blood of Christian children – the Blood Libel. As Bohuslav knew only too well, this was an accusation Hitler had levelled at Jews too.

'Indeed,' the man said. 'So here, from Tower Wharf in 1290, 1,461 Jews left by boat never to return. Jews were then banished from England until Oliver Cromwell invited them back when he took over as Lord Protector in 1653. We've been here ever since.'

Cooper Lewis was a young man who made his living planning and running historical trips around London. Proudly Jewish, he specialised in Jewish London history as well as Irish London, Jack the Ripper tours and Ghost Walks. Bohuslav had been looking for some Jewish London tours online and had initially come across a guide called Leo Lowe, who was all booked up. Lowe it had been who had recommended Cooper.

Standing on the pavement on the side of the road across Tower Bridge, Cooper pointed out the main building inside the Tower site, the White Tower.

'It was basically a fortress,' he said. 'And of course a prison and place of execution. As for the bridge . . . built much later, in 1886, and no connection to London Jewry as far as I know. Like everyone else, Jewish Londoners used and still use it. But, as I said in my text, we've an opportunity to go into a part of the bridge very few people get to see – and it is something, I hope, you will not want to have missed.'

'No.'

One of two bascule chambers were open for viewing, apparently. These were the huge cavities into which the bridge's massive counterweights swung when it opened to allow shipping into and out of the Pool of London. They were rarely open to the public; Bohuslav had apparently got lucky.

Cooper smiled. 'Do have to warn you, however, that there are a lot of steps down to the chamber. They're narrow and steep and there are one hundred and fifteen of them. Health and safety: if you think you might have a problem getting down there and then getting back up again, you should tell me now.'

'No,' Bohuslav said. 'I don't think so.'

Cynthia and her sister Madeleine arrived back at the house exhausted. As she put her key in the front door, Cynthia said, 'Give Lionel a bit of a shock. I told him we'd be back about five. We're not what we were, are we Maddy?'

'Oh, I don't know,' Madeleine said. 'You maxed out a credit card and I've spent my entire clothes allowance for the year. I think we've done well.'

'Yeah, but it was so hot in there, wasn't it? Thank God for Caffè Concerto!'

They went inside and Cynthia called out to her husband. 'Lionel!'

He didn't reply. Cynthia rolled her eyes. 'Probably gone to sleep in front of the racing,' she said.

The two women walked to the kitchen, which was when they noticed that something was wrong. There was what looked like flour all over the worktops and all of the cupboard doors were open. Lionel only very rarely did anything more than make sandwiches, tea and coffee in the kitchen.

'God Almighty!' Cynthia said. 'What's this? Lionel!'

Still nothing. Leaving her sister in the kitchen, Cynthia Richmond walked back down the hall, headed for her husband's study.

At first she couldn't see anything amiss. The TV was on, there was an empty plate on the coffee table. Clearly Lionel had fed himself. But then, as her eyes adjusted to the relative darkness of Lionel's study, she began to make things out, things that were not right. Like the standard lamp fallen on its side, its bulb apparently blown; like all the drawers in her husband's desk pulled out, their contents scattered across the floor.

And then she saw her husband. Lying behind his chair. His shirt had been pulled up to his chest to expose his belly, which had been ripped open. Blood, intestines and chunks of something black and glistening hung out of him.

Cynthia fainted.

FIFTEEN

There was a bloke at the top of the stairs leading down to the bascule chamber. Bohuslav and the man he was with had walked right past him without a word, but Lee felt uneasy about him. He'd no idea why, beyond the fact that he had no official badge or anything to denote what he was doing there. Lee himself wasn't sure what *he* was doing there either. He'd followed the Czech into a lesser-known part of the bridge, and now here he was hiding round a corner from a man he had a vague feeling of unease about.

He was four-square, the man at the top of the stairs. He reminded Lee a bit of Hungarian leader Viktor Orban. An overweight, belligerent would-be dictator, Orban's look was not a good one, and whenever he saw him on the telly, Lee always got the impression he was a thug. Ditto this man, although while the guy was big, with large fists and a definite weight advantage, Lee was taller, slimmer and hard in that way only ex-professional soldiers can be. In other words, he didn't mind getting hit.

But there was getting hit and there was walking into a fucking shitshow, and he didn't want to do the latter. In addition, nothing was going on. Kovar was on some sort of tour, that was all. Lee would just have to hang around and see what developed. Then Viktor Orban left his post and followed the Czech and the other man.

'Invoices,' Vi said as she held a sheaf of thin, almost transparent paper up to the light. 'Formaldehyde.'

'Eeeww!' Mumtaz said.

'Gallons of the stuff,' Vi continued.

'We know Jaggers employed embalmers,' Mumtaz said.

Vi frowned. 'Funny Rudolf Baruch never set up as an embalmer when he came here, I think. Personally I don't see the point but it's quite a rare skill. He could've made some money.'

'The Atkins's and the rabbi said Rudolf was sick. Maybe he couldn't work?'

'Maybe.'

They both carried on sorting through the mountain that was Jaggers's company paperwork until Mumtaz said, 'Vi, going back to Rabbi Dreyfus again, he must've got in contact via Pipps's dad, right?'

'Yeah. Lionel,' she said. 'Got a funny vibe off him.'

'Yes, I remember.'

'What did you think about the rabbi warning us off Bernie?'

She sighed. 'We can't let him down now, Vi. Lee told me

the cops are going to check on you and me at night from time to time, but I don't know what else we can or should do. I mean, if this is anti-Semitism we have to front it out, don't we. We have to do that for Bernie and his Czech family, if not for that journalist Kovar.'

'What's he like?' Vi asked.

Mumtaz stopped sorting. 'Obsessed with the story of Rudolf Baruch, or rather fixated. Obsessed implies some level of derangement. He wants to know the truth, but some of the things he told us require the kind of suspension of disbelief I find hard. He reckons there are people who protect the golem, magicians who know how to control it. He's also of the opinion that other people, basically Nazis, are bent upon getting hold of it for their own, less public-spirited purposes.'

'If I hadn't seen the rise of far-right groups on the streets myself, I'd say that was laughable,' Vi said. 'But I have and it's far from funny. It's also been made normal. Look at all the press the far right get these days and look at the shit people can be made to believe. Not that any of that should concern us. If we don't stick to what we can see with our own eyes, we're buggered. Deepfakes notwithstanding.'

They both went back to sorting, but then Mumtaz stopped and said, 'Vi, are undertakers usually embalmers too?'

'I dunno,' she said. 'I think some are.'

'But not all?'

'No. It's a separate thing. Why?'

'Well, assuming that Rudolf Baruch was embalmed, I wonder who did that and whether they knew he was an embalmer himself?'

'I can't see how that's important, Mumtaz, but . . .'

199

'No, me neither – but it just occurred to me, and I feel strange about it for some reason.'

The old man's sister-in-law took charge. The wife just kept on being sick. Eventually a constable took her out into the garden. Then the pathologist arrived.

Chief Inspector Susan Quinton of Thames Valley Police hadn't known the alleged victim, Lionel Richmond, but she'd known of him. A retired lawyer, he was a bit of a leftie, gave money to local good causes, into prison reform, rich. Unlike his wife, he was Jewish and so there could possibly be an anti-Semitic aspect to this crime. It was certainly what she was sure any psych profiler would describe as 'personal'. It had been a long time, thank God, since Susan had seen that much blood. A cursory inspection of the corpse had revealed a jagged, deep incision to the right side of the torso, as well as a very obvious head wound. The house, which was proper Millionaires' Row fare, had been turned over – although it was going to be a while before they could discover whether anything was missing. SOCO couldn't as yet ascertain how entry to the house had been achieved. There'd been no sign of forced entry. Maybe Lionel Richmond had known his killer? Maybe one of his old clients had come back to take revenge on him for putting them away? Where anyone in the legal profession was involved, that was always a possibility.

'I've called Lionel's son, Alex,' Madeleine Price, the sister-in-law, told Susan. 'He's on his way. He said he'd tell his sisters.'

'Thank you.'

'There's also Lionel's brother, Reginald. But someone will have to go out to him.'

'He in a care home or something?'

'No,' she said. 'He's a strange one. Doesn't do the modern world at all. No internet, no phone – not even a landline. I've never met him but Cynthia told me he lives in a shed.'

'A shed. Where?'

'In London. I've no idea where. I'm sure Lionel must have his address somewhere.'

The bloke and Viktor Orban did not have Bohuslav Kovar with them when they came out through the door. Wordlessly they began to walk towards Tower Hill. But where was Kovar?

Lee had seen pictures of the bascule chambers. Vast brick and metal spaces, marvels of Victorian engineering, but also dark. There had been, he'd read, some exhibitions and performances down there at some point, when the bridge wasn't open. When it was, it was into the bascule chambers that the massive counterweights that raised the bridge went, presumably filling or almost filling the space. He pushed the door leading to the staircase and found himself confronted by utter blackness.

The kids on remand didn't know anything – or they claimed not to. They'd all had visits from family and their briefs in prison. Tony Bracci had requested visitor lists and there was nothing about those that struck him as being remiss. Neither Gabe York nor any of his people had been near or by. But then they wouldn't. Tony knew some of Gabe's old lieutenants, but from the footage they'd got from Belvedere he'd managed to discern that the crew used on that job were all slim and probably young. Not the brick shithouses usually employed by drug lords. Perhaps this lot were kids, as in new kids recruited to county lines?

Gabe had acted weirdly when they'd spoken about the golem. He was a man who feared no one, but he'd looked spooked. Tony'd let him stew. Then he'd ring him the following morning. At that moment his phone rang. It was Vi Collins.

Tony smiled. 'Hello, guv,' he said. 'What's happening?'

'Tony, Jaggers the undertakers,' she said. 'You know anything about them?'

'You, or rather Mumtaz, got in touch with Robin Jaggers, didn't you? Ask him.'

'He's not picking up,' Vi said. 'Listen, Tone, it's about embalming. Do you know whether Old Man Jaggers did his own embalming or whether he employed someone else?'

'How would I know that?' he said. 'Christ, it took us long enough to find out their old place was now Greggs at the Green Gate. Why?'

'Because Mumtaz's got this thing about the possibility of Jaggers's embalmer being the one who swapped Rudolf Baruch's body for the golem,' she said.

'So?'

'So, if we can find out who that was and whether they've any living relatives, maybe we can find out why he did it. Old Man Jaggers and his son are both dead, and the boy Robin doesn't know anything. It's worth a shot.'

'All I know is that the old chapel of rest and the embalming lab still exist behind Greggs.'

'Can you get in?' Vi asked.

'Not without a warrant, no,' he said. 'Place looks as if it's not been used for years. There's a load of wood and other shit piled up against the outside.'

'Embalmer's name could be on something in there.'

'Yep.'

Tony had wanted to go inside the little building himself. But Greggs was a big company with lots of money and so if he went in there without a good reason or paperwork, it could all end very badly indeed. But he wasn't going to go in there, was he . . .

Eventually Vi said, 'Cameras?'

Tony sighed. 'Pointed towards the back of the shop,' he said. 'One security light. The little old shack is in darkness.'

'Well, that sounds . . .'

'I can't stop you, I know, guv,' Tony said. 'But—'

'If anything happens, it's nothing to do with you,' Vi said.

'No, I didn't mean . . . Look, just don't do anything . . . mental,' he said.

'I don't know what you mean, but noted,' Vi said.

When she finally ended the call after a few pleasantries, Tony was left alone to wonder why he always allowed himself to be gamed by her.

Lee used the torch function on his phone as he made his way down the uneven steps leading to the bascule chamber. It was a long way down. He called out, 'Bohuslav! Mr Kovar!'

But no one responded, so there was no way he could get out of going down there. Christ, it was awful! He began to feel his skin crawl, his brow sweat. Not only did he not like spiral staircases, but he wasn't that keen on the dark and he was frightened about what he might find when he did eventually track down Kovar. As far as he knew there was only one way in and out of the chamber below, so the Czech had to be in there somewhere. But in what sort of state?

As he climbed down, Lee felt his knees tremble. The irony was that had he still been drinking, he would have been fine with this. He'd never so much as twisted his ankle when he'd been a drunk. Wobbling down escalators on the Tube, mucking about running along the tops of walls . . .

'Bohuslav!'

If the man didn't answer him soon, Lee would have to get help. He'd have to call the Old Bill, but what would he tell them? Then he heard what could be a groan from somewhere down below and so he stopped and called out again, 'Bohuslav! Mr Kovar!'

This time the noise from below was louder and was most definitely a groan. It sounded like one of pain. The Czech could be dying down there. Lee pointed his phone down the spiral staircase and, holding on as tightly as he could to the handrail, he began to run.

He hadn't wanted to let them in. Bloody coppers! What the hell did they want with him?

Reg had been coming back from one of his periodic litter picks around the periphery of his garden when they'd appeared. There'd been a lot of used condoms. He'd been holding one when they'd turned up. He'd put it in the bin outside the back door and then they'd all gone inside. Then they'd told him to sit down. What was this?

Reg thought back to his meeting with 'Terry' at St Magnus

the Martyr, and started to wonder whether what he'd told him could be actionable in some way.

'Mr Richmond,' the man copper said, 'I'm afraid we have some bad news.'

'What? I'm busy in the garden,' he said. 'People use my property like a knocking shop. If I don't clear it up, it stinks.'

The woman copper sat down. Reg hadn't asked her to but it wasn't a hill he was going to die on.

'We understand you have a brother,' she said. 'A Mr Lionel Richmond?'

'Yes,' he said. 'What about him?'

'I'm afraid I have to tell you he's dead,' she said.

Dead? Lionel? He was eight years younger than him. Reg frowned. 'No. Lionel? Lives in Gerrards Cross. Likes a drink but otherwise he takes care of himself. He can't be dead.'

The two officers looked at each other and then the woman said, 'I'm afraid there's no mistake, Mr Richmond. Lionel is dead. His body was found by his wife in his study.'

She attempted to reach a hand out towards him but Reg recoiled. 'No . . . How?'

They looked at each other again and then the man said, 'That's what we have to find out, Mr Richmond.'

'What? Whether he had a heart attack or what?'

Reg began to tremble. Something was poking at him from the back of his mind. Old Menachim's face, the strange sounds that had squeezed under his bedroom door when he was a child, Lionel pushing to find things out . . .

'I'm afraid, Mr Richmond,' the policeman said, 'that we think your brother may have been unlawfully killed.'

Murdered. Why? And why did Reg feel so guilty?

'There was a break-in,' the policewoman said, 'at his house. At the moment our colleagues at Thames Valley Police are working with the idea that theft was the motive for the attack. I'm so sorry for your loss, Mr Richmond.'

How much time passed before anyone spoke again, Reg didn't know. All he could feel was his stomach contracting into a knot, his breath coming shallow and short. He watched the coppers look from one to the other and then the woman asked him, 'Mr Richmond, do you know whether your brother had any enemies?'

What a fucking question. Unable to contain his anger, Reg yelled, 'He was a brief for God's sake! A good one! Of course he had fucking enemies!'

'Do you—?'

'No, I've no idea who they might be. Ask his clerk,' he said. 'I hate to point out the bleeding obvious but as you can see, we live very different lives, my brother and I. He's always embraced the world, I choose to reject it. Given what's happened, I think I probably made the right choice.'

'Sir—'

'If my brother is dead, then there's no justice in this world. None. I always told him that being a brief wouldn't change anything and it didn't and I'm right!'

Reg began to cry. His tired old head sank towards his kitchen table as he howled his pain like a dying wolf.

They'd beaten him up. The one who'd looked like Viktor Orban had pushed him up against a wall while the other one, the so-called tourist guide, had kicked and punched him until Bohuslav Kovar lost consciousness.

206

'But before they started, the tour guide man told me to go home,' he told Lee. '"Go back to Prague and never come back, or we'll kill you."'

As soon as they'd managed to get out of the bascule chamber, Lee had hailed a cab. The Czech needed to see a doctor and so they were headed for Accident and Emergency at St Thomas's Hospital on the Westminster Bridge Road. In order to allay the cabbie's fears about Bohuslav's bloodied face and hands, Lee had spread some newspaper he'd found in a bin underneath the Czech as he'd sat down.

'How did you get to know this Cooper bloke?' Lee asked.

Cooper Lewis was, Bohuslav had told him, a registered London guide. And he was Jewish.

'I found the name of a Jewish London guide online, but he didn't have any time,' Bohuslav said. 'He gave me this man's name and telephone number.'

'So what were you doing in the bascule chamber?' Lee asked. 'Tower Bridge isn't a place to do with Jewish London, as far as I know.'

Bohuslav gasped. His ribs hurt and Lee felt certain he'd at best bruised them heavily, at worst had them broken.

'He said it was a special thing,' Bohuslav said. 'Something you don't see often and he could get me in. It sounded interesting.'

'Well, it was that alright!'

'What?'

'Nothing,' Lee said. 'Look, I'll take you to the hospital and we'll get you checked out – but then you've got to talk to me, Bohuslav.'

'I have . . .'

'You've got to tell me everything,' Lee said. 'No more holding stuff back, no more bullshit.'

'I've told you everything,' the Czech said. 'Everything I can I have told you.'

Lee leant forward so that his head was close to Bohuslav's and said, 'So now you're gonna tell me everything you can't. Because unless you do that, I can't keep you safe and, more to the point, I can't keep my staff safe either. And if anything happens to them I promise you, Mr Kovar, you won't just have to worry about a deranged tour guide and a bloke cosplaying Viktor Orban of Hungary. Do I make myself clear?'

There was nothing here. Stuart Zell perched himself on a wall outside Newham General Hospital and smoked a cigarette. Were Bernie Bennett having an affair with Mr Black's daughter they'd be together on their days off, but they weren't. He'd been to East Ham and then gone home and she was working her clinic. He'd only seen them speak once and that had to be well over a week ago. She'd asked him to clean her office floor.

And yet Stuart was reluctant to tell Mr Black he was delusional, because he needed the work. In spite of his mother having left the house in Boundary Road to him and even taking into account that he'd stopped drinking, Stuart was still skint. He knew why. Thanks to not exactly advertising his services in anything like a professional manner, he got very little work; that coupled with an Only Fans internet addiction meant money was tight.

But that didn't alter the fact that Bernie Bennett wasn't having an affair with either Black's daughter or anyone else as far as Stuart could tell. He was simply a rather lonely widower trying to make a living in a harsh and unloving world.

Stuart wasn't a bad man. He'd told the police what he was up to and why, and now he'd have to go and tell Black he was wasting his money. He'd had no enquiries for months and so God-alone-knew how he was going to pay his utility bills. But he'd have to find a way, because if the leccy went off then he'd lose the internet and thereby lose contact with Double Trouble and her amazingly bendy body. He'd have to remortgage the house – again.

Zell got down off the wall and began to walk towards the Green Gate.

SIXTEEN

'DI Bracci?'

'Yeah.'

Tony had been leaving the office to go home when his phone rang. Shit.

'This is Chief Inspector Susan Quinton from Thames Valley Police.'

'Oh, right,' he said. 'What can I do for you, Chief Inspector Quinton?'

'I'm working on a suspected murder in Gerrards Cross,' she said. 'Do you know it?'

'No,' he said. 'But Thames Valley's a bit posh for me.'

She laughed.

'Anyway,' she said. 'The victim, a Mr Lionel Richmond, was attacked and killed in his own home. On the face of it, looks like a break-in gone wrong. But the level of violence used seems to point at something more personal. Mr

Richmond was a barrister and so . . .'

'Could have enemies.'

'Absolutely. But a cursory glance at his phone has thrown up a name I want to run by you.'

'Oh?'

'It caught my eye because I was on a diversity course with someone who has the same name some years ago.'

'Wasn't me, was it?' Tony asked. 'The Met have done a few things with your lot.'

'No,' she said. 'But you're right that we've sometimes attended the same courses. No, this was DI Violet Collins, who I'm told has retired.'

'She has, yes. And you say her name was in this victim's phone.'

'And her number,' she said. 'Violet's an unusual name these days and so I thought, maybe . . . Do you have her number, DI Bracci? So I can compare it to the one in the phone?'

'OK.'

Tony brought up Vi's mobile number on his phone and listened while Quinton read from Lionel Richmond's mobile. The number was the same.

Tony said, 'I see Vi quite a lot even though she's retired, but I've never heard her talk about anyone in Gerrards Cross. I mean, she is single . . .'

'Mr Richmond was happily married. Or at least that's what we've been told so far,' she said. 'I remember Vi being quite a character.'

He laughed.

'But thank you for confirming that for me, DI Bracci. I can now contact her and find out how she knows this man.'

'You know Vi's straight down the line, don't you, Chief Inspector,' Tony said.

When the call finally ended, Tony wrestled with the idea of warning Vi about this. Should he? She was, he knew, involved in this golem investigation with Hakim and Arnold – but this murder was something else.

It was getting dark, they were tired, and they'd not found anything else pertaining to Rudolf Baruch's funeral or Jaggers's embalmer. They'd finally made contact with Robin Jaggers that afternoon, and he'd told them that his grandfather hadn't been an embalmer. He'd always employed one or two to work for him. It sounded as if they were taken on in a casual fashion.

Yawning, Mumtaz said, 'I think I'll have to go home soon, Vi. I'm pooped.'

'Me too,' Vi said. 'You know, because Jaggers employed casual embalmers, I'm wondering whether we'll ever find anything about them. Different times, maybe it was cash-in-hand work. If records exist they're with the embalmers, or rather their families. Or . . .' She paused.

Mumtaz looked up. 'Or what?'

'The old chapel of rest and embalming lab still exists behind Greggs on the Barking Road.'

'Yes,' said Mumtaz – and then suddenly realising what Vi had in mind, she added, 'Oh.'

'Cameras round the back point at the shop,' Vi said.

'We can't . . .'

Vi's phone began to ring and she picked it up. Looking at the screen, she mouthed at Mumtaz, 'It's Tony Bracci.'

'Hiya, Tone,' she said. 'What—'

'You with Mumtaz?' he interrupted.

'Yeah.'

'Put me on speaker,' he said. 'I need to speak to both of yous.'

Vi did as he asked and Mumtaz leant forward so that she could hear.

'Vi, do you know a bloke called Lionel Richmond? Lives in a place called Gerrards Cross in Buckinghamshire?'

Vi and Mumtaz looked at each other. That was Pipps's father.

'Yeah,' Vi said. 'Why?'

'Because I've just had a call from Thames Valley Police about him,' Tony said. 'He's dead.'

Again, they looked at each other.

Tony said, 'Murdered in his own house. Could be a break-in gone wrong, but he had your number in his phone and so Thames Valley are going to tap you up at some point. What's going on, Vi?'

She sighed, looked at Mumtaz and said, 'Maybe we need to talk, Tone.'

'Where are you?' he asked.

'We're just about to go to my flat, Tony,' Mumtaz said. 'We can meet you there in about twenty minutes.'

'OK,' he said.

After she ended the call, Vi said, 'I was gonna go back to my place.'

'I'd rather you stayed with me,' Mumtaz said. 'Vi, it's getting worrying. Something's ramping up here.'

'Pipps's dad was rich,' Vi said. 'Chances are someone broke in . . .'

'Vi, you told me yourself that when you brought up Rudolf Baruch's name with Lionel Richmond, he behaved oddly.'

Vi looked down at the floor.

'And anyway, Tony's already involved via the break-in at Belvedere, if you're concerned about the police and all this. Let's go back to my place and talk to him.'

They eventually emerged from St Thomas's Hospital at just after 10 p.m. In terms of A&E waiting times, they'd not done badly. Eight hours from admission to Bohuslav Kovar walking out of there carrying a packet of painkillers. He had broken two ribs but current medical practice was no longer to bind the torso, instead letting the breakages heal on their own. But the Czech was still naturally shaken and, for a while, Lee did wonder about saving their chat for the morning – but he also didn't want to risk either losing his man or undermining the promise Bohuslav had made to him. He was going to tell Lee everything and he was going to do this when they got back to Lee's flat.

Lee hailed a cab to take them to Forest Gate. It was proving to be an expensive day. When they got in, Lee made tea and settled Bohuslav in his living room. Chronus, Lee's mynah bird, looked at their visitor briefly and then went back to sleep. Lee lit a cigarette while Bohuslav launched into his story.

'As I told you before,' he said, 'I have been fascinated by this story all my life. It is one of those that seems to have no solution.'

'Unless the authorities in Prague dig up the old lady's grave,' Lee said.

'They won't. It's too much work, too expensive. Also, if they discover that the diamond is a fake, what can they do? Which brings me to the family of Mathilde Zimmer.' He paused to breathe and then said, 'I have been working for her great-great-grandson, an American called Adam Sachs. He and his family want the Acorn.'

'I suppose they're entitled to it,' Lee said.

'Yes, but even if it was found they would have to wait . . .'

'And this Adam Sachs don't want to wait, right?'

'He doesn't. I think he has money problems.'

'But he's paying you?'

'Sometimes.'

'Mate . . .'

'Lee, I want to do this also. I know he's not a good man. But I don't believe he is a bad man either.' He leant forward. 'The problem is that there are other things happening here too.'

'Like what?'

'The golem,' he said. 'When it was found, I came to the UK. Golems are big news in Czechia. I reported a story but, at the time, I could not get too many details. It was later I found out that this man, Bernard Bennett, was the grandson of Rudolf Baruch. I decided to come back to the UK when Sachs contacted me. He knew of Bennett too. I don't know how. Maybe the story was reported in America?'

Lee shrugged.

'One thing I have always known, even before I knew of this golem, is that there are people who protect them.'

'Golems?'

'Yes. You know the story I told you about the golem in the Old New Synagogue in Prague? People have been looking in that attic for centuries to find the golem of Rabbi Loew, but they never find it. This is because there are people who protect such things.'

'Jewish people?'

'Some. They do it because such a powerful thing cannot fall into the wrong hands. If a person without knowledge were to activate the golem . . .'

'Hang on,' Lee said, 'are you telling me that you believe this thing can actually be brought to life?'

The Czech looked at him as if he were insane and said, 'Of course!'

Temporarily stumped, Lee folded his arms over his chest.

'And it would cause havoc,' Bohuslav said. 'It would bring down fury on the Jews. Now, at this time, when the world is gone crazy, can you imagine that? We would be done.'

'So you want the diamond and the golem?'

'I want to find the truth,' he said. 'These people who protect the golem, maybe they stole it from this police store. I do not know who they are. In my country there is talk of people maybe in power, maybe in the Church who do this.'

Lee thought about internet conspiracies; all sorts passed through his mind. The assassination of JFK, the moon landings, crazy stuff about Jews ruling the world. Was Bohuslav just one of those?

'Bohuslav . . .'

'And there are other people!' He was in his stride now and, Lee felt, teetering on the edge of craziness. 'Nazis—'

'Bohuslav—'

'Lee, you must listen! You see how all these Nazi things come back now. People saying there was no Holocaust. People say the Jews want to take over the world. This is bullshit! But millions believe it. Even in my country that was occupied by the Nazis. What is wrong with people? I told you, if such people have the golem they can use it as proof that we mean Christians harm. They are mad!'

'Yeah, but Bohuslav, do you know who any of these people are?'

He became quiet for a moment and then he said, 'Those men who beat me today, they tell me to go home or they will kill me. I do nothing in your country except what I told you. Why would those men want to kill me? All I think is that I search for what they are searching for themselves.'

Vi Collins shook her head. 'Fucking hell,' she muttered. 'His family must be in bits.'

Tony Bracci had told Vi and Mumtaz about Thames Valley's theory regarding the death of Lionel Richmond.

Chief Inspector Quinton had told him, 'Our pathologist said it was as if whoever attacked him was trying to take out his liver.'

'Quinton reckons there are some similarities between this and a ritual murder she worked on years ago,' Tony said. 'They're getting a profiler in.'

'Christ!'

'Which brings me to you two,' Tony said. 'Or rather you, Vi . . .'

'I'm involved too, Tony,' Mumtaz said. 'We met Mr Richmond's daughter Philippa when we went to Stepney Green in search of any remaining family Bernie Bennett might have there.'

Tony lit a cigarette. They were sitting outside in Mumtaz's garden. She'd made a little seating area beside the back wall.

'Pipps, as she calls herself, told us that her father came from Stepney Green and still attended the Congregation of Jacob Synagogue whenever he could. She offered to ask her father about the family called Freedland, who are or were Bernie Bennett's grandmother's family. Pipps and Vi swapped numbers. Then Lionel called her to tell her he didn't know anyone called Freedland.'

'But when I came out with the name Rudolf Baruch, he went a bit weird,' Vi said.

'Was that the only time you had contact with him?' Tony asked.

'No. Lionel said he'd speak to his older brother on my behalf about the Freedlands. So then he called me again to let me know his brother didn't remember them.'

'Then there was the business with Rabbi Dreyfus,' Mumtaz said. 'Out of the blue I got a call from one of the rabbis connected to the Congregation of Jacob Synagogue, Rabbi Dreyfus, who had been told by someone that we were looking for this Freedland family. He had some information for us. We saw him this afternoon. This morning we met a man who told us where the Freedlands had lived and a little bit about Rudolf's wife Chani and her brother Saul. The rabbi expanded on this, and also he called Rudolf Baruch the Golem of East Ham, as if the man and the thing were one and the same.'

'Then he warned us off,' Vi said. 'Said that as far as the golem was concerned, things were in hand and we were to back off. In hand how, we didn't find out.'

'But when we told him we'd been followed, he told us to go to the police,' Mumtaz said.

'Ah, yeah, but he also said that it "might be too late",' Vi said.

'And so you didn't tell me but Lee did,' Tony said. He shook his head. 'Lionel Richmond's death may have nothing to do with what feels to me a bit like something my kids read on Facebook, but then again it just might. Thames Valley will contact you, Vi.'

'Fair enough.'

'But in the meantime, until we know some more, I think you should do what the rabbi said.'

'Tony, Bernie is employing us . . .'

'Yes, I know you lot are always skint, but look, I'll speak to Lee.'

'About what?'

'About,' Tony said, 'the fact we've now got a death – maybe. And also about a theory I have about the golem.'

Mumtaz frowned. 'What's that?' she said.

'That,' Tony replied, 'come out of my thinking about the Belvedere break-in again, and a little visit I made to a bloke involved in the Cyprus Place investigation this morning.'

Stuart had told him that the coppers knew he was following Bernard Bennett, but the old man either didn't hear or he was choosing to ignore him. Even when Stuart said, 'I've only ever seen him in the same room with your daughter once!' he'd only smiled.

Mr Black lived in Plaistow on that weird road that ran between the Barking Road and Tunmarsh Lane at the Green

Gate. Scrappy Edwardian houses – in the case of Mr Black's gaff, complete with dirt front garden and a knackered old Ford up on bricks. Inside, it was like backstage at a failing theatre in Blackpool – curling playbills on the walls, dirty chandeliers, crystal balls and a load of badly made replicas of Ancient Egyptian artefacts. Mr Black had been Ramesses, High Priest of Thebes, a mind-reading act back in the day. The day being the 1950s and 1960s and, as he never stopped reminding Stuart Zell, once on the telly in the 1970s.

'I met Roy Castle and Bernard Manning when I did that show,' he said, citing two very popular entertainers of the 1970s. 'I told Bernard that he should stop thinking so much about birds or he'd get himself in trouble!'

By 'birds', Mr Black meant women. Stuart Zell, born in the 1950s, could remember when women were called 'birds' all the time. His mother had not approved.

'Mr Black, I'm trying to be honest with you,' Stuart told the old man. 'Rosamund and Bernard Bennett are not in a relationship.'

'You telling me I'm daft, boy?' the old man asked.

'No, but—'

'But nothing,' he said. 'I know she's having it off with that cleaner, because she as good as told me so herself.'

What did that mean? Mr Black made little sense. When Lee Arnold had made him go to the police, he knew his story about why he was following Bennett was going to sound deranged – because it was. Funny though, that when he'd told Lee, Stuart had felt it sounded sinister. That it was weird was undeniable. Why, if his daughter had told him about her 'affair' with Bennett, did Black want him to be followed anyway? Had Dr Rosamund meant this 'affair' to be some sort of joke? If she had, then Stuart was inclined to talk to her about it because it was costing her old man money. But then that was money he currently needed . . .

'Anyway, I'm paying you, aren't I?' Black said. 'Do as I ask and I'll keep on paying you. The only thing I want out of this is some indication that Bennett is a gold-digger. For all her qualifications, my daughter doesn't know people at all. She wouldn't know if a man was using her! But I do and Bennett is. I want to protect her kids, my grandchildren.'

It was pointless and so Stuart just nodded. The old man smiled.

'So you go out there and you get me some dirt on Bennett, I'll pay you handsomely and we'll all go home happy,' he said. 'And don't forget, Mr Zell, I can see inside your mind – so don't you be trying to cheat me or anything, will you?'

Stuart panicked. What was this? 'But Mr Black, Bennett will know about me. Lee Arnold, who I told you about—'

'Mr Zell,' Black said. 'How about I pay you enough money so you don't have to remortgage your house? Then you can indulge your little online fantasies . . .'

Stuart gasped. 'How do you know about that?'

'As I say, I can read your mind.'

'No, that's impossible.'

'Is it?' Black said. 'Can you guarantee that is the case? Mr Zell, I know everything – and so you tell me where Bennett goes and who he meets, what his routine looks like, and I will ensure you don't have to beggar yourself.'

* * *

221

Lee took the call in his car.

'Where are you?' Mumtaz asked.

'Prince Regent Lane,' he said.

'Why?'

He looked at Bohuslav in the passenger seat.

'I'm taking Mr Kovar to his hotel to pick up his things. There was an incident today and so he's coming to stay with me for a few days.'

'An incident?'

'Tell you later,' he said. 'What's going on?'

'I'm at home with Vi and Tony and we need you, Lee,' she said.

'What, me without Mr Kovar or with? Because he was beaten up pretty badly earlier today, which is why I'm putting him up.'

'Beaten up?'

'We're not sure why,' he said, 'but we suspect it has something to do with the diamond/golem.'

'Then he'd better come with you,' Mumtaz said.

'What's Tony doing there?' he asked.

He heard her take a deep breath and then she said, 'Lee, this has all gone way beyond Bernie Bennett wanting to find his dead grandfather. Someone has been murdered and there's a chance he was killed because of this case.'

The church was even spookier at night. Its forbidding grey facade, the fact that it hid in the shadow of London Bridge, that its main door was open . . .

After recovering from the initial shock of Lionel's death, Reg had taken a taxi to Monument Tube Station. The police

222

had told him they'd take him to Gerrards Cross in the morning, but for the moment there was nothing he could do. His nephew had formally identified the body, so there could be no mistake, which was why he was here.

Reg hadn't expected the place to be alive with candlelight. There had to be hundreds of them – in front of the main altar, the side altars, gleaming up into the eyes of painted saints, illuminating dark pictures. He'd not expected this. But then what had he expected? And what did he do now he was here? Did he just call out Terry's name and see what happened? Or did he sit down on a pew quietly and wait?

As he fought to hold back tears for Lionel, Reg remembered what his mother used to always say when his father locked himself in the living room with all the old men with the side-locks and the black coats and the furry hats. She'd said, 'No good will come of it.' And Reg had always, deep down, known why. The low chanting, the ceremonies, the promises his father had forced him to make, the promises the old men had forced upon his father. Unlike his father, his mother had been an atheist. 'There's no one there, Menachim!' she'd told him once during one of their frequent rows. 'You and them other old fools talk to nothing. Don't you think that if there was a God, He'd do something to help us?'

Reg had agreed. But he'd never said anything and he'd agreed to his father's request. Rudolf Baruch was a danger to them all. So he had done what he'd promised, but now Lionel was dead. And while he didn't know why, he suspected that the coming of Rudolf Baruch into their lives was not unconnected.

One hour bled into two and no one came. His mind a

223

whirlpool of guilt, fear and grief, he jumped at every sound. Slight creaks from the pew he sat on, the spitting of a dying candle. He had a notion that someone was watching him, but he also knew he was very far from being in his right mind. Terry wasn't going to come because he/they had finished with Reg. And then he remembered how Terry had threatened him, saying if he didn't find out about those women who had spoken to Philippa about the Freedland family, they'd contact his brother. He'd done as they had requested but he still felt cold when he thought about it. Why would a Christian priest do something like that?

Reg knew why he hadn't followed this up – it was because he was old. Too old; he should have died years ago. Now what was he? Fucking useless. He'd lived his life in the shadow of his father's muttered commune with the unseen, working in basements, screening his face from the world behind trees, saving every penny 'just in case' as his father had put it. Listening for that name. Scanning every newspaper, listening to snatched conversations, tensing his shoulders against something he didn't understand. And now here he was, alone in a church at night, crying for his lost little brother and trying to work out what he might do next.

And then it came to him.

SEVENTEEN

Sitting beside Gabe York on his posh glass balcony overlooking the River Thames was, Tony Bracci felt, a bit like having tea with a boa constrictor. Though he was outwardly passive, even welcoming – the tea was very nice and Gabe was smiling – there was a vicious unhinged urge to strike this man. And if he gave in to this urge, Tony knew that Gabe could dismantle him. The words he used were key, words Tony had rehearsed with Lee Arnold in the tiny hours of the morning, trying not to make them sound as if he was threatening Gabe. Because he was and what was more, he was on shaky ground as he was alone and what he was doing was unofficial.

'So we're talking past tense here,' Tony said.

'Would you like another cup of tea, DI Bracci?' Gabe asked. 'It'll only take me a minute . . .'

'No. No, thank you, Gabe,' he said. 'I know that in the past you've always had your ear to the ground, when it comes to other businessmen like yourself and the people who work for them.'

'I don't know what you mean.' Gabe carried on smiling, taunting. He knew.

'Alright, Gabe,' Tony said, 'let's try this another way. The kids on remand in the Cyprus Place . . .'

Gabe picked up his phone. He had his brief on speed dial. But he just held the phone up, because that was enough and he knew it.

Tony said, 'The chances of two crews being involved in the Belvedere break-in are slim.'

'Anything's possible in an infinite universe.'

'True. But let's look at that break-in, shall we. And don't say "let's not", Gabe, because I didn't sleep last night and I'd hate for me to nod off and accidentally kick a hole in your lovely balcony . . .'

'Bracci—'

'I won't!' Tony shook his head. 'But you and I both know that the chances of two or more crews breaking into Belvedere on the same night are slim, right? Which means that whoever half-inched a lot of the physical evidence in the Cyprus Place investigation also, probably, nicked the golem too. And while you and me can agree that at the present time you have absolutely nothing to do with Cyprus Place, or in fact any other county lines operation, we both also know that your name has come up.'

'Erroneously.'

'Some forensic—'

Gabe held his phone up again and said, 'Allegedly.'

'Allegedly,' Tony said. 'But you know things can change

very quickly in this game, Gabe. Whispers and rumours, you know what it's like. But I think we can agree that whoever took the evidence also took the golem. Which is something I find odd.'

'Why?'

'As you say, why,' Tony said. 'I mean, Belvedere's a big unit . . .'

'I wouldn't know.'

'Course not. But it is. So my question is: why take the Cyprus Place evidence and the golem? I mean, that place is full of all sorts – and so if you're trying to cover up that the Cyprus Place stuff is the target, there are a lot of things you could take that are much more portable than a six-foot-tall statue of a long-dead bloke. Makes no sense. But then I thought to myself that maybe it was the other way round. Maybe the Cyprus Place stuff was stolen to cover up the theft of the golem. And that, I thought, might very well lead us to a different kind of crew entirely.'

Gabe said nothing, but he was obviously thinking.

'Now I imagine that whoever did this job, assuming the golem was actually the target, picked up the Cyprus Place stuff either with a view to giving it to any interested parties, for a fixed fee, or maybe using that in order to blackmail interested parties. Now I know that you don't know any of this. But it occurs to me that whoever set this up could have a vested interest in disappearing that crew. I mean, those with vested interests could be one person, one firm or two, even three firms. It was a complicated job that must have required some technical skill. They certainly knew about forensics because we've so far found nothing we can use to trace these people. And now with this death . . .'

'What death?' Gabe asked.

'Bloke with a connection to the golem,' Tony said. 'Out in the sticks somewhere. Really nasty business. Really nasty.'

'Our father was what we call a Mekubbal,' Reginald Richmond told an astonished Chief Inspector Susan Quinton. 'That is a Jewish mystic, a Kabbalist.'

They were sitting at the table in Lionel's huge luxury kitchen. Reg was taking the police officer into territory she clearly neither understood nor believed.

'Before he died, my father gave me an envelope he told me I mustn't open until I heard a certain name. Then I was to open it and obey the instructions inside,' Reg said. 'I was to tell my younger brother Lionel this name and bequeath this envelope to him upon my death.'

'The name . . .'

'Rudolf Baruch,' he said. 'Lately also known as the Golem of East Ham. Back in March in a cemetery in East Ham—'

'Yes, I know the story, Mr Richmond. I read about it,' she said. 'And coincidentally I've recently spoken to an officer in Newham. This golem is missing, I understand.'

'It was taken,' Reg said. 'People believe it has magical power.'

'Magical power?'

'I know! Mad, eh? It doesn't. What it does have though is power in people's minds. As a symbol of Jewish resistance and also as a symbol, to others, of Jewish manipulation of the occult. It can play into the fantasies of those who wish to demonise Jews. I didn't know what it was about, this Rudolf

Baruch. I had no idea that name was something to do with a golem. I try to live away from the world. The thing was found in March, but I had no idea. Then the name, Rudolf Baruch, appears on the lips of a woman who says she's trying to find a family called Freedland. This came to my brother via his daughter from a woman called Violet Collins.'

'I know her,' Quinton said. 'She's an ex-copper.'

Reg told her about his visits to St Magnus the Martyr and his meetings with Terry.

'And you've no idea who this man is?' she asked.

'No. I told you. He wore priest's clothes.'

'Why would a priest be involved with Jewish, what? Magic?'

'I don't know.' Reg said. 'But what I'm trying to make you see is this could be a factor in my brother's death.'

'According to Mrs Richmond, her husband had received death threats in the past,' Quinton said. 'One of the reasons he retired from the Bar. So we're looking at those he defended in the past. That said, Mr Richmond, there does seem to us to be a ritualistic aspect to this crime and so we have contacted a psychological profiler, who will want to talk to you.'

Reg shook his head. 'I blame myself,' he said. 'I should've thrown that envelope of my father's away years ago. My poor mother, who didn't have time for what she called my dad's superstition, always said that no good would ever come of my dad mixing with a load of muttering frummers.'

'Frummers?'

'Religious types,' Reg said. 'None of those old men my father used to lock himself away with lived in the real world. Their whole lives revolved around the Torah, folk tales from

Eastern Europe, and the ghosts and demons that had haunted their persecuted ancestors. But I went along with it. I put my head in the sand. I should have come to you, the police. That Terry, he wanted to drag my brother into this and so I did what he wanted, I gave him the names of Violet Collins and her friend. I should not have done that. I should not have believed Terry. I should have protected my brother. But I didn't. I didn't and now all I want is to die. All I want is to die.'

Bernie put his phone down on the kitchen table and spooned another mouthful of Mrs Igwe's lime cake into his mouth. Yesterday she'd baked him a vanilla cake decorated with tinned peaches. She was a bloody good baker and if this went on, Bernie would soon be twice his current weight. But who cared?

Laughable though it was, ever since Lee Arnold had told him about Dr Black's father paying another PI to follow him because he was worried Bernie was having an affair with the gynaecologist, Bernie had felt uneasy. He didn't know Dr Black's father! He barely knew her! And he'd heard she was married, *and* she was a deeply unpleasant woman who always had a scowl on her face. Lee had also warned him.

'We don't know how or why, but it may be that the death of a man in Buckinghamshire is connected to people looking for the golem,' he'd told him. 'So be aware of your surroundings and don't let anyone in the house you don't know.'

The police had called too. Meanwhile his grandfather's body was still out there, somewhere. He wished he'd never started this quest. So far he'd fallen out with his daughter, he'd been stalked and his house had been trashed. Was it worth it? His arm was throbbing today and Bernie wondered, not for the first time, whether that break he'd sustained all those years ago was ever going to properly heal. All this stress certainly wouldn't do it much good.

Bernie finished his mug of tea, picked up his keys and his phone and left for work. Thank God he was working nowhere near the gynaecology department!

Another text from her father.

Mumtaz. I need to talk to you. There is something you should know before you do anything silly regarding Lee. This is important. We need to talk. Baba.

She sighed. He meant well but her father just didn't understand. It was wonderful that he, a man brought up in poverty in Bangladesh with no formal education, should be so committed to his children's happiness. A lot of men of her father's age just saw their daughters as problems to be married off as soon as possible, exclusively within the community. But then Mumtaz's marriage to her now-dead husband had been arranged and it had failed spectacularly. Baharat Huq, her father, still carried a huge weight of guilt about that. He also knew that she loved Lee Arnold, and that he loved her. But just the thought of becoming one of those tragic women married to a Westerner, who didn't know who she was any more, made her feel sick. She'd rather be alone. Mumtaz liked living alone – although the last few days sharing the flat with Vi, while stressful, had been comforting too. Vi could be outrageous and she was funny. It was also nice to see her so energised by being involved with the Bennett case. Vi needed to be 'doing'; retirement was not suiting her.

Currently, Vi was sitting at what was usually Lee's desk across the other side of the office, talking on the phone to Thames Valley Police. Until she'd received her father's text, Mumtaz had been looking at the British Institute of Embalmers' website, preparatory to giving them a call about whether any of their members had ever worked for Jaggers in Plaistow. Founded in 1927, the Institute was a training and support organisation. Whether they had records of previous members, possibly going back to the 1940s, she had yet to find out. Everything during the 1940s must have been so confused, given how life was upended by the Second World War. She couldn't imagine it. The war lived in her head next to that pain-filled space occupied by stories she'd heard her grandparents tell about the Partition of India in 1947. So many had died in the explosion of sectarian violence that had happened after independence from Britain. And the British had done nothing to stop it, something her grandparents could never forgive. Millions had died.

Distracted, Mumtaz decided that she would give in to this need she felt to pause now. She'd not slept the previous night and felt slightly sick. Lee and Bohuslav had tried to find the tour guide website that had led the Czech to his attacker, but it didn't exist any more. No surprises there. Now Lee was grilling Bohuslav about his involvement with the American Adam Sachs, Mathilde Zimmer's descendant. The diamond Sachs sought, the Acorn, was far more historic and valuable than Bohuslav had initially told them. It had been given to Mathilde Zimmer by her friend the Empress Elisabeth of Austria-Hungary and there was a connection to the Empress's son, Crown Prince Rudolf, who had killed himself and his mistress in the imperial hunting lodge at Mayerling. It was a famous story, although not one Mumtaz had heard before, and had even been made into a film starring the Egyptian actor Omar Sharif. The Acorn, it was thought, had witnessed the death of the crown prince and his lover.

When Vi finally got off the phone, she said, 'You know, I've been thinking about how much of all this Bernie Bennett knows. About the diamond.'

'Bohuslav Kovar told him about the diamond. He told all of us,' Mumtaz said.

'Yeah, but what did Bernie know before that?'

'Nothing,' Mumtaz said. 'Why? Do you suspect him?'

'I don't know. Or rather yes,' Vi said. 'I know that's because I'm a cynical old cow. But I also know that, in my experience, most murders eventually boil down to greed. Bernie's not exactly minted, is he?'

'It's a theory, sir,' Tony told Superintendent Michael Ross. 'But on the basis that we've got nothing else, I think what I did was the right thing.'

Ross, who was a pale man at the best of times, became marble.

'DI Bracci, had you seen fit to tell me you were going to confront Gabriel York with your "theory" I may have considered it, but you've just presented me with a *fait accompli* that now requires me to wait—'

'Sir, I don't know what, if any, arrangement Gabe had with the Belvedere raiders—'

'If any!'

'Yeah, but looking at this from the point of view of the

driver being Cyprus Place, we weren't getting anywhere,' he said. 'Of course, that's Gabe's goal. But what if we assume that he teamed up with people who wanted into Belvedere for other reasons, like the golem.'

'Who would want that?'

'We don't know. But if we can find out, then maybe we'll get a lead on Cyprus Place,' Tony said. 'Gabe felt something when I said that he might get blackmailed.'

'Gabriel York's too clever to get blackmailed.'

'Is he? I dunno, sir,' Tony said. 'There's something about this golem that disturbs people. And don't forget Gabe's originally from Jamaica. Come from one of those born-again Christian families. They believe some wild stuff, and also the golem's a human figure. Voodoo.'

'Tony . . .'

'All I ask is that we give it a chance.' Tony said. 'Give Gabe time to think. Let me have two officers to obbo. Just two. One of them can be me! Let's follow him, see what he does. It was the heroin stashed in Plashet Cemetery that set me thinking. I thought, like, "Who does that?" If you're going to nick evidence, you don't split that up just because some of it's worth a bob or two, especially if you're nicking on behalf of someone else. Not unless you've got a big habit or you're pretty sure you won't get caught, or you've got something on your client. And none of that smack had been used. Weighed exactly the same as what was recorded when we confiscated it. What skaghead you know can do that?'

Ross rubbed his face. 'Voodoo? Seriously?'

Tony shook his head. 'Maybe not actual voodoo. But crims are superstitious, sir.'

'Are they, DI Bracci?'

'Yeah. All the old crims had their lucky hammer, lucky knife . . .'

'Why do I get the feeling you're talking about Ealing comedy films from the 1960s, DI Bracci? I don't think your average drug dealer has a lucky gonk in his box of tricks. Maybe a lucky bong . . .'

'Sir, yesterday a foreign reporter investigating the golem story was beaten up by two men at Tower Bridge.'

'Oh. Why don't I know about it?' Ross asked.

'Victim didn't want to take it forward, sir. I heard from PI Lee Arnold.'

'Oh.'

'And then the murder in Gerrards Cross. There's a connection to the golem, which Thames Valley are taking seriously.'

Ross nodded. He was far from convinced but then he was, by his own admission, focussed almost exclusively on knife crime, which had been creeping up in Newham for some years. He had even been reported as saying to one local paper that he was 'fixated' on this activity. In a way he was right to be, considering knife crime in the borough generally affected the young.

'Sir, all I ask is to give my idea a go,' Tony said. 'If I come back to you tomorrow with my tail between my legs, then we'll know I was wrong.'

Adam Sachs was forty-five and as well as being a Broadway theatrical producer, also owned a string of apartments across Manhattan, most of which were rented out to tourists via

Airbnb. His father, Anthony Sachs, Mathilde Zimmer's great-grandson, had also been in property in New York, although Wikipedia described him as a 'magnate'. Lee wondered whether he had been in the same league as Donald Trump's property-owning father. Anthony Sachs, when he'd died in 1999, had owned, rather than a string of apartments, whole blocks.

'Looks as if this Adam Sachs could do with some money,' Lee told Bohuslav.

The Czech had only got out of bed an hour before and was still bleary-eyed after his ordeal the previous afternoon.

'I don't know,' he said. 'He pays me – mostly. I have no complaint.'

'Maybe he's borrowing money?'

Bohuslav shrugged.

Lee, unlike his guest, had hit the streets early. He'd watched Bernie Bennett go to work and observed him washing floors on the maternity wards. From there it had been a short distance to the gynaecology department and the office of Dr Rosamund Black. He'd waited for the consultant to finish with a patient and come out, briefly, into the corridor. A large woman, probably in her sixties, Dr Black had the sort of face that looked unaccustomed to smiling. She was also incredibly rude and high-handed to the nurse working for her. And while Bernie Bennett wasn't exactly a catch, he did appear to be quite nice – unlike Dr Black.

As he'd left Newham General, Lee had thought he'd seen Stuart Zell in the car park. But he had been too far away to tell. If he was still following Bernie, then he had to ask why. Stuart had been rumbled.

* * *

236

'Bohuslav,' Lee said, 'do you believe that Rudolf Baruch came to the UK with the Acorn?'

'Honestly? I don't know,' he said. 'How can anyone, except maybe a surviving relative like Bernie Bennett. But he says he knows nothing.'

'You think he really does?'

'Again, I do not know,' he said. 'Had it been Levi Rozenberg and not Rudolf Baruch who came to this country, it would be easier to find the truth.'

'Why?'

'Because Rozenberg was a Mekubbal, an occultist,' he said. 'He was one of many wise men in Prague at that time. Baruch was just an apprentice embalmer.'

'But Rozenberg died in one of the camps, right?'

'Theresienstadt. His family died in Auschwitz. Baruch's family died too. It was only Rudolf who got away. I have chased these phantoms all my life, Lee, but I am still no closer. Not in reality.'

'Bohuslav, have you ever considered that it was actually Rozenberg who came here and not Baruch?'

'Of course,' he said. 'There are legends told of Levi Rozenberg in my country, you know. He could bring the dead back to life, it was said. He could move matter through space and time.' He laughed. 'I even looked at the possibility of Levi Rozenberg having first disappeared and then reappeared the Acorn. I spoke to many rabbis who know Kabbalah – Jewish occult.'

Lee suddenly felt sad. Bohuslav was a good-looking, youngish, intelligent man and yet he'd wasted his life on this nonsense. Because it was nonsense. Elaborate and mystical, it was nevertheless a conspiracy theory, just like the ones that had proliferated ever since the death of John F. Kennedy. Like the people who still, in the face of huge evidence to the contrary, believed that Elvis Presley was alive.

And yet there had been a statue in Rudolf Baruch's grave, his body was still missing, Bohuslav had been beaten up and a man in Gerrards Cross was dead.

'Bohuslav, can we go back to this tour guide, Cooper Lewis?' Lee said.

'I didn't know him. I found a website for a Jewish London guide – the one we looked for but could not find – a Leo Lowe.'

Lee remembered the name. While Mumtaz, Vi and Tony had talked about the death of Lionel Richmond, Bohuslav and Lee had looked for this guide. But without success.

Something was niggling at him. Lee asked, 'Was there anything that made you pick that guide rather than any of the others? I mean beyond the name.'

Bohuslav frowned. 'What do you mean?'

'Leo Lowe. Sounds made up to me,' Lee said. 'If I can explain, my business partner Mumtaz is qualified in psychology. Some years ago she used her training to work out how someone had been manipulated by what looked like random stuff in a suspect's environment. In fact it wasn't random at all. It had all been carefully placed to influence this person, unconsciously. It's called forcing. Can you remember anything about Lowe's advertisement?'

'It said he was an expert on Jewish history in London,' Bohuslav said.

'Did it name any sites?'

'Some synagogues. I don't know the names. Some cemeteries.'

'Were there pictures?'

'Yes. But I can't remember what they showed. The receptionist didn't point it out.'

'The receptionist?'

'At my hotel. I asked him if he knew of any Jewish guides, and he brought the list up on the computer for me.'

Kam Shah had volunteered for the obbo, so Tony knew there'd be no slip-ups. Unlike some officers he could name, Kam wouldn't fall asleep in his car, mainly because he routinely drank heroic amounts of coffee. He was also one of the best drivers Tony had ever come across, although what the locals would make of an Asian bloke sitting parked up in his car for hours on end eating an endless stream of biscuits he didn't know. Not that too many people were about. Once a bustling riverside manor full of dockers and lightermen and rough pubs, Wapping was now largely gentrified, providing lofts and wharf apartments for the rich. No one who was anyone, it seemed, did much walking about.

Tony had positioned himself inside the entrance to Gabe York's apartment building. He'd flashed his badge to a man who called himself a concierge and then positioned himself in the small room behind the reception desk. The door was open and so he could see who came in and went out without being an obvious presence. If Gabe made a move, he'd see him. If the drug dealer went straight down to the car park underneath the building, Kam would pick his car up in the street and follow.

Tony's phone vibrated in his jacket pocket, and he took it out and looked at the screen. It was that woman from Thames Valley Police.

'Chief Inspector Quinton,' he said. 'What can I do for you? Got to keep my voice down.'

'Understood,' she said. He didn't have to explain. 'Tony, I've been on to the City of London Police about a church called St Magnus the Martyr. Do you know it?'

'By London Bridge, yes,' he said. 'What about it?'

She told him about Reginald Richmond and the priest known only as Terry he'd met there, and why he'd met him.

'The thing is, there is no priest at St Magnus fitting Richmond's description of this man,' she said. 'Also, Reginald says he spent last night in the church waiting for "Terry". Apparently when Mr Richmond had first met this man, he'd threatened to involve his brother Lionel. The head man at the church, called the Cardinal Rector, told City of London that they never have the church open at night. He's very concerned.'

'Christ!'

'Tony, what is this?'

'I dunno, mate,' he said.

Then he saw Gabriel York walk past the reception desk and go through the door down to the car park.

'I've gotta go,' he said.

'The only other receptionist is Maureen,' the man said. 'Woman. Fifties. Looks like she's chewing on a wasp.'

'Are you sure?' Lee asked.

'No, mate, I'm blind, can't you tell? Of course I'm bloody

sure,' the receptionist at the Eastside Hotel said. 'No young man here. Wish there was, take the strain off me.'

Lee and Bohuslav left. Once outside Lee lit a fag and said, 'So we've got a young man, not an employee, who brought up a screen with the name of Jewish London guides on it but didn't direct you to Leo Lowe.'

'Yes,' Bohuslav said. 'He didn't. I chose it.'

'Why?'

'Randomly,' he said. 'I promise you! I just looked down the list and I chose a name. I wanted a tour so that I could know more about the Jews of London. Why a golem here? I mean, why? In Czechia there is a tradition, but not here.'

'And yet if we assume that the golem was switched for Baruch's body in 1940, before his funeral, then it could have been someone, maybe from your country, trying to protect the city,' Lee said. 'We were being bombed by the Nazis every night back then.'

'But why a golem?'

Lee shrugged.

Then Bohuslav frowned.

Lee said, 'What is it?'

'Lowe,' he said. 'It was Rabbi Loew who made the first golem, in Prague.'

'There are a lot of people in the UK called Lowe, Bohuslav. It's a common name.'

'Yes, but . . .' He sat down on a low wall outside a shop. 'Lee, what you said about Mumtaz and how she solved a case using – what did you call it? Unconsciously influencing? Loew in German means lion. To explain, we Jews have a tradition we call *kinnui* – it is where you substitute a European name

241

for a Hebrew name. Loew is used for the name Judah in this system. And so to give the maker of the first golem Rabbi Judah Loew his full name, it means Lion, Lion, double. And this was common. So Leo Lowe . . .'

'Is Lion, Lion too,' Lee said.

'And so such a name would attract my eye,' Bohuslav said. 'Of course it would. I have been following signs that might point to Rudolf Baruch and the Acorn all my life. I have studied Kabbalah, and whoever made this name knew that and they know Kabbalah too. But then if they are the people who protect the golem, they would.'

'He's going home on the bus,' Stuart Zell told Mr Black.

He'd been hanging around in the vicinity of Bernie Bennett while he cleaned Newham General for bloody hours. Now the man had finished his shift and was going home, and Stuart was following him in his car.

'So see him go into his house and then knock off for today,' Black said. 'Looking through your logs, he rarely if ever goes out at night, does he?'

'No . . .' Well he certainly didn't go out with Dr Black, that was for sure! Bennett didn't go out and the only people whom he'd observed visiting him in the evening were the African woman next door and Lee Arnold's mum, Rose. When the cleaner's house had been trashed, Stuart had been watching him up at the hospital.

He still felt uneasy about that. If he'd been on Shipman Road at the time, Stuart liked to think he might have tried to stop whoever had done it. Even though he knew there was no way he would have done anything much except drive away.

Had Mr Black paid someone to do it? His hatred for Bernie, though irrational, was clearly real to the old man.

And then there was the small matter of Stuart's debts.

He watched Bernie go inside his house and shut the door behind him. Then he drove home.

EIGHTEEN

As well as being very much into his new life of fitness, family values and cleanliness, Gabriel York still, it seemed, visited at least one of the dens of iniquity he had once run before he went straight. Now owned by a man who had once been an enforcer for the drug dealer, The Sweet Spot nightclub in Hackney Wick was outwardly bog-standard, but was actually a front for some serious crystal meth dealing. Everyone knew, including the police. But on the basis the place no longer belonged to Gabe, they were giving the 'new man' some rope with which to hang himself.

Gabe had been accompanied by two young white men. Were these some new 'clean' enforcers maybe? He didn't have his wife in tow and so it appeared that he was simply having a boys' night out. But was he? Tony had felt he'd rattled Gabe's cage at least a bit when he'd gone to visit him and talked about the theft of the golem. Now, as he got out of his car, the drug dealer did look grave. When he and his very young lads walked into the club, it didn't look as if Gabe was going in there for a dance and a few beers – he didn't drink these days.

Tony had put his dancing shoes away sometime in the early 1990s, and so there was no way he was going to be able to follow Gabe in there. He called Kam.

'You've got the shiny suit on, Kam, so you've drawn the short straw,' he said. He heard Kam sigh.

'You know I hate these places.'

'Yes, but you're twenty-eight, Kam, and I'm a hundred and fifty. It's a no-brainer I'm afraid.'

It had been an exhausting day. Physically he'd had to make the journey from Highgate to Gerrards Cross, attempt to console his sister-in-law, his nephew and niece – Reg wasn't good at emotions – and then make his way home again. All against the backdrop of his own guilt and grief. On top of that he was thoroughly shaken. Lionel's death felt like a curse, like their father reaching out from the grave to infect his sons with his occult madness all over again.

Reg sat down at his kitchen table and poured himself a big glass of gin, which he topped up with a very small amount of tonic. He didn't just want to sleep, he wanted to obliterate himself, and this seemed like the best way to do that. Whenever trouble arrived, Reg had always hidden. In his bedroom, in his various shops and flats, and now here in what was little more than a garden shed.

Like his mother, he'd never believed as his father had. All that mumbo jumbo. All that awful secrecy. He should have thrown that letter away. Why hadn't he? Reg knew. As he drank, his mind loosened to the truth. He'd never be able to either hide from or outrun what he was. He'd seen the film the British had taken of Bergen-Belsen. There had been a reason the Jews had hidden in their books of magic. To build an invincible avenger out of mud! A golem bound by spells and incantations to make sure it never happened again. That was worth risking everything for, dying for.

'Reg?'

He knew the voice, and he turned as quickly as his old body could manage to face him.

'You need to lock your door,' Terry said.

He came and joined Reg at the table. The old man didn't even try to stop him.

Looking at the bottle of gin, Terry said, 'Mind if I join you?'

Reg shrugged. Terry went to the kitchen cabinet where Reg kept his glasses and took one out. He moved as if he knew the place.

He sat down and poured himself some neat gin. 'Your brother wasn't meant to die,' he said.

'So why did he?' Reg said.

'I think it was because he was asked some questions he couldn't answer. I don't know, I wasn't there.'

Reg looked up. 'Who are you?'

Terry took a sip from his glass before saying, 'My father knew your father. He was one of the men who used to meet at your father's flat.'

'You're not a priest.'

'I am,' he said. 'But not at St Magnus.'

'So why meet there?' Reg asked.

'We always have. It's holy ground.'

'You're a Jew, it's a church, how can it be holy to us?'

'It was holy to my father and yours,' he said.

'Explain yourself.'

He'd had enough of this. Lionel had been right – he should have got a phone years ago. If he'd had one, he would have called the police by now. Or he'd be dead.

Terry said, 'You're not the only one who was given an envelope by your father. A lot of ears listen. That the name Rudolf Baruch came to your brother's attention was . . . chance . . .'

'Lionel is dead,' Reg said. 'I should grass you up to the police.'

'And you can do that,' Terry replied. 'When this is over.'

'When what's over?'

'When we find the golem and deliver it into safe hands,' Terry said. 'Until that happens, we are all in danger.'

It had been a lot to take in. It had also been unbelievable and weird. Vi Collins had left to go home by the time Lee and Bohuslav arrived at Mumtaz's flat. As they sat in the garden so that Lee could chain-smoke, the Czech told Mumtaz about the name Leo Lowe and how he'd worked out what it meant to him and why it had attracted him.

'You were set up,' she said. 'But by whom?'

'I would say by people involved in the occult,' he said. 'Jewish people. But that makes no sense, because I am only here to try to solve a mystery and maybe find the Acorn.'

'A fucking great diamond strikes me as something people'll kill for,' Lee said.

'All of this is bound up with the golem,' Bohuslav said. 'And I told you how important that could be to some people. To separate the golem from the diamond is not possible because they are connected by Rudolf Baruch. Anyone interested in one of these things will be interested in the other.'

'But you know that there are people whose aim is to protect the golem?' Mumtaz asked.

'All golems,' he said. 'Wherever they are.'

'You don't know that,' Lee said. 'That's your belief.'

He was becoming angry. Anything bordering on belief or religion unsettled him. It was one of the reasons Mumtaz always gave her father for no longer being with Lee. He'd offered to convert to Islam, but that meant nothing because he believed in nothing and that wasn't going to change. That was him.

'There have been stories, for years,' Bohuslav said. 'Long before I was born. You don't have to believe them, Lee, but if you deny they exist—'

'Bohuslav,' Mumtaz cut in, 'Lee and I were employed to find out about Bernie Bennett's father and hopefully discover his body. This search has taken us into territory we never imagined we would visit.'

Lee, slumped in his chair, lit another cigarette and went into himself. He was angry – with how this investigation was progressing, and with Mumtaz for continuing to shut him out.

'All I want is to know,' Bohuslav said. 'The truth.'

Lee grunted – scornfully, Mumtaz felt.

She said, 'When we were at Bernie's house, you said something about Nazis wanting to get hold of the golem . . .'

'Hitler was fascinated by the occult,' Bohuslav said. 'He stole from synagogues and temples. He believed that the Jewish people had power. He tried to collect their most precious things because he wanted to use them to take over the world. He was insane. But after so much time, the world finds itself with these sorts of people again. I am sure that such people see this golem here and they want it.'

'But you don't know,' Mumtaz said.

'I don't know but then what do I miss, eh? I am a foreigner in your country and there is a lot I do not understand. Like the connection between the name Leo Lowe and Jewish tradition. I only work that out when I have a long time to think. Who knows what else I have missed. Being followed? Simple connections that would come to you in a moment . . .'

Bohuslav felt Lee's hand on his arm and looked around at him.

'Then again,' Lee said, 'you can sometimes be a born and bred London rat and miss things too, mate. Take it from a London rat who knows. Names, mate. It's all in the names.'

This was the sixth circle of hell! Kamran Shah liked music and a bit of a dance from time to time, but this was enough to crack your skull. The volume! While he could appreciate the lure of alcohol, even though he didn't drink himself, he'd never really 'got' drugs until this moment. Everybody seemed to be on something and with good reason. It was the only way you could survive in an environment like this. Apart from the shrieking, pounding music there was also the stifling heat, the press of too many sweaty bodies in a small space and the smell of the toilets. He'd lost Gabe York and his buddies, couldn't see them anywhere.

His immediate problem, however, was how he was going to survive. Everyone except him was carrying a bottle of water and so he went up to the bar. If he didn't get something with which to cool himself down, he was going to pass out. He joined the queue for the bar which, mercifully, moved quickly on account of most punters just buying water. The barman, a young white lad very obviously off his tits on something, yelled, 'What?'

'Bottle of water please, mate,' Kam said.

He took what turned out to be a lukewarm bottle from underneath the bar and said, 'Ten quid.'

Bloody hell. But Kam paid up and then began to move through the crowds. He had no idea where he was going, but he knew that these places usually had some sort of smoking area outside – and while Gabe was famously a non-smoker, anyone with any sense would be out there, especially a man of Gabe's vintage. It was just a case of finding it.

He'd finished his water by the time he got across the dance floor and found himself outside the toilets. Although it was dark in the club, whenever anyone opened one of the bog doors, he was blinded by neon light – and the smell of urine. This was pleasure?

Smiling when he realised how much his internal dialogue sounded like his father, Kam accidentally knocked into a girl who was only just about wearing a tiny Lycra dress. He apologised, but she ignored him. He pushed past her, this time without apology, and it was then that he saw a door open and then close on something that wasn't a toilet.

* * *

'The desecration of Rudolf Baruch's grave was a random act of vandalism,' Terry said. 'Those who knew where the golem was were content to leave it on the basis that if necessary, it could be unearthed.'

'To do what?' Reg asked.

'The golem was created early during the Second World War in order to protect this nation should the Nazis arrive on our shores. And make no mistake, Reg, this was a job that was properly done, by a man of power in conjunction with other learned men both Jewish and Christian. But in those days, back in 1940, German spies were everywhere and so it was decided to bury the golem somewhere safe. In a grave. And while I don't know how that was achieved, I do know that from that time onwards, the name Rudolf Baruch became code for the golem.'

'I hope you know that you sound like a crackpot,' Reg said. The gin had taken the edge off his fear now.

'Yes. But rather a crackpot than dead.'

'I want nothing to do with this, Terry or whoever you are,' Reg said. 'When I opened that envelope I made a mistake.'

Terry glared at him. Was Reg correct in thinking that his eyes were black?

'Your life, Mr Richmond, has always been all about that envelope,' he said. 'Like it or not, that was always your destiny.'

'Oh, and I suppose Lionel's death was his destiny?'

Terry shook his head. 'No,' he said. 'No, that was not supposed to happen. But you see, when the golem was dug up in March we lost control of it. It went into police storage and, while we laid plans to recover it, someone got there before us.'

'Who? The Nazis?'

'Yes,' he said.

'Stuart, I want you to concentrate,' Lee Arnold said into his phone.

Zell had been in bed, so he said, when he called. Now he was hysterical.

'When I left him, he'd gone into his house. I swear!' he said when Lee asked him where Bernie Bennett might be.

At first Lee had phoned Bernie, then he, Bohuslav and Mumtaz had driven to Shipman Road where they'd discovered he was out. Lee had even jumped over Bernie's back fence just to make sure, but the house had been silent and dark. Then remembering that Stuart Zell was probably still following Bennett, Lee had called him.

'Do you think he might have made you, Stuart?' Lee said. 'Maybe gone to have it out with your Mr Black?'

'He doesn't know Black,' Stuart said.

'Hardly knows his daughter, does he?' Lee said.

Mumtaz was speaking to Bernie's neighbour, Mrs Igwe's daughter. She'd knocked on her door to find out whether she might know where Bernie was.

'Mr Black's protecting his family,' Stuart said.

'And you buy that do you, Stuart?' Lee shook his head. 'And while not wishing to be offensive about either of them, neither Bernie nor Rosamund strike me as good catches. Know what I mean?'

'Dr Black is a well-paid consultant. Her father doesn't want her to give what should be her kids' inheritance away to her lover.'

'Lover! It's bollocks, Stu, and while I accept you're not the sharpest tool in the box, even you must be able to see that, surely.'

'I . . .'

Mumtaz returned shaking her head. The daughter didn't know anything. Her mother was out.

'Where does Black live, Stu?' Lee said.

'I can't give you his address. That would be betraying client confidentiality.'

Lee rolled his eyes. Then he said, 'Don't you think it's a bit strange that Mr Black is paying you to do a barely plausible obbo on a nothing like Bernie? I mean I know you're skint, Stu. But that's nothing new, is it.'

'Professional standards, Lee!'

He sighed. 'OK, Stu,' he said, 'pretend I'm the Old Bill. I used to be, so it's not too much of a stretch. Pretend I'm the Old Bill and tell me Black's address.'

While Kam was inside The Sweet Spot, wrestling with an internal dialogue that sounded like his father, Tony Bracci was standing outside the club doing battle with his own father's voice. As he saw people leave the club, obviously intoxicated men staggering into their performance cars, young girls wobbling about on high heels, clutching their enhanced breasts, he could hear his dad say, *Drink driving? Fucking disgraceful! That girl! Her there in the pink? Her mouth looks like a duck's bill. Here, love, your mouth looks like a fucking duck's!*

It was desperate being past it – even if the young were indeed fucking ridiculous.

Kam had only called him once so far, to tell him he'd lost Gabe and his crew but was about to go outside into the smoking area. Unless there was an office somewhere in the club, this was the only place he could imagine they might be. Tony had raised the possibility of Gabe and co being in the 'bogs' but Kam didn't think that was possible, given how particular Gabe was. Tony had asked him what he meant.

'Imagine a swimming pool, but instead of water, filled with piss,' Kam had said before he ended the call.

Once Kam had told him he was in the smoking area, Tony had walked around the building until he heard voices over the clattering music inside and saw smoke billowing up from behind a wall. It sounded like there were a lot of people outside. In the morning that comparatively small space would be carpeted with dog-ends and, if his nose wasn't playing tricks on him, roaches from cannabis joints.

Five or so minutes later, Kam texted to say he'd eyeballed Gabe and one of his gorillas. He reckoned the other one was probably in the bog. Tony was just about to text back when it all kicked off beyond the wall.

Reg said, 'Go to the police.'

Terry didn't answer.

'I'm an old man, leave me alone,' Reg said as he got to his feet. The room was spinning a bit now and he wanted to go to bed. 'I've no idea where your golem is. Plus I don't believe a statue can come to life. Get help, Terry.'

'I'm asking for your help, Reg.'

'I meant psychiatric help,' Reg said. 'The only real thing in all this is that my brother is dead and I'd like to know why.

And don't go off on one about secret stuff or any of that, because I'm done with it.'

'Reg, you must have noticed rising anti-Semitism in this country . . .'

'So people never learn? So when countries experience hard times it rears its ugly head again? What do you want me to do, eh? Anyway, I'm going to bed now. You're welcome to carry on boozing on your own if you like, or you can go. I really can't give a damn either way.'

He began to walk towards his bedroom. He'd almost made it when Terry said, 'Reg, there's something else . . .'

'Spare me!'

'The golem,' he said. 'Some people believe that when it was made something was incorporated inside it.'

Reg knew he should ignore him but he paused just long enough for Terry to say, 'A diamond. Huge. Priceless. It isn't true, not as far as we know. But these people . . .'

Reg looked round. 'Nazis?'

'Yes. They believe it. Or rather they believe the golem may be one of its possible hiding places. This jewel, the Acorn, belonged to one of the richest women in Prague,' Terry said. 'It was taken out of the country and brought here when Rudolf Baruch escaped to Britain in 1938.'

And suddenly, all the mumbo jumbo stripped away, this made some sort of sense.

There was an old Ford Mondeo, no wheels, up on bricks in the front garden of the house Zell had told Lee was Mr Black's. Augurs Lane, which ran between the Barking Road and Tunmarsh Lane, created a strange triangle of land which, together with the junction of the Barking Road, Prince Regent Lane and Greengate Street, made up an area called the Green Gate. There had once been a pub of the same name here, which had since become a Tesco Metro. Lee could remember when on the corner of Augurs Lane and the Barking Road there had been a big toy shop his parents had never been able to afford to take him to.

Now Augurs Lane was dark and quiet. In common with all the other houses in the street, Black's place exhibited no light. Not many cars were parked on the roadside and so Lee managed to park easily. When he, Bohuslav and Mumtaz got out, he realised he could hear faint music from the house next door. Ignoring it for the time being, Lee approached Black's house and rang the doorbell. The man was old and so, especially if he was in bed, he'd have to give him time to get down the stairs. Lee gave him five minutes and then rang again.

In the silence that followed, Bohuslav whispered, 'What do you think this man has done?'

'I'm not sure,' Lee said. 'But he was having Bernie followed for a reason. He chose Stuart Zell for a reason too, mainly I think because he's always skint.'

'Skint?'

'Poor,' Lee said.

Nothing emanated from the building. Mumtaz, who had been observing the house next door, said, 'They're playing Bangla music.'

'Do you want to give them a tug?' Lee asked.

She nodded and then knocked on the door. After a minute or so a man opened it and said, 'Yes? Do we disturb you with the noise?'

He was dressed in an impressive gold silk kurta jacket and salwar trousers and looked, to Mumtaz, as if he was at a wedding, possibly his own.

'I'm sorry to disturb you,' she said. 'We're looking for your neighbour.'

'Mr Black,' he said. 'Oh yes. He's an old man, mostly in his house. Maybe he is asleep now?'

'We've knocked and he doesn't respond,' Mumtaz said. 'We really need to speak to him.'

'Oh.'

'You said he is mostly in his house. Can you tell me whether you know where he might go if he isn't at home?'

He thought for a moment and then said, 'He has a storage place here.'

'Where?'

'Mmm. Behind the shops on the Barking Road,' he said. 'There are outbuildings, old ones.'

'Can you show me which one is Mr Black's?' she asked.

'No. He just tells me he has one,' he said. 'There are many garages and things. Mr Black worked in the theatre years ago. He keeps things from those days in there, I think.'

'Thank you,' Mumtaz said. The man went back to his celebration.

Mumtaz looked at Lee and said, 'One of the shops he's talking about is Greggs.'

'Where Jaggers used to be.'

'Exactly. Vi wanted to try and get into the old chapel of rest round the back of Greggs yesterday. She thought we might find something about Jaggers's embalmers in there,' Mumtaz said. 'Maybe discover who embalmed Rudolf Baruch.'

They all looked at each other for a moment and then Lee said, 'I'll be honest, I still don't really know what this is. But if Black is Jewish . . .'

Lee had come to this conclusion when they'd all been back at Mumtaz's flat. When Bohuslav had talked about Jewish naming traditions, he had remembered what his mum had told him about how some Jews had been given surnames by immigration officials when they arrived in the UK. Colours and place names had featured heavily.

'If Black is Jewish then it may mean absolutely nothing,' Mumtaz said. 'Let's face it, he can't be Rudolf Baruch's embalmer because he's long dead. Black was a variety star. We still don't know who Rudolf's embalmer was.'

'Black followed Bernie for a reason,' Lee said.

'Which may have nothing to do with the diamond or the golem.'

'And yet he has a unit here,' Lee said.

Mumtaz had never seen Lee like this before. His default position was always one of cynicism. But when he'd made that connection between what his mother had told him and Black back at the flat, something had changed. She wasn't sure she liked it. But for the moment there was nowhere to go but onwards.

'Come on then,' she said to the men. 'Let's find this alleyway, access road or whatever it is.'

Tony Bracci had been obliged to call for back-up. Some twat in the smoking area had a gun. Twenty years old and determined to prove himself, he'd got the weapon out to show off and somebody's girlfriend had lost her shit and

258

screamed. Then it had all kicked off. And while the weapon hadn't been fired, that was only because Kam had been there to take control of the situation.

Now The Sweet Spot was a crime scene, everyone was being searched, and Tony Bracci found himself standing next to Gabriel York.

'Never thought I'd find you in The Sweet Spot again, Gabe,' he said as he supervised the search of a man who he feared was just about to shit himself.

'I still come here occasionally,' Gabe said, smiling. 'In part it reminds me why I'm no longer here every night.'

Tony laughed. 'Too long in the tooth for this music are you, Gabe? I know I am.'

The bloke in front being searched slumped and there was suddenly a terrible smell.

'Oh, dear,' Gabe said.

'Some people, eh?' Tony said. 'What can you do? You can't follow a vindaloo with a bottle of Jack Daniel's and hope to come up smiling, can you?'

'No.'

It was then that Kam ran over to Tony and pulled him to one side.

'Guv, can't find those lads Gabe came here with.'

Tony felt cold. They had been obboing Gabe, but his heavies were and always had been an extension of him. He turned to the drug dealer and said, 'Here, Gabe, where's your mates gone?'

'Mates?'

'Those two handy-looking sorts you came here with,' Tony said.

Gabe frowned. 'Have you been following me for some reason, DI Bracci?'

'Just answer the question, Gabe, mate,' Tony said. 'Were you?'

'I was talking at some point to two very interesting young men. In fact I did, I remember, give them a lift here. But I wasn't with them, DI Bracci. That's an error on your part, I'm afraid. I repeat: have you been following me? Because if you have, I will need to speak to your superiors about that. I'm a private citizen, going about my business . . .'

This flood of what Tony knew was bullshit was distracting him from what Kam was doing, which was going out to see where the young men might have gone. Tony and Kam had already been distracted from what was really going on once; they didn't want to make the same mistake again.

Once outside the club, the two men split up and then met up again at the back of the building. All either of them could see were coppers – and rats. Trendy though it might be in the twenty-first century, Hackney Wick was still one of those places where people fly-tipped and rats felt at home.

Tony, breathless, shook his head. 'Fuck all,' he said.

'Gabe's car's still in the car park,' Kam said. 'So they must've walked out of here.'

'Or got a taxi.'

'Maybe. Uber or something. He certainly brought them here from his flat,' Kam said. 'Any theories, guv?'

'No.' Tony lit a cigarette. 'No, this time Gabe has excelled himself. I just can't tell you how. Or why.'

* * *

260

This man was a neighbour from hell. Although he kept the doors of his garage shut while he worked on his Ford Capri, his attempts at panel beating were loud enough to wake the dead, let alone those people who might be trying to sleep. Lee and Mumtaz both hammered on his door for over five minutes before they managed to get his attention. When he finally opened his garage door and popped his head out, the PIs and Bohuslav Kovar were surprised that no one else had turned up to tell him to shut his noise.

'What?' he bellowed. Then immediately on the offensive he added, 'If she sent you from the chicken shop, you can tell her to fuck off!'

The alleyway behind the Barking Road was a confusing place. Full of parked cars, dustbins, garages, sheds, cracked hardstandings. It wasn't easy to see which yards, vehicles and dustbins belonged to which shops and offices on the Barking Road. Some shops had fences, some didn't; some parts of the alleyway were choked with weeds, shit and struggling saplings.

'Sorry, mate,' Lee said as the man's furious eyes glared into his. 'Wrong garage.'

'No shit?' the man said, then he shut the door and began banging again.

Mumtaz said, 'Tony told us that the old chapel of rest behind Greggs is brick-built and has planks of wood stacked up against it.'

'That garage is brick-built,' Lee said.

'Yes, but—'

'Ssshh!' Bohuslav put a finger to his lips. 'I can hear something.'

261

'Yes, banging,' Lee said.

'No, no, no, no, no!'

The Czech made his way past the garage, picking through some foliage until he came to a brick-built outhouse. There were planks of wood on the ground outside. He pointed at the building and then said, 'Here.'

Lee walked in front of Mumtaz, but it was she who saw the light inside the building, before he did. She tapped him on the shoulder and told him. Bohuslav meanwhile stopped and put his ear to a crack beside a boarded-up window. Voices. As he'd heard before. Or rather, human sounds – grunts, a whimper, then a groan.

NINETEEN

'The name of Rudolf Baruch's grandson was kept out of the press back in March,' Terry said. 'We knew it was a man called Bernard Bennett. We'd had eyes on him for a long time, but it was always believed he would never get involved. Now it seems he's taken it into his head to employ private detectives to try and track down Baruch's body and find out more about him. Your brother unwittingly became involved.'

'That's no comfort to me,' Reg said.

'It wasn't meant to be. I'm simply telling you what happened. Then the golem was taken from the police storage facility in Kent. Nothing to do with Bennett, everything to do with those who want the golem – and a crime syndicate,' he said. 'So money's involved.'

'Money's always involved,' Reg said. 'As soon as you mentioned that diamond . . .' He shook his head. 'So what now?'

'Now, we wait,' Terry said.

'What for?'

'A phone call or a text,' he said.

'And what then?'

'Then I will have to leave you, Reg. Then I will probably, maybe, never see you again. Unless of course you know where the golem is. Do you?'

Reg said, 'No, I don't. Why would I?'

'Because your father made it, Reg,' Terry said. 'He fashioned it from clay, he imbued it with wisdom and he gave it life. The golem is in your blood.'

Pastor Khumalo had been on good form. Calling down the Holy Spirit had affected a lot of people in the prayer meeting. Talking in tongues, fainting away when the mightiness of the Lord's grace came upon them, so many souls had been saved! Mrs Igwe, who had walked all the way home from the church at the Green Gate, was both exhausted and elated when she got home. Her feet were swollen, and so she had sat down in the living room and was rubbing them when her daughter Andi came into the room in her pyjamas.

'What you still up for, Andi?' she asked her. 'You got school in the morning.'

'Just not tired, Mum,' she said. 'Dunno why.'

'Pity I didn't take you and your brother to the meeting,' Mrs Igwe said. 'It was inspirational to see so many souls brought to Jesus this night.'

'Mmm.'

'So if you been up all this time, did you see Mr Bennett come home?'

'No.'

'I see him on Prince Regent Lane on my way to the prayer meeting,' Mrs Igwe said. 'He was with a friend and so I don't interrupt.'

'Some people came round asking whether he was in,' Andi said. 'They rang the bell and couldn't get him to the door. An Asian lady it was who came. I told her he was probably out. Why?'

Mrs Igwe stood, painfully.

'Because he's had a bad time,' she said. 'With the break-in. I think I'll go and check that he's OK.'

For a long time, all he could see was a man's back, his white shirt stuck to his spine with, presumably, sweat. Then as the man moved partially out of the way, Lee managed to see something that looked like the side of a sink and, on the opposite wall, a row of top hats. The Asian guy who lived next door to Mr Black's house had told Mumtaz the old man stored his theatrical stuff in his unit.

Lee heard a woman speak. She said, 'Do you want me to make a start?'

A man said, 'No,' and then silence rolled in.

The gap Lee was looking through was tiny. That both Mumtaz and Bohuslav were trying to look through it too was making it even more difficult.

He was just thinking about how the groans he'd heard earlier had stopped when the man in front of the crack moved. Suddenly Lee could see that what he had thought was a sink in the middle of the room was something much more sinister. Made of white marble, it was an old-fashioned autopsy slab complete with a gully around its edge for the collection of bodily fluids. It was not empty. A thin, white man, naked, his face turned away from Lee, lay unmoving on the slab. Who was he? Was he alive or dead? On the floor around the slab, Lee could see what looked like sawdust. It reminded him of going with his mother to old-fashioned butcher's shops in his youth. They had always put down sawdust to cover up blood.

As yet, he couldn't see either the man who'd had his back to him or whoever he had been talking to. He'd thought that sounded like a woman. Unless it was the man on the slab. But now that he looked again, Lee couldn't actually see that he was breathing. Completely absorbed in this scene, what Lee also missed was Mumtaz and Bohuslav being attacked from behind.

Then whoever they were came for him.

Terry's phone beeped. He had a text, which he read; then he stood up.

'So that's you now, is it?' Reg asked him.

'I fear so, yes.'

'So are there going to be any more deaths? Or is this an end of it now?' Reg said.

'I hope it's the end, really,' Terry replied.

Reg shook his head. He still wanted to die, but he'd accept some sleep as a poor substitute. Lionel, his only sibling, had gone – and all he was left with was a story about his father and his mediaeval beliefs. His mother had always said that 'mumbo jumbo' wouldn't end well.

Terry was almost out of Reg's place when he called him back and said, 'So if you find this golem, what are you going to do with it?'

266

Terry smiled. 'Put it where it should always have been.'

'Where's that then?' Reg asked.

'Holy ground, Reg. In holy ground.'

A face, pink and narrow, topped off with straw-coloured hair, loomed into his line of sight. Smiling, it was a young face, clear and clean and yet with breath that smelt old and stale – like a dinosaur's fart. Lee Arnold groaned. Then he thought about Mumtaz and tried to get up and look for her. The face moved away and a foot came down and planted itself on his chest. He was lying on a floor, surrounded by what looked like sawdust. And his arms were tied behind his back.

He heard a woman's voice say, 'It's getting crowded in here.'

An older man's voice said, 'My father used to work in here when half this space was used as the chapel of rest. Him and usually two assistants.'

'Be that as it may, I can't work with all these people getting in my way,' the woman answered.

Lee moved his head and finally saw Mumtaz. She was tied to a chair and her eyes were closed. Pushing down on an urge to scream and utter threats against whoever these people were, Lee considered the other people in the room. There was the blond boy, who seemed to have a twin, unless he had double vision. No, it was just a very similar blond boy – suited, smart. A fat old man in a black suit who was sitting on a stool and a dowdy woman he thought he knew.

Concentrating, Lee went through what he could remember about what he'd been doing before he came or was brought here. They'd come to see Mr Black, the man Stuart Zell had been employed by to watch Bernie Bennett. But Black's reason for employing Zell, because he thought his daughter was having an affair with Bernie, hadn't added up. They'd come here to confront Black and . . . of course: the dowdy woman was Rosamund Black.

One of the blonds bent down and put the muzzle of a gun against Lee's cheek.

'You alright are you, pal?' he said. Then he smirked.

The old man looked at the blond with ill-disguised loathing and said, 'This isn't a game. I know scum like you won't be able to understand that. But decorum, please, until we've finished. Then you can go and, I don't know, kick some homosexuals or whatever it is you people do.'

Now the other blond smirked.

The old man looked at Rosamund and said, 'Do we really need these people around?'

'They'll need to clean up,' she said.

She walked over to the autopsy table and picked up one of the body's wrists. The arm stayed in the air.

'He's not even sedated yet, Dad,' she said. 'I can't operate until the blood's stopped ripping around his veins like a racehorse, or we'll all get covered.'

Lee Arnold glanced up and found himself looking into the slackened face of Bernie Bennett.

He was dying. Bohuslav Kovar moved his hand away from the stab wound in his stomach and held it up. It dripped blood. He was dying and all he could think of, even now, was the Acorn. He'd wasted his life. He was forty-four. Most men his age had a family, a proper career – as opposed to some bizarre hobby that didn't even pay his rent. They had friends and lovers and enjoyed simple pleasures. All he'd ever done was wonder how a long-dead man had managed to smuggle a diamond out of Czechia during the Second World War.

Wasn't there supposed to be some sort of light that appeared when someone was close to death? Where was it? Maybe that was just a myth, like St Mikulas, the golem or God? Maybe instead your brain presented you with all your failures in life, a film of all your worst moments, crimes and sins. Waste was a sin. His parents had been reluctant communists in the old Czechoslovakia. Though Jewish, his mother's parents had converted to Catholicism after the Second World War and young Bohuslav had secretly been brought up in the latter faith. So many secrets.

But then how else did a nation live under Soviet rule without losing even the slightest sense of who they really were? In Bohuslav the layers of obfuscation were complex and deep, and although he could now feel himself coming and going, in and out of consciousness, he was also painfully aware of how that trauma had put a brand on his soul. He was still 'theirs' – whoever ruled with an iron fist this day, month, year. That was never going to change. And while it didn't, did it even matter what he'd done with his life? Had he been a doctor, would it have made any difference? No . . .

'What happened?'

The voice was foreign and very far away. The words made no sense. Then there it was again, but even more indistinct this time; and then it was just a whisper, like the hiss of a snake in absolute darkness.

* * *

The two blond men left the small building, shutting the door behind them. Lee saw Black follow them with his eyes, the expression on his face one of loathing. Catching Lee's eye, he said, 'The people one must get into bed with sometimes . . .'

Lee was about to ask him who they were, but Black answered before he had a chance.

'Criminals,' he said. Then he smiled. 'Oh well.'

Licking his lips so he could speak, Lee said, 'What've you done to Mumtaz?'

'The woman?'

She was still tied to a chair, her eyes still closed.

'Sedated,' Black said. 'We couldn't do you, according to my daughter. Not enough of the old jollop.'

That was an old word. Lee could remember his grandmother talking about jollop – it was what some people used to call medicine.

'Are you squeamish, Mr Arnold?'

'Depends what you plan to do, Mr Black,' Lee said. 'See, unlike you I can't read minds, so I don't know.'

Black shuffled his large behind in his chair in an attempt to get comfortable. His daughter, Lee noticed, looked at him with disgust.

'I've been watching you, Mr Arnold,' Black said. 'I thought at the time what a pity it was you and your lady friend decided to work for Bernard Bennett. I'd only just found him myself.'

'What's Bernie to you?' Lee said.

'Bernard Bennett stole from me,' Mr Black said.

'Stole what?'

Rosamund Black had taken a box out of a large bag on the floor. She opened it and took out a pair of plastic gloves.

She was a surgeon and she was going to operate . . .

'Well, in reality it was his grandfather who stole from my father,' Black said.

Lee remembered what Bohuslav had told them about Mathilde Zimmer.

'The Acorn.'

'Yes,' the old man said.

'So you're related to the man in America? Your real name's Zimmer?'

'No.' And then Black laughed. 'No, my real name is Franz Rozenberg. And my father used to work in this very building.'

Lee shook his head. It hurt. 'Levi Rozenberg died in a concentration camp.'

'No. He came to this country in 1938. I came with him.'

This was madness.

'No. Where's the fucking golem, Black?' Lee said.

'You, my friend,' Black said, 'are lying in it.'

They killed them both. Silently and efficiently. They threw their bodies in the back of their van.

And while it was utterly futile to comment in any way on this, Father Steven muttered to his companion, 'They are the worst of us.'

The other man pulled a black balaclava over his head and said, 'No they're not.'

He was right. There were those who did and those who gave orders to do, and Steven knew which one he was. He was far worse than these hired thugs far better than those they had killed. He looked at the body of the Czech journalist still on the ground and said, 'Help me get him in the van.'

They lifted up the body carefully, placing it gently beside the two blond boys. Bohuslav Kovar would be buried with dignity.

Lights flickered inside the small building and they heard voices.

Father Steven bowed his head for a second. Anyone watching would have probably interpreted this as a moment of prayer. Those who knew him would have known better. God was nowhere near what was about to take place here. But then that was because any notion of a loving God was about to be subverted, inside that little building they were about to enter – and that had to be stopped.

Father Steven pulled his black balaclava over his head and the four men walked towards the building. But when they arrived at the door, Steven held up a hand to stop them. Voices from inside were bringing back a past he had only ever heard about in the tales his father had told. Tales that had made him do this work.

Lee couldn't believe his eyes. He wanted to shut them, but he couldn't. Because it was revolting. He looked over at Mumtaz, who was now beginning to come round. He heard her groan. He said, 'Mumtaz, don't open your eyes! Please.'

Rosamund Black was cutting slowly. She was a surgeon and so all her movements were precise. As she cut she swabbed blood from the wound, which ran sluggishly. Bernie groaned. Sedated he might be, but he could still feel pain. Rosamund pushed down on Bernie's elbow joint as she cut deep into his forearm. Lee looked over at Black, who said,

'Can you feel anything?'

272

'No. Not yet.'

'What are you doing?' Lee yelled. 'For Christ's sake!'

'Mr Arnold, please don't shout,' Black said. 'I will explain. You see, back in 1938 in Prague, when Rudolf Baruch was apprenticed to my father, things were bad for the Jews. A lot of people wanted to leave, including my father and Rudolf. The problem was they couldn't get hold of their money. Jews couldn't. So when Mathilde Zimmer died and her body was given to my father for embalming, they made a plan.'

'Can you stop cutting into Bernie's arm!' Lee shouted.

His daughter stopped what she was doing.

Black said, 'You're an impatient man, Mr Arnold. Rosamund . . .'

She began cutting again.

'Mathilde Zimmer was a dreadful old woman who hated her family,' Black said. 'So she stated in her will that when she died she wanted to be buried with her greatest treasure, the diamond her friend the Empress Elisabeth had given her – the Acorn. Of course, when my father and Rudolf embalmed her she was naked, but when they came to check their work and dress the old woman for burial, they were given her clothes and the diamond to tie around her neck. They knew that when they left the body for the final time, before the family came to view it, they would be thoroughly searched, right down to their skin. And so they confided in their mortuary assistant, a Christian called Janos Horak whose father was a jeweller. He made a copy of the Acorn, which Janos brought into work with him that day.'

'So they switched the paste diamond for the real one,' Lee said. 'How did they get the real one out?'

'That was something the Czech journalist Bohuslav Kovar spent his life trying to find out,' Black said.

'So where is he now?'

They all looked up at Mumtaz, who added, 'He was with me, Bohuslav . . .'

'Oh, I don't know anything about that,' Black said. 'Except to say that those criminals we're obliged to work with must have found a way to shut him up. Anyway . . . We find our heroes switching the real Acorn for the fake Acorn. So how did they manage to evade the search they were put through at the end of the process? Rudolf, who was slightly more fleshy than my father, cut his arm open, as you can see my daughter is doing here, placed the diamond inside his flesh, and my father stitched him up. Rudolf's "accident" was not commented upon and he and my father left. My father picked me up from school and we began to walk home. When we arrived on our street the fascists were there. Local men, they were pulling people out of their apartments, beating them, stealing. A man and some boys were already dead. The police just watched. My father was supposed to take our family to meet Rudolf. Janos had a car – he was going to take us all to the Austrian border. Janos knew people who could help us there. But instead we hid. I watched as my mother and sisters were taken away. My father took our papers and put them on dead men. We spent that night in our neighbour's coal cellar. Rudolf left Prague, never to return.'

Lee felt a slight change in the atmosphere. A tiny breeze.

He had to stop this. 'Mr Black,' he said, 'if you stop this now, there's a chance you can explain yourself. Given what you went through . . .'

Black laughed. 'Don't be silly, Mr Arnold,' he said. 'You and I both know that's a lie.'

Rosamund stopped cutting. 'Dad . . .'

'Oh, not you as well, Rosamund!' he said. 'You and I will take the Acorn and go. Why the hell do you think I did a deal with the Devil? They get paid and they clear up—'

'Not if they're dead.'

It was a deep, male voice and it was calm. Lee saw the door open and found himself looking at boots.

There were four of them, all in black, their faces covered by balaclavas. Franz Black felt his heart sink.

He said, 'What took you so long?'

Only one of them spoke. He said, 'We were the ones who did a deal with the Devil, your father.'

Franz looked down at Lee Arnold, lying in the ruins of the golem, and he said, 'You do know that now these gentlemen are here, none of us are going to get out of here alive, don't you?'

As if to underline this point, the leader of the small group said, 'Your Aryan friends are dead. There's no one coming, Franz.'

Rosamund Black dropped her scalpel. It made no noise when it hit the floor, its fall broken by the powdered body of the golem.

'Your mannequin is destroyed,' Black said.

'We heard you.'

'You can understand why I had to search it once I'd got my hands on it.'

'No. You knew the diamond wasn't inside the golem.'

'Did I? My father never trusted you.' Black said. 'Superstitious lunatics, he called you. All high and mighty, muttering to your ridiculous gods, wearing your ridiculous clothes. You gave Rudolf's body to my father in exchange for putting that abomination in his grave.'

'Nobody gave Rudolf Baruch's body to Levi Rozenberg,' the man said. 'He died in an air raid and was given to your father to embalm by his family. When Levi ripped Rudolf's body to shreds looking for the Acorn, he came to us. He had to put something in that grave and our forebears had to find somewhere that was safe.'

'And look how we've both come away with nothing,' Franz Black said as he opened his arms wide to encompass that small room. 'I do not, as yet, have my diamond, and your golem lies underneath your feet. Never going to protect you now, is it?'

'You'll never know, will you?' the man said as he took out a pistol.

TWENTY

He'd taken some of his father's books and put them in a box when the old man had died. His mother had been all for burning them.

'How the fucking hell are we ever going to beat the ruling classes when we're being held back by fairy stories?' his mother had said the day after Menachim's funeral. 'Take them if you must, Reggie. But don't ever look at them, they'll rot your bleeding mind!'

And he hadn't – until now. Still unable to sleep, Reg Richmond put the cardboard box on his kitchen table and began to take out his father's books. Bound in leather, maybe even calfskin some of them, their covers were cracked and some were mouldy and they were all written in Hebrew.

Reg picked one up and opened it. Dust flew out. He remembered how his parents had fought when his father had wanted him to go to Hebrew School and his mother had objected. She, as usual when it came to her children, got her way. How had his parents ever got together? They'd been so different. She'd spent her life complaining about him. But then he remembered that one afternoon he'd come home early from school and found them both in bed. They hadn't been making love, but they'd been cuddling and laughing and she had kissed his father's fingers. Later that day, when the men in the fur hats had arrived and Menachim had locked himself away from the family, she'd spat on the floor outside that room.

Now he knew, in part, what his father had been doing, did it make him feel any different about the old man and his mother? Reg had always and would always love his mother. But his father? Now he knew that his father and those other men had made the golem, did that make his feelings for Menachim any clearer?

In a way. Just as his mother had always been convinced she was doing the right thing when she went to her Labour Party meetings, his father had believed that through Jewish mysticism he was helping to build a better world. When he, together with those other men, had made the golem it had been done with the aim of protecting not just the Jews, but the whole United Kingdom. That's what Terry had told him. Those religious men, Menachim and some Christian priests, including Terry's Uncle Bertie, had done their bit for the war effort just like the people who had driven ambulances, become air-raid wardens and joined the Home Guard. They had pushed back against Hitler in the way they knew best. They had magicked the bastard. And it had worked.

* * *

Rosamund Black was shaking so much she couldn't get out a single word. But then he shot her, just like he'd shot her father, and then she was still.

Lee looked up at Mumtaz, who was desperately trying to hold back tears, and said, 'I love you.'

'And I love you,' she answered.

The man with the gun approached the old autopsy table and took hold of Bernie's wrist. Then he looked at the wound in his arm and nodded at one of his group.

'Can you stitch him up?'

'I'll look in Rosamund's bag of tricks,' the other man said.

'Good.'

Then the first man squatted down and looked into Lee's eyes.

'You're not going to die, Mr Arnold,' he said. 'And neither is Mrs Hakim. Believe it or not, we're the good guys. My colleague here is going to stitch Mr Bennett up now. Then two of my lads are going to clear up all this shit in here while you, Mrs Hakim and Bernie, if he's awake by then, are going to come with me.'

'I've just seen you kill two people, in cold blood,' Lee said. 'Do you think I'm going to let you walk out of here with Mumtaz and Bernie? Do you think I trust you with their lives?'

'You don't have a choice, Mr Arnold,' he said. 'At the most basic level, we have guns and you don't.'

He was right. But he was also a killer, albeit one who had probably saved their lives. But who was he? Who were they? They weren't the police . . .

'Where are you taking us?' Lee asked.

'Out into the country,' the man said. 'It'll be light soon

and so we'll have to get a move on.'

'Where?' Lee reiterated.

'Out Epping way. You know it?' the man said. 'Of course you do. We're going to the cemetery Philomena O'Mara goes to, to visit her mother's grave and meet her brother, Micheal Ryan.'

The man started to untie Lee's hands and feet. 'You know Phil O'Mara?'

'No,' the man said, 'but I do know Micheal Ryan. I've spent a lot of time with Micheal.'

Once free, Lee picked his way over to Mumtaz and untied her. Although still terrified as well as confused about the allusion to one of his clients, Lee pulled her up into his arms and said, 'I won't let you die.'

She clung to him, her nails digging into the flesh on his back.

And the men around them dressed in black all stopped for a moment and looked at them. Eventually the main man said, 'You know, you're very sweet together.'

The young man who had brandished the gun in the smoking area was a complete unknown. Called Jordan Simpson, he came from a tower block in Silvertown and fancied himself a bit of a player. He wouldn't say where he'd got the gun, and so Tony assumed someone who was actually a player had given it to him. Every so often he noticed that Jordan would look at Gabe and smile. Gabe didn't smile back.

The boy was proving his mettle. A lot of firms used unknowns for little jobs like distraction. Kam was bagging up the gun for delivery to ballistics, but the chances of it being a known weapon were slim. Jason would be bailed, tried, banged up for a bit – or not – and then he'd be given another job to do, slightly higher up the pecking order. If he was an idiot, he'd serve more and more time as the years progressed; if he wasn't, he'd become a 'face' and end up directly or indirectly killing someone.

Tony saw Gabriel back to his car.

'I don't suppose I'm going to find out where your two mates went, am I?' Tony said.

'I told you, I don't know them. I picked them up. Gave them a lift.'

'That's a bit limp, if you don't mind my saying, Gabe,' Tony said. 'I saw a few Ubers come and go. But of course, I couldn't scope out all the exits on me own, could I?'

Gabriel said nothing. He pressed his key fob and his car lights flashed.

Although the Gabriel York who'd been a Yardie back in the 1980s was long gone, having been replaced by this slick, fit, media-savvy gentleman some years ago, Tony had never experienced Gabe as a man afflicted by depression. But that was how he seemed to Bracci now – depressed.

'Well, I'll leave you with it now, Gabe,' Tony said. 'You know where I am.'

He began to walk away when Gabe called him back. 'DI Bracci?'

'Yes, Gabe?' Tony lit a cigarette. He was knackered now and wanted to get home, have a shower and put his head down.

'Do you believe in evil?'

'Evil? What, you mean like in the Bible, rivers of fire and all that? Not really, mate,' he said. 'Why?'

'But you do believe that some crimes are worse than others, right?'

'Who doesn't? Murder's worse than a bit of shoplifting, innit? I knew this old bird years ago, used to go shoplifting for Jesus. Go through every stall on Queen's Road Market nicking stuff for the Lord. I asked her once what he did with it all, and she told me he gave it to the poor. 'Course, she was the one what give it to the poor herself. Nicest woman you could hope to meet and yet I had to nick her. And yet I've never successfully nicked you, have I Gabe?'

'I've done nothing wrong, DI Bracci.'

'Is that so?' Tony walked back towards him and pointed his cigarette at his face. Gabe wrinkled his nose. 'But I was about to, wasn't I, Gabe? That was your smack those kids on Cyprus Place were shipping out to those pretty little villages in the West Country, weren't it? That little lad Tommy Carvalho never left Newham in his life, but suddenly turns up in Zennor – a village in the middle of nowhere in Cornwall, which is itself in the middle of nowhere.'

'Nothing to do with me,' Gabe said.

'And yet you look so down, don't you Gabe?' Tony said. 'I'd almost say you look as if your conscience is pricking you, if I thought you had one.'

'I do.' Gabe breathed in deeply and then said, 'Some people sometimes find themselves in positions where they do deals they then go on to regret.'

'*Caveat emptor*,' Tony said. 'Buyer beware. You'd never think to look at me that I done Latin at school, would you. Gabe, we both know you've got something to tell me, something to do with what happened here tonight. So you have a think about that while I run some tests on that gun, and we'll see where we are in a little bit. I mean, nobody died, not here, did they?'

The sun was just peeping over the M25 motorway when they reached a nondescript copse. Not that Lee, Mumtaz and Bernie would have had any idea where they had been going, on account of being blindfolded. Bernie, still experiencing the after-effects of sedation, had also been given painkillers which had put him to sleep. As he climbed out of the van, Lee was struck by the similarity of this scene to the one in the film *The Great Escape* where a group of captured Second World War British officers were executed by the Nazis in a wood. There was even a hole in the ground in the shape of a grave.

Some other men had joined the leader of the group and his sidekick now. Similarly disguised, Lee imagined they had come to replace those people who had been in the process of cleaning up Black's workshop when they left.

'This isn't a cemetery,' Lee said, referring back to what he'd been told earlier.

'I lied,' the man said. 'We are in Epping. But where though, eh?' He walked up to Lee, closing in. 'We are not responsible for Bohuslav Kovar's death. He was an ordinary man who became involved in something extraordinary and he died for it. He is owed a respectful burial.'

Two men brought a body bag out of the back of the van and Mumtaz gripped Lee's arm.

'Do you think that Bohuslav is really in there?' she whispered.

'I don't know,' he said. 'I don't know anything.'

And his confusion only increased when the man in charge conducted a funeral ceremony in a language Lee only later realised was Latin. Still held at gunpoint by the man's accomplices, Lee and Mumtaz looked on uncomprehendingly while some of the men crossed themselves while others filled in the grave.

When it was over, Lee looked up into the trees. It was a beautiful morning. He was in the countryside, with Mumtaz, and he didn't want to die. But he was going to. He'd seen the other pit they'd dug about ten metres behind Bohuslav's grave. It was bigger than the first, clearly designed for more than one person.

As he watched the leader of the group put away his prayer book and come towards them, his gun drawn, Lee pulled Mumtaz close so she wouldn't see.

Then there was pain. And then there was nothing.

Although she had her number, Vi Collins hadn't called Pipps since her father's death. Now she put that right. Sitting out on her balcony looking at the Abbey and watching the sunrise, she called the young woman.

'So sorry to hear about your dad, love,' she said.

The pain in Pipps's voice was hard to hear. 'He never had enemies, my poor dad,' she said. 'Everybody liked him and yet his death was so . . . vicious. You know, they cut him almost in half. Who would do such a thing? What kind of people are these?'

Vi only had sympathy to give. And a listening ear. She feared that Lionel had died due to some connection he had to Rudolf Baruch and the golem. Vi had pulled away when

284

the Czech journalist had become involved. She didn't like cases that involved things that bordered on the 'spiritual', because she didn't understand and didn't want to. Mucking about with 'healing' candles was one thing, but ancient rites involving spells and magical symbols were quite another. Both her parents had told stories about what could loosely be termed the occult, her father particularly. When she'd been a child, she'd had a wart on her hand. Her father had muttered something over it and then buried a piece of meat in the ground. He'd told her that as the meat rotted, so would the wart – and it had. Like her siblings, Vi had gone to Sunday school at the local Methodist church when she was young, where the teacher had told her that practices like 'wart charming' were devilish. She'd wondered for several years afterwards whether her hand actually belonged to Satan.

When she got off the phone, it rang almost immediately. Looking at the screen, she could see that the caller was Lee Arnold. She took the call and said, 'Hello gorgeous, what can I do you for?'

His voice had been slightly strangled, thick and rasping.

'Vi, we're in the garden at the back of the Abbey, can you come and get us?'

'Us? Who you with?' she asked.

'Mumtaz and Bernie Bennett,' he said. 'I can't explain. Just come.'

Reg had fallen asleep in his chair when there was a knock on his front door. He got up slowly and shuffled towards it. A familiar face smiled at him and so Reg ushered the visitor in.

'Thought I wasn't going to see you again,' Reg said. 'You

want tea or something stronger?'

Terry sat down at the table and said, 'Gin?'

'Yes, I've also found some orange squash,' Reg said. 'What do you want?'

'Gin and orange is fine.'

Terry was looking at the books on the table, quietly mouthing the Hebrew titles to himself.

'You know these books?' Reg asked as he poured Terry's drink.

'Some.'

Reg sat down. 'I know I asked you whether you're a priest and you said you were. Are you actually a rabbi?'

'No,' Terry said. 'I'm a priest. Reg, I've come here to tell you that the search for the golem is over.'

'You found it?'

'In a manner of speaking. The person who had it smashed it to powder.'

'Why?'

Terry drank. 'There's no one reason. As I told you, there were several interested parties. In this case the motivation was greed.'

'Were these the people who killed Lionel?' Reg asked.

'No.'

'So who destroyed the golem?'

Terry smiled and said, 'Your father and his colleagues needed to find somewhere safe for the golem when invasion seemed imminent. Your father knew this embalmer. In and out of graveyards, this man told Menachim he could bury it for him. What your father didn't know until he and his colleagues delivered the golem to this man's laboratory was that the embalmer intended to put it into the grave of a man whose body he had desecrated.'

'Why had he desecrated a body?'

'Looking for the Acorn. The dead man was called Rudolf Baruch and he had stolen the Acorn from the dead body of a rich woman called Mathilde Zimmer, along with his colleague Levi Rozenberg back in their home city of Prague in 1938. They were embalmers. They took the stone in order to fund their escape from the Nazis, but they became separated and the jewel was with Rudolf Baruch.'

'Why?'

'In order to steal it, Rudolf had hidden it inside his body. Two years later, when Levi was given his body of course he recognised him. He looked for the stone.'

'But surely Rudolf had used the diamond to fund his escape?'

'Probably yes,' Terry said. 'But Levi didn't believe that. And so your father's people and my grandfather watched and waited, and when history threatened to repeat itself last night we intervened.'

'How?'

'Levi's son found Rudolf's grandson,' Terry said. 'And the timing could not have been worse.'

'Why?'

'You're a Jew. You must've seen how extreme ideologies have been taking hold. When the golem was found, they began to show themselves. Get hold of that, prove that the Jews do magic, worship the Devil! And of course find the Acorn too. So it was a race,' Terry said. 'Between us, our extremist friends and Levi Rozenberg's son. And in the middle of all that, almost entirely oblivious, was your brother.'

'Why not me?' Reg asked. 'I mean, you saw, you can just walk in here.'

'I don't know,' Terry said. 'It's not like the 1930s now. People who would have been called Nazis back then are now often seemingly quite normal, respectable people. They're also in some cases, like this, enabled by organised crime – for a price, of course.'

Reg drank. 'Is my family in danger?' he asked.

'Now? No,' Terry said. 'The criminals have got what they wanted and the Rozenbergs have gone.'

Reg frowned. 'Gone where?'

But Terry didn't reply and Reg felt cold. If Terry was one of the 'good guys', then he'd hate to come across one of the bad ones.

'You've kept your head down all your life, Reg, nothing will happen to you,' he said.

Reg leant back in his chair, exhausted. 'But you have no golem, so what do you do now? With no hero to protect us, what will we Jews do?'

Terry stood, smiling. 'Things are in hand, Reg,' he said. 'Don't worry about that. You bury your brother, see your family and get a new lavatory fitted. I'll be in touch.'

'When?'

'When our work is finished,' Terry said. 'Now I must call the police.'

'The police? Oh Christ, the police!' Reg said. 'They're still investigating Lionel's murder. What do I tell them?'

'Whatever you like,' Terry said. 'Those who killed your brother are already dead.'

'You know this for certain?'

Terry smiled. 'I do.'

He'd done it, he'd killed them.

Reg shuddered. 'Do I tell them about you?' he asked.

'I wouldn't,' Terry said, smiling again. 'They might section you.'

And then he left.

Vi put a towel down on her bed and then they lay Bernie on top of it. Blood was still oozing from the bandage that covered his wound. He went back to sleep immediately. Lee shut Vi's bedroom door, and he and Mumtaz joined Vi in the living room.

Once they'd all sat down, Vi said, 'So anyone care to explain why you've brought Bernie Bennett here with a fucking great gash in his arm?'

Lee and Mumtaz looked at each other. Mumtaz put the bottle of antibiotics they'd given her for Bernie on Vi's coffee table. Whoever they'd been, they'd thought of everything.

When no one spoke, Vi continued, 'And you look like shit, Arnold. What the fuck have you been doing?'

Between them, Lee and Mumtaz told her what they'd experienced. She interjected a few times to wonder out loud whether they'd been on drugs when all that had taken place. It was a fair assumption given the content of what they were saying.

When they'd finished, Vi said, 'What now, then?'

'I pick up my car from outside Mr Black's house and get down the station,' Lee said.

'And say what?'

Lee shrugged. 'They killed people, Vi.'

'We both saw it,' Mumtaz said. 'What else can we do?'

Vi leant back in her armchair and lit a cigarette. 'What I don't get,' she said, 'is why you're still alive. I mean, I know you never saw the faces of these men, but they took you to somewhere in Epping where they buried three bodies. You could, potentially, identify that place.'

'Yeah.'

'But why?' she said. 'Why take the risk of letting you live?' She took her phone out of her pocket and said, 'I'm gonna ring Tony.'

Was this a good idea? Lee didn't know and was too tired to really care. But Vi didn't get through. 'Engaged,' she said as she put her phone back in her pocket.

TWENTY-ONE

Just like the anonymous caller had said, there were two sites. They started with the larger of the two. Because his days of wielding a shovel were long behind him, Tony Bracci watched a team of much younger officers move what proved to be a lot of loose earth off two almost identical bodies. Kamran Shah hunkered down to get a better look.

'Gabe York's two kids from last night,' he said.

'Oh, well that's a nice little find, isn't it,' Tony said. 'Handsome.'

Kam stood up. 'Gabe never left with them, guv,' he said. 'We're his alibi.'

'Yeah. But as well as you being able to positively ID them, we've also got footage from the club, proving they were there, with him,' Tony said. 'So headache for Gabe, whichever way you swing it. To be honest with you, Kam, I wonder whether he even knows. I mean, these kids buggered off to do something last night . . .'

'Thanks to the kid with the gun.'

'Yup.'

Tony walked over to the other, smaller site and instructed two of the team to get digging. Kam joined him.

'Any theories about our caller?' he asked Tony.

'Burner phone,' his boss said.

'Yeah, but what did he say?'

'That we'd find three bodies at this location.'

'That was all?'

'That was it,' Tony said.

'I wonder what the story is, guv?' Kam said.

Tony lit a cigarette and said, 'Fuck knows.'

Vi took Bernie, Lee and Mumtaz home. She dropped Bernie off first, then Lee, much to Mumtaz's relief. Ever since they'd said they loved one another, she'd not been able to meet his gaze. But then when she and Vi got to Mumtaz's flat, they found her father standing outside, waiting for her.

Another problem.

'Oh God, what does he want?' Mumtaz said as she got out of the car.

'I'll leave you to it,' Vi said and drove off.

Baharat Huq was a small, elderly man. He wore traditional *salwar kameez* and had a neat grey beard and carried a small leather bag. When he saw his daughter, tired, her clothes torn, he said, 'Where have you been? I've been worried.'

Mumtaz shook her head. 'Not now, Baba.'

'Mumtaz, you look as if you've been sleeping on the ground!'

She invited him in and, although all she wanted to do was go to sleep, she made them both tea and sat down with him in her living room.

'I have been trying to get some time with you,' he said. 'I've texted, as you told me to do, but Mumtaz, I need to tell you something and it just won't wait.'

She put her head in her hands. 'Oh, Baba!'

'No, not "Oh, Baba",' he said. 'This is important!'

He put the leather bag he was carrying on the coffee table and put his hand inside. He took out a small brass figure of a Hindu deity.

'You know what this is?' he asked.

'It's a Hindu god,' she said. 'Why have you got it?'

'It is a representation of the Hindu god Lord Shiva,' Baharat said. 'In the form of the Cosmic Dancer. See how he dances in the circle of life?'

Mumtaz was aware of such things. When the Bangladeshi community had first opened 'Indian' restaurants in and around Brick Lane back in the 1970s, many of them had decorated them with Hindu deities, particularly Ganesh, the elephant god, because they attracted white customers. Unable or unwilling to realise that most of the Asians in the area were actually Muslims, these people liked the idea of 'Indians' and 'India' and exotic gods.

'You know how I got this?' her father asked her.

'No. Maybe from Uncle Sadiq?'

Her mother's brother, Sadiq, had owned an Indian restaurant back in the 1980s. It was now long gone, and Uncle Sadiq and his family had moved out to Harlow at the beginning of the century.

'No, not from Uncle Sadiq,' Baharat said. 'From my father, your grandfather.'

'Oh.'

Mumtaz knew that her grandfather, Zayan Huq, had lived through the violent Partition of India when the country had split into two – India, and East and West Pakistan – at independence from Britain. West Pakistan and East Pakistan (the latter later becoming Bangladesh) had become a single Islamic state while India had remained predominantly Hindu. As the colonialists had withdrawn, communities had clashed over the newly drawn maps that had been agreed, not by the people, but by their leaders and the British. Thousands had died and Mumtaz knew that her grandfather, whose mixed Hindu and Muslim village had been on the Indian/ Bangladeshi border, had been obliged to leave his home and move to the capital, Dhaka. Consequently, Mumtaz was now in fear about what her father was going to tell her. Had her grandfather looted this from an empty Hindu home? Had he maybe killed someone during those turbulent times?

'When he was a boy, my father had a friend called Hamza,' Baharat said.

Her grandfather had a brother called Hamza, but this was the first time she'd heard about a friend. But it was a common name.

'So?'

'So they always played together and went to school together,' her father said. 'Then Partition. Life becomes frightening and the boys no longer go to school, their families no longer go in and out of each other's houses. One day when the boys are playing down by the river, Muslim soldiers come. They take all the Hindus remaining outside the village and they shoot them. When the boys return from the river, some of the houses are on fire. And so they run to Hamza's house, where they find the soldiers talking to his father, who is crying. One of the soldiers is harsh with him. They tell him they had to kill the Hindus because it was, he said, "them or us". Then one of the soldiers sees the two boys and he asks who they are. Hamza's father told him they were his sons, Hamza and Zayan. And then my father, whose real name was Zevesh, realised that his whole family were dead.'

'What do you mean?' Mumtaz asked. 'I'm not following.'

'My father was a Hindu,' Baharat said. 'He was called Zevesh and he was saved from death by the family of his best friend Hamza Huq. From that time on, the two boys who had always played as brothers became brothers. My father, Zayan Huq, was a Muslim now and, as you know, he lived as a Muslim until the end of his life. This Lord Shiva is all that remains of his Hindu life and when he told me that story and gave this to me, he told me to treasure it always and I have. Mumtaz, if you go to Lee, it will not be the first time we have had non-Muslims in this family. And unlike my father, neither of you will have to change for the other. I know you fear becoming someone who does not know who she really is, but none of us know that, do we? I don't think we do. And in answer to a question I know you have in your mind now, my father was always a good Muslim, but he was a good Hindu too. Just before he died, he told me he wanted to go back to his old village and so I took him. We found the ruins of the temple where his family used to go. Alone in that place he made the Hindu Prayer for Peace. He still remembered it. He still knew himself. Mumtaz, follow your heart. You will never lose who you are.'

At first, Mumtaz didn't know what to say. She didn't know how to feel. Her grandfather had always been a gentle, kind, pious man. She'd only seen him once when she'd visited Bangladesh with her family when she was ten. But she'd liked him and her Great-Uncle Hamza who, her father had just told her, was not related to her at all.

'But how did he live knowing that people like the Huqs had killed his family?' she said.

'The Huqs were good people,' her father said. 'They saved him. He knew all Muslims were not like the soldiers who killed his family. The same happened on the other side too – Hindu soldiers killed Muslims. And he was never forced to change his religion. His new father, Ali Huq, went to the home Zevesh had once shared with his family, and he picked up Lord Shiva here and he gave it to him. The Huq family spent a long time on the road before Ali finally got a job in Dhaka. They were poor, sometimes desperate, but they always carried Lord Shiva with them so that my father, Zayan now, could still be connected to his past. Those were desperate times, Mumtaz, but . . .'

'Baba, how could he not hate Muslims?' She was almost in tears now. She was exhausted and emotional and this story of both hatred and mercy was breaking her apart.

'Because as he always told my brothers and sisters and me, hate must stop,' Baharat said. 'If you do not put an end to it, it will end you. The world now boils in hate, as we can all see, Mumtaz. Be a light in the darkness, like your grandfather. Love those who love you, whoever they are.'

* * *

296

'Mumtaz and me were the last people to see him alive,' Lee said. 'Apart from his killers. Two blond lads—'

'Identified as Owen and Christian Stewart,' Tony Bracci said. 'Essex Police know them, or knew them. Nasty little pair apparently, on the fringes of several far-right firms.'

Lee had picked his car up from outside Mr Black's house and driven straight to Forest Gate nick.

'But they didn't kill Black and his daughter,' Lee said. 'I've no idea who they were. But they knew about the golem and Bernie Bennett, and they were killers.'

'All of these people were killers, Lee.'

'Yes, I know,' he said. 'But these were professionals. They killed quickly and in cold blood and they'd come apparently prepared for every eventuality. They even had antibiotics for Bernie.'

'Tell me about that again?' Tony said.

Lee had happily let a duty brief sit in on his interview, which was also being performed in the presence of Kam Shah.

'Black told me that when his father, Levi Rozenberg, got hold of Rudolf Baruch's body, he cut it open to look for this diamond, the Acorn. He didn't find it, unsurprisingly. He probably sold it to get to this country. But then when he saw Bernie with a huge scar on his arm, Mr Black got the idea that Bernie had hidden the jewel inside his body too.'

'How did Mr Bennett get his scar?'

'Years ago, running along a corridor in Newham General, he went through a plate glass door. He put his arm up to save himself, but by that time it was too late.'

'So the jewel isn't . . .'

'No, it's not in his arm!' Lee said. 'Christ, Tone, I saw them poking about in there . . . Anyway, Bernie never knew his grandfather. He didn't know about the Acorn at all until poor old Bohuslav told him about it.'

'You got any idea about these people who killed Black and his daughter?'

'No. All I can tell is that they knew a lot about the golem and the diamond, and they told us they were the good guys.'

'The good guys?'

'Made no sense to me either,' Lee said. 'But inasmuch as they saved our lives, I suppose they were right. Tony, ex-Inspector Collins has been working with us and she's of the opinion that the death of Lionel Richmond over in Gerrards Cross could also be significant to this investigation.'

'It could be,' Tony said. 'But for the time being, I'm trying to tie up as much as I can here.'

Kam said, 'We've managed to source a Czech speaker for liaison with the authorities in Prague about Mr Kovar.'

'And I need to get Gabe York in here,' Tony said. 'I'd bet my pension on the idea he and his firm did the Belvedere job, but I still don't know why he took the golem or for whom. And while from what Essex have told me, the Stewart brothers are distinctly low-rent, I know not to underestimate these far-right organisations.'

'Bohuslav Kovar warned about anti-Semites possibly getting hold of the golem and using it for their own purposes,' Lee said. 'And someone was following him. Tried to warn him off when he visited Tower Bridge.'

'How did your "good guys" react when Black told them he'd destroyed the golem?' Kam asked.

'Showed no emotion,' Lee said. 'It was just like a

professional hit. But then . . .'

'Then what?' Tony said.

'When they buried Bohuslav Kovar, the leader of the group conducted a sort of a funeral service,' Lee said. 'In Latin.'

'He was a Catholic,' Tony said.

'He was Jewish.'

'He might have been an ethnic Jew, but he had a chain round his neck with a pendant instructing anyone who might find him dead to call a Roman Catholic priest. In English and what I imagine is Czech.'

Lee sat back in his chair and said, 'How did that bloke know that?'

'Maybe he read the pendant like we did,' Tony said.

'Maybe.' Lee shrugged. 'But then the Latin . . . People don't know Latin much now, do they? Not even doctors these days.'

'So maybe he's some sort of academic,' Tony said. 'Or a priest.'

'A priestly assassin.'

'Wouldn't be the first time,' Tony said. 'You ever heard of the Crusades?'

Lee pulled a face.

'We will have to take statements from Mrs Hakim and Mr Bennett,' Tony said. 'I know he's got antibiotics, but I imagine Mr Bennett still needs medical treatment.'

'Bernie just wanted to get back to his own home,' Lee said. 'But yes, he'll have to see a doctor. I expect he might need therapy too after what he's been through.'

Tony nodded. 'And now you ought to be getting home, Mr Arnold,' he said. 'I know where you are if I need you, and thank you for coming in and doing this for us. Tech are looking at CCTV from the Green Gate around Black's place and we've got a couple of potential witnesses.'

He stood up, closely followed by Lee, who stumbled.

'Kam,' Tony said to his sergeant, 'can you drive Mr Arnold home in his car? I think it's all finally caught up with him.'

His brother's living room was vast. Much bigger than the whole plot on which his home stood. It made Reg feel exposed. He didn't like it.

Chief Inspector Susan Quinton said, 'We understand from an ex-DI over in the London Borough of Newham that your family may have some information about a Jewish artefact called a golem. One was found in Plashet Cemetery, East Ham back in March. It was recently stolen from the Met's storage facility down in Kent.'

Reg had thought a lot about what he was going to say while in the taxi that had taken him from Highgate to Gerrards Cross. His brother was dead and there was nothing he could do about that. Terry had intimated that he'd either had a hand in or had in some way approved the deaths of those who had killed Lionel. Reg, for better or worse, had decided to believe him. He was an old man – who cared what he thought? And if those people were dead, then they couldn't do anyone else any harm. Killing them was more than the police would do. He already had a kind of justice.

'I know nothing of how either the golem came to be in East Ham or down in Kent,' Reg said. 'My brother told me that a woman had been asking questions relating to the golem—'

'Ex-DI Collins?'

'Yes,' he said. 'But her queries were actually more about the grave in which the golem had been buried, if I'm honest.'

'That's the grave of Rudolf Bennett?' she asked.

'So I understand. But what you have to understand, Chief Inspector Quinton, is that I was just a child when my father and his colleagues created the golem.'

'What did he tell you about it?'

The best way to deflect any questions he didn't want to answer was for Reg to give the police some, but not all, of the truth. In this reality his father had told him about the golem and what it meant, which he'd already described to Quinton.

'Just what I told you. It is a traditional talisman against persecution.'

'It can,' she lifted her hands up and made inverted commas with her fingers, '"come to life" . . .'

'My father believed in the occult, Chief Inspector,' Reg said. 'It seems whoever took the golem did too. Maybe whoever killed my brother. I don't know.'

'We've still a lot of evidence to sift through, Mr Richmond. As I told your brother's widow, some of his neighbours have CCTV cameras. We've already got footage of a few people we've yet to identify.'

'Thank you.'

Then she said, 'Just one more thing, Mr Richmond. And I'm sorry, I do have to ask this . . .'

'Do I have the golem myself?' he interjected. 'No, Chief Inspector Quinton, I don't. Unlike my father, I don't believe in magic, Jewish or otherwise. I'm just an old man who simply wants to live out his life with the minimum of fuss. That's all I've ever wanted.'

TWENTY-TWO

It was dark now but Bernie still didn't feel like sleeping. He'd nearly died and he still didn't understand why. Maybe when he was interviewed by the police he'd find that out. All he knew was that it had something to do with that diamond Bohuslav had talked about. But he didn't have it. He'd told that old man and those boys he had with him that he didn't have it. Why had they thought it was inside his arm?

Lee Arnold had wanted him to go to A&E, but he'd told him 'fuck that'. He knew how long you had to wait to get seen in there. And he had antibiotics. His arm hurt, but what hurt more was that his only child hadn't called. He'd parted on bad terms with Kelly the last time she'd visited – but then they often did, mainly because of bloody Darren.

Mrs Igwe had come round shortly after he got home, and she'd made him tea and given him cake. She was more like family than Kelly. But unlike Kelly, Bernie couldn't confide in her. For a kick-off, if he did tell her, she'd think he'd lost his marbles.

The discovery of the golem had upended his life. It had made him curious about his family in ways he'd never imagined. He'd wanted to know so much, and yet now he realised that by knowing just a little he'd made a mistake. The past had come back to punish him, or so it seemed, and for something he had never been part of.

Dr Black and her father were dead, Lee had told him. But he didn't remember that. He'd been injected with a sedative, Lee had said. All he remembered now was the pain and, when that had disappeared, graves in a wood somewhere. Bernie was sleepless, and he knew it was because he was scared to drift off in case he dreamt about it. Eventually he got up and went downstairs. The place was still a fucking tip after the break-in. They'd been looking for that diamond.

He cleared some paperwork off a chair, sat down and put on the TV. The local news was on and there were pictures of police going into that brick shed he'd been taken to. The reporter was saying that it was empty and that they were still looking for two people, a Mr Black and his daughter, a consultant at Newham General Hospital. You could just see inside the little building, and Bernie noticed that the floor was covered in what looked like sawdust.

He hadn't expected to be taken to a pub. When the police had turned up at his apartment to take him away, Gabe York had imagined he'd be taken to Forest Gate Station. But instead, Tony Bracci and his DS Kamran Shah had brought him to the old West Ham United supporters' pub on Green Street, The Boleyn.

Bracci led them to a table in a corner while Shah went to the bar and bought them three soft drinks.

Eventually Bracci said, 'We've come here for a little chat before I formally interview you, because I think we need to talk about what's going to happen back at the station.'

Gabe sipped on a pint of lime and soda, which he didn't like, but his mouth was dry. He said, 'Talk about what?'

'Well firstly, I need to tell you a few things,' Bracci said.

'What things?'

'Open your lugholes and you'll learn something,' he said. 'Alright, Gabe, the two blokes you took from your gaff to The Sweet Spot last night . . .'

'I told you, I picked them up.'

'Where?' Bracci smiled. 'Gabe, they were in your apartment. Don't try and mug me off. They were in your apartment and you brought them to the club. You knew we were watching you, but at the same time you had to get them out of your apartment to go and do the little job their bosses had boxed off for them down the Green Gate. So you arranged that little incident at The Sweet Spot to get them out from under, which was good – just a pity your story about picking those boys up somewhere or other wasn't. It's not like you, and I have to say it disappoints me. Now Gabe, I'm sorry to have to tell you that those boys, Owen and Christian Stewart according to Essex Police, are dead. Broken necks, the both of them. In their early twenties. Tragic.'

'I didn't know them.'

'No, you probably didn't, Gabe,' Tony said. 'I get that. This is what happens when you go into business with other firms.'

'I'm not in business, as you put it, with any other firm. I'm legit, DI Bracci.'

'Oh yes!' Tony put a hand up to his head. Kam, watching the performance, smiled. 'Of course they're not a far-right crime syndicate, are they, Gabe! They're a respectable political organisation! Christ, I'm a fucking div aren't I, me?'

Nobody spoke for a moment and then Tony said, 'I thought you were cleverer than that, Gabe. You've managed to work the system all these years, playing the game intelligently, and now this? Having said that, I have to admit that until I spoke to Essex, the Britannia Party were only very marginally on my radar. Couple of swivel-eyed sorts contesting a few councils in Essex. And to be fair, it's not them I'm talking about. Nutters, but what can you do? Well you can, if you get the opportunity, have a go at the people who stand in the shadows, behind this lot. And that's where you come in, Gabe.'

Gabriel felt his stomach turn.

'Can't say I understand it,' Bracci continued. 'You've got a bit classy in your old age, Gabe. Getting involved with bullet-headed racists? But then Essex told me about just how big the big money coming into Britannia is, and while I still can't really square that with you as you are today, you were a greedy tyke when you were a kid, weren't you? And now you're getting old.'

'I think, DI Bracci, that we should go to the police station now and I should call my lawyer,' Gabe said. 'That is my right.'

''Course it is, Gabe,' Kam Shah said. 'But DI Bracci and I thought you'd like to have a little chat first, on the basis that Essex Police have been watching a bloke called Harry Crowley for some time now.'

Gabriel felt his face flush.

Bracci said, 'Not that Crowley's his real name, is it Gabe? That was Smith until he became interested in the occult. Changed it in honour of his hero Aleister Crowley. I knew nothing about the bloke, but apparently he had a direct line to Satan back in the 1930s. All sorts of rumours about raising the dead and ceremonies involving the blood of virgins. Called himself the Great Beast. Some say Hitler was a fan. But then he dabbled didn't he, in the occult.

'Smith slash Crowley wanted the golem bad, didn't he. And so at one of them Rotary Club or fucking charity gala whatsits you attended with him and a load of other respectable concerned citizens you mix with these days, you had a chat about Belvedere. You had an interest in getting in there because of the Cyprus Place evidence, ditto Smith and the golem. But to break into Belvedere, you would have to do know what you're doing.'

'I don't know what you're talking about,' Gabe said.

'No? Well, let me enlighten you,' Bracci said. 'You went to a fundraiser for Britannia in Loughton last month. You took Tim.' He frowned. 'I was dubious about this when Essex told me, because I know you keep your boy well away from your businesses and associates. But then when I thought about it, from the little we know about the Belvedere break-in, one thing seems to have been key – whoever did the job knew a lot about technical security systems. And while I'm pretty sure that Mr Smith slash Crowley could have sourced someone with that sort of knowledge all on his own, why would he do that when one of his friend's sons is an expert?'

'Tim's an honest man,' Gabe said. 'He would never—'

'Every man has his price, Gabe, and you and I both know that were the Cyprus Place evidence brought to court, you were going down.'

'So why didn't you arrest me at the time, Bracci?'

'Because, Gabe, we wanted to get the lot of you,' Bracci said. 'Including your wife.'

Nausea began to creep up on Gabe. He felt hot and so he took a long slug from the hated lime and soda water. Was Bracci bluffing or did he . . . Gabe couldn't even consider it.

'But that fell apart when Belvedere was raided, didn't it guv?' Kamran said.

'It did, Kam,' Bracci said. 'And Gabe, I've no doubt that all that evidence was destroyed almost immediately. But of course, some of the crew you and Smith used for the job were as thick as shit – good in a fight, I get it, but also greedy and frankly fucking stupid. Because I'm sure you didn't sanction the taking and then burying of some of that smack we had in Belvedere, did you? No. And to bury it in the graveyard where we found the golem? Not a good idea unless you're a seventeen-year-old meathead who wants to get a bit of extra dosh to have his shitty old VW Golf lowered.' He leant across the table towards Gabe. 'Whatever happens, the little Cyprus Place kids are going down. They were caught red-handed. But they've not grassed, ditto the daft kid with the gun at The Sweet Spot. But unless you want me to come for your Timothy and your wife, Gabe, you'd better sing me a song about Smith slash Crowley and these Britannia nutters.'

Gabe began to speak, but Bracci stopped him. 'Because

believe me, much as you might not want to go inside after your very long career outside, it's you or your boy – and so I suggest you throw yourself on your sword. Britannia and those behind them are a matter of national security, so you sing loud enough and maybe you'll get away with it. But don't sing at all and your family's over, mate, because unlike the knobs behind Britannia, you're not titled and you don't have friends in high places.'

There was a knock at the door. Lee had been half asleep on the sofa and hadn't heard it until Chronus the mynah bird squawked. Lee looked at his watch. It was almost 2 a.m. Whoever was outside knocked again and so he got to his feet and went to the front door.

'Mumtaz?' he said when he saw her.

'Can I come in?' she asked.

'If you like.' He stood aside to let her into his flat. When Chronus saw her, he put his head underneath his wing and went back to sleep. They knew each other well and, although he didn't exactly let her pet him, Chronus felt safe with Mumtaz.

'Take a seat,' Lee said as he flung himself down on his sofa. But Mumtaz stood.

'Lee, I've come to apologise,' she said.

He yawned. 'Apologise for what?'

'For locking you out,' she said.

They'd been here many times before during the course of their on-and-off relationship. The threat of death had made them express their true feelings, but was that any basis upon which to build it yet again?

'We nearly died,' he said.

'That's not the only reason I said what I did.' She sat down opposite him. 'My dad came to see me today.'

'That's nice.'

He knew that Baharat Huq wanted them to be together. But he also knew that wasn't enough.

She told him the story her father had told her about her grandfather.

'But what has that got to do with us?' he said. 'My grandfather was Jewish. It doesn't affect my life now. I'm not sure what you're getting at, Mumtaz.'

She swallowed. 'I felt that being with you might change me,' she said. 'This job means that you meet a lot of people. In my case those people are mainly women because that's what I do. I try, where I can, to help women who are in bad marriages, whose daughters are being abused, girls who want to love those their families do not approve of. I also meet other women who feel they've lost themselves. They've married or have relationships across cultural lines and they feel like traitors, they feel cut off, they don't feel like themselves any more.'

'Mumtaz, I told you right from the start that I would always respect your culture and your religion,' he said. 'You come with that, it's part of you, just like my support for West Ham United is part of me. We take these things on and we don't change them. I don't know why you won't believe me, but that's the truth. Christ, you're an intelligent woman! Why would you, after going through the hell of an abusive marriage when you were younger, pick a man who'd do that all over again to you?'

'Because sometimes that happens.' she said. 'I've seen it.'

'And you thought I could be capable of that?' He was angry. 'So you come in here and what? Tell me you've changed your mind?'

Mumtaz could see how it looked. She began to cry.

'No, Mumtaz,' he said. 'I told you that however you want to live your life is fine by me. I'm sorry about what happened to your granddad. I'm happy it made you come to the realisation that you have. But I can't just suddenly behave as if everything's alright again. If you really do want to be with me, then we will give it another go, but I can't go through this again. Do you understand?'

She said nothing.

'Do you?'

She stopped crying. 'Yes.'

'And it will take time,' he said. 'I'm not sure I'm ready. And I'm not sure you are either.' He swallowed. 'What I would like is for us to be able to be normal and honest with each other again. You and me, we used to work alongside each other really well. We had each other's back. We joked around . . . If we could get back to that, it would be a start.'

She nodded.

'And don't think I don't love you or want to punish you, because I don't,' he said. 'I want you more than anything or anyone I've ever met. I'd die for you, Mumtaz. To be honest, I feel like I'm dying a little bit now because I just want to hold you and never let you go. But although I don't see my daughter very much, she's still in my life and I have to be there for her. Also Mum. Since Roy died I'm all she's got. I can't get myself messed up again. I can't.'

And then he began to cry, and Mumtaz walked across the room to put her arms around him. Lee did not try to stop her.

The police found the bodies of Black and his daughter inside the old man's house. During their first inspection of the property, they'd thought that a door at the back of the old man's bedroom led to a cupboard. But on closer inspection now, after pulling a wall of boxes and clothes out of the way, the police found a small room.

'It's a shrine, sir,' Scene of Crime Officer Roland Blunt told Superintendent Ross, when he arrived.

'A shrine to what?' Ross asked as he put on a pair of nitrile gloves and slipped plastic covers over his shoes.

'Well, actually more of a crime board really,' Blunt said. 'Newspaper cuttings, photographs, notes.'

'So let's have a look,' Ross said.

Blunt led the way into a strange world. Black and his daughter sat in chairs, their clothes covered in the dried blood from the gunshot wounds that had killed them. On the walls were hundreds, maybe even thousands of cuttings related to, notes on and pictures of the diamond they'd been looking for. The Acorn, lost during the Second World War. Or was it? Ross looked at a picture of Mathilde Zimmer's mausoleum in Prague. It was a huge edifice. Fashioned in what he imagined was top-grade marble, it represented the last gasp of a Jewish civilisation in Central Europe that had all but disappeared during the Holocaust. It was terrifying.

'God, how do you explain this?' he said.

'Man next door said Mr Black was a quiet bloke, kept himself to himself,' Blunt said.

'Well clearly he was obsessed with this nonsense!' Then looking at Rosamund Black's corpse he said, 'Don't understand her though. How does an intelligent person, a surgeon, become involved in something like this?'

'He was her father, sir,' Blunt said.

'Even so.' He shook his head. 'But then again, the search for treasure has obsessed people for centuries. Some of Hitler's loot is apparently still missing.'

'This could be part of that,' Blunt said.

'Maybe.'

Tony Bracci was in the process of interviewing Gabriel York about his connection to the break-in at the Belvedere storage facility down in Kent. Criminal he might be, but it was still baffling that someone with York's intellect had become involved with far-right thugs. But then, money. It was behind most acts of criminality if one broke it down. Less obvious was who had put an end to Black and his daughter's lives, and who had let Lee Arnold, Mumtaz Hakim and Bernard Bennett live. They too were dangerous. And where was the golem? Had it, just like the Cyprus Place evidence, been destroyed – or had it simply disappeared?

TWENTY-THREE

Six months later

'I wish you people wouldn't do so much at night,' Reg said as he climbed painfully out of Terry's car and walked around the hoarding that currently surrounded the Church of St Magnus the Martyr.

'People wouldn't understand if we did our business during the day,' Terry said.

'Not sure I do either,' Reg said.

Terry had told him a few days ago that an important ceremony was going to be taking place at the church. He hadn't said what it was but, in spite of increasing pain from his arthritis, Reg Richmond had wanted to attend.

Once on the other side of the hoarding, he could see that the main door of the church was open. Inside he could see lots of people, some of them wearing the same fur hats and side-locks he remembered his father's fellow Kabbalists sporting when he'd been a child. Underneath the bell tower, flagstones had been lifted and a hole had been dug.

A young priest walked up to Terry and said, 'Can we start now, Father Steven?'

'Yes. But please bring a chair out for Mr Richmond. It's cold tonight and we can't expect him to stand.'

'Yes, Father.'

The boy left. Reg said, 'Steven?'

Terry smiled.

'Do you remember, Reg, when I was with you at your home during that terrible night after Lionel died? I told you that this, the footprint of St Magnus Church, was holy ground?'

The young priest arrived with a chair and Reg sat down. 'Yes,' he said. 'I think I may have thought about it at the time, but I've given it little attention since. Why?'

People, most of them men, began to file out of the church and arrange themselves around the bell tower.

'And when we first met here, you were looking at the model of Old London Bridge?'

'Yes.'

'I told you that an alchemist called Chaim Falk had lived on the bridge in the eighteenth century.'

'He made a golem,' Reg said. 'The Golem of London. If it ever existed.'

'It did,' Terry said.

'You sound very sure.'

As people continued to file out of the church, Terry explained.

'Although not directly bombed during the Second World War, St Magnus sustained a lot of damage,' he said. 'This

314

courtyard was ruined. It was a terrible mess of earth and underground pipes and paving slabs. There was also what one of the priests thought at first was a body. However, it seemed to be in reality some sort of idol. Horrified, he contacted his friend, Father Edward, who was priest at St Etheldreda's Church in Holborn. A learned church historian, Edward was well known for his connections to many different faith communities across the capital. He was also my uncle and when he arrived here it was said he was in a state of enormous excitement. The priest who had called him, a Father Sebastian, had covered the thing up with a piece of corrugated iron. When he removed it, my uncle almost fainted. Here was the London Golem of Chaim Falk! In his excitement my uncle reached down and attempted to pull it from the ground. But it fell apart in his hands. You can imagine how he felt.' He shook his head. 'That golem had been protecting London for two hundred years and now, in a moment, it was gone. And at a time of great danger.'

People lit candles and the cold, black night sky was illuminated by warm, yellow flame.

'And so Father Edward went to his friend Menachim Reichman in Stepney, and he told him what your father already knew. That a golem existed in the sacred ground of this church, but he, a man who had considered himself good, had inadvertently destroyed it. Menachim Reichman told him not to worry. He told him that he would make sure that London would not be without its golem for long.'

'Which was when my father and the others created the East Ham Golem.'

'They did. But by that time this part of the city was in ruins

315

and so they had to find somewhere else to put it, somewhere in a more distant part of London. It lay in Plashet Cemetery for decades until it, in turn, was destroyed.'

'Who did that?' Reg asked. 'Why?'

'Greed,' Terry said. 'But here, look, it's back, Reg. Not created by your father, but by others like him. And like the original, it is made from London clay.'

It was tall, the mud man, and heavy. It took ten men to carry it to its new home underneath the courtyard flagstones. And when they lowered it into position, great care was taken to make sure that it didn't break. Reg looked at its face, rudimentary, with slits for eyes, a mouth open as if waiting for the breath of life; its lumpen arms and legs, kneeless and roughly hewn. In a way it was beautiful and when the Kabbalists began their rituals of blessing, Reg found that he was moved to tears.

Mumtaz didn't know what woke her up. But suddenly she was wide awake, even though she could see that it was still pitch black outside. Slipping silently out of bed, she made her way to the kitchen and then opened the back door and went down the wooden staircase into the garden.

At first she couldn't see anything, but as her eyes adjusted to the light level outside, she saw the face of a fox peep through the hedge. For just a second they looked at each other, woman and fox – and then the animal left, jumping over the wall into the cemetery behind.

Mumtaz sat down on one of her garden chairs. For a long time after the East Ham Golem case had been closed, she'd imagined she'd seen a person watching her from the garden.

Now, all these months on, she had started to wonder whether any of that had even happened. Bernie Bennett was back at work and, she'd heard, could regularly be found next door at Mrs Igwe's house joining the family for dinner. Unfortunately, relations between Bernie and his daughter had worsened since Kelly's husband had been questioned by police about his involvement with the Britannia movement. Vi Collins had told her it was all part of the golem taking its revenge – but then she'd laughed. The golem was long gone, destroyed by Mr Black in his endless search for the Acorn diamond. He had actually felt entitled to it, which was strange because it had never really belonged to his father. But then maybe taking ownership of things was just what humans did. They conned themselves into believing that what they wanted they were also entitled to.

Life had settled into a familiar rhythm again after the golem. For her this meant working – currently on a historical missing person case – visiting her family and her stepdaughter, and living her life in her flat. She thought about her grandfather Zayan – or Zevesh – a lot these days. She wished he'd lived longer so that she could really have known him. She just hoped that now he was at peace with all his deities.

As she walked back up to the flat, Mumtaz touched the statue of Shiva that had once belonged to Zevesh, and then she returned to her bedroom. In her bed, his head slightly to one side, completely asleep, was Lee Arnold. Snoring loudly, as usual. She got into bed beside him and kissed his head.

BARBARA NADEL was born and brought up in the East End of London and now lives in Essex. She has a degree in psychology and, prior to becoming a full-time author, she worked in psychiatric institutions and in the community with people experiencing mental health problems. She is also the author of the award-winning Inspector Ikmen series, now a major BBC crime drama, The Turkish Detective.

@BarbaraNadel